Praise for **Blackbirch**
Book (

I devoured this book! The intrigue grabs you from page one, and this
air of mystery and magic carries throughout the whole story.

★ ★ ★ ★ ★

Blackbirch: The Beginning has the kind of smart, sharp prose that
makes it stand head and shoulders above the usual YA read.

★ ★ ★ ★ ★

...a cliffhanger ending that made my jaw drop...

★ ★ ★ ★ ★

Blackbirch: The Beginning is the kind of book that will make you stay
up late reading it and then invade your dreams.

★ ★ ★ ★

K.M Allan weaves you into the story at a visceral level - creating a
sense of place and a feeling of dread that follows you right through to
the closing pages.

★ ★ ★ ★

Source: Goodreads

Available in paperback and ebook - kmallan.com/blackbirch

Blackbirch
Book Two

The Dark Half

K.M. Allan

Published by K.M. Allan 2020.

This is a work of fiction. Similarities to real people, places, or events are entirely coincidental.

BLACKBIRCH: THE DARK HALF

First edition. July 2020.

ISBN: 9780648773023

Written by K.M. Allan.

For Donna.

My evil twin and dark half.

ONE

Josh Taylor stumbled for the nearest door, finding it buried in the far wall of The Playhouse interior. As he yanked it open, and the room tilted, a wave of energy shoved him. He rode it out, letting the momentum carry him into the darkened alleyway.

Sarah Randall followed, lowering herself to his side when he came to rest on the hard pavement. The hem of her dress dirtied as it dragged across the dusty ground, smudging the pale pink material as she kneeled. Her blanket of long blond hair swept across her blurred face before he was hit again, forcing his eyes shut. Was the invisible force trying to crush him? He pushed his fists against his forehead as the pressure swelled.

Sarah's presence slipped away, snuffed out by the energy and the darkness of his closed lids. He was alone against the elements, completely at their mercy. His skin cooled as ice seeped into his limbs, and a palm pressed against his cheek, making him wonder if it was his own. His fingers were so cold it was hard to tell. The hand warmed, weakening the wave and giving him back his strength.

He lifted his chin and opened his eyes. It was Kallie. Her petite hand outstretched, resting gently on his skin as if it was where it belonged.

"Just breathe," she murmured.

Josh sucked in a lungful of air. When he exhaled, the scattered remains of the energy wave broke and her features sharpened, her brown eyes shining at him, their shade darker than he expected.

"It's real life, not a dream," he reminded himself, watching Kallie's brow furrow. Dammit, she'd heard him, and it caused a flush of heat to wash through his cheeks. Her hand slipped from his skin, taking the warmth and the faint blue glow of her energy with it. She'd been using her power on him?

"What was that?" he asked.

"That was my fault." She stood. "I was channeling my full strength of energy to find you, not realizing you didn't have your veil up."

"My what?"

Now her cheeks flushed. "Sorry. A veil. It's like a filter between you and the weight of the magick. It'll stop it from becoming too much."

"That would have been good to know." He rubbed where her palm had been, and his fingertips tingled.

"Ah hum."

Sarah's throat cleared loudly, reminding Josh she was there. He watched her rise to her feet and grip Kallie's hand, giving it a shake.

"I'm Sarah."

"Kallie Jacobs."

"This is the girl I was telling you about," he said to Sarah as he stood. "I'm Josh." He held out his hand. Kallie's gaze had followed him as he straightened, her head tilting up. When his fingers found hers, a spark of energy burst between them, sending a ticklish jolt through his body.

"Just picture a veil being pulled between you and everything else." Kallie smiled as she withdrew her touch. "It'll stop that from happening when we're close."

"That wasn't so bad." Josh grinned, not caring that he probably looked like an idiot. He pictured a veil like she said, and the intense buzz simmered down.

"That's better, right?"

"Yeah." She could feel what he'd done?

Sarah leaned into him. "When you say, 'this is the girl I was telling you about,' do you mean the girl from your weird dreams? The one who we agreed wasn't real?"

Kallie laughed. "You didn't think I was real."

"It's a long story, but obviously you do exist." Everything about Kallie was the same as his dreams. Her long, dark chocolate waves, her warm olive skin. She was even wearing the same clothes; black boots, blue jeans, and a fitted white shirt. The only thing missing was the ash and bloodied hands. "You said you were using your power to search for me?"

"Yes."

"I guess you beat me to it then." A smile found its way to his lips. The dreams they'd shared had been fleeting yet comforting, a confirmation neither of them was alone. Kallie experienced them trapped in a tiny room with him as her only connection to the outside world, and he was positive she felt the same way, yet she didn't react to his words. Maybe she didn't remember? "We promised to use our energy to—"

"Find each other," she finished his sentence. "I know." Her eyes darted to Sarah before returning to his. "I'm glad I could."

Ahh, so she hadn't forgotten their promise. She just didn't want to talk about it in front of others.

"Your energy exploded into the world yesterday," Kallie told him. "It made it easy to find you."

Yesterday was when Josh fought Arden Flynn in the clearing, when he'd used his power for the first time. "You sensed it?"

Kallie nodded. "I did. In a very big way. What were you doing?"

"Saving our lives," Sarah said.

Kallie's lips parted. "What?"

"We were attacked," Josh told her. "And I was forced to use my power."

"Attacked? By who?"

"A man named Arden." Josh paused after the word 'man', knowing Arden was far from it, but now wasn't the time to explain the reality of the monster he'd been. "He's dead."

"Did you kill him?"

Kill him? Did she think he was a murderer? "No. Another girl with us did."

"Using magick?"

"A knife." Memories of Arden grasping for the blade plunged into his back forced their way into Josh's mind. "Arden was the one with power, not the other girl."

"He had power, but she could get close enough to kill him?" Kallie's eyebrows arched.

"I was keeping him occupied. He didn't see her coming."

"I must thank her then, if she kept you safe for me."

Kallie's choice of words reminded him of what his mother had done. How she'd traded her life for his. "Did you know my mom before she died?"

His hands clenched while he waited for her answer. "Her name was Laura Taylor." He needed to know his mother's role in all of this.

Kallie's head shook. "I'm sorry, I didn't."

Josh's shoulders dropped at her answer; his palms stung by the sharp pinch of his nails. Sarah tilted her head at him, but he didn't want her sympathy. Just like he didn't want his disappointment to be so obvious. He focused on the ground.

"I knew your aunt," Kallie continued. "Melinda Tucker."

"My aunt?" His head shot up. "What does she have to do with magick?"

"That's the first of many questions I'm sure you have. I can only tell you what I learned from Melinda. I didn't know your mom was also gifted."

"It doesn't seem like anyone did." Maybe he wouldn't get all the answers he wanted after all.

"Uh, guys?" Sarah tapped Josh's shoulder. "Maybe we should have this discussion somewhere *less* public?"

He followed her pointing thumb to the far end of the alleyway where a movie session had let out from The Playhouse's twin theater. They were standing in the middle of the path from it to the parking lot.

"I'm happy to answer what I can," Kallie offered, stepping back to the side door and picking up a backpack. "Anywhere you want."

Anywhere, huh? Where exactly did people go to discuss the secrets that had ruined their life?

Turns out it was home. Well, at least the modest two-story Josh shared with Sarah and her mom, Grace—his guardian.

She was at work, running the Blackbirch Bookstore, so they had the house to themselves. It was a good thing. Grace would ask a million questions about Kallie and he had too many of his own.

"Max will never talk to me again," Sarah mumbled from the armchair after they'd settled in the living room, her scowling mouth lit by the glow of her phone screen. It was her first sentence in the last ten minutes not littered with her fun new habit of dropping f-bombs. She must be calming down.

"She left her boyfriend at The Playhouse?" Kallie quietly asked Josh.

He felt her weight shift next to him on the couch and admired her profile in the light of the lamp on the corner table. She was beautiful. And definitely real.

"No, her friend. But it's okay, Max won't stay angry at her."

"He's not answering my calls or texts!" Sarah jiggled her phone.

"So, he doesn't know about the magick, but she does?" Kallie asked.

Josh glanced at Sarah. Her scowl had melted, but her attention remained glued to the screen, studying it like she expected her stare to conjure a text. "Yeah, she knows."

"And she's okay with it?"

"More or less."

An impressed expression crept across Kallie's face, as if the concept that someone could know about their magick and accept it was new to her. There was so much he wanted to ask.

"Ah, Sarah?" He waved at her, gesturing for her to put her phone away.

"Right! Question time. Sorry." She placed her cell in her lap.

"What would you like to know first?" Kallie smoothed her hands along her jeans.

A few hours ago, Josh had ruled out finding anyone to answer his questions. Now that he had the opportunity, where did he begin? He knotted his clammy fingers together, trying to put his jumbled thoughts into something understandable. He should start simple. Work his way *into* the crazy.

"How about you tell us how you became gifted." He used the description she'd given his aunt and mom.

Kallie straightened, rocking the cushions of the couch. "A few months ago, a fire destroyed the house I lived in and it killed my mom."

The breath left his body. She'd lost her family too?

"It wasn't a typical fire. It chased me out of the house and cornered me, the smoke killing me as well."

Kallie's words were delivered with a steady voice; her story repeated like it hadn't happened to her. It was a form of denial Josh knew well and one that almost made him miss the significance of her statement.

"I'm sorry, did you just say the fire *killed* you?"

Kallie nodded.

"What?" Sarah looked up from her cell screen.

"The fire was started by power," Kallie explained. "Although I didn't know that at the time.

Josh knew all about magical fire. He'd seen it in the clearing, spewing from the hands of someone he once thought he could trust. Had the scarred monster gone after Kallie too? "Arden could shape his energy into flames. He used his fire as his weapon during the car accident that killed my parents."

"I'm sorry to hear about your family." Kallie's tone softened. "Fire was the gift of the man who attacked you?"

"Yes. We can both take comfort in the fact that he's dead."

Kallie reached out and patted his hand, giving it a squeeze before she let go. "Arden wasn't the one who set fire to my house. A man named Cade did."

"Wait, so there's another magick-fire-maniac out there?" Sarah asked. "That's just great."

"Yes and no. Cade was using power, but it's not a part of him like us and this Arden person."

Josh scowled. "What do you mean?"

"The magick you and I have, when it's in a human, is incredibly powerful and manifests itself into gifts unique to the person who possesses it. The power Cade has is limited. He found it trapped in a crystal and can only wield it from that crystal and others he adds to a specially made wooden staff."

"So he's not gifted?" Sarah asked.

"No. His magick isn't as strong, but it still causes damage."

"Like the fire that killed you and your mother?" Josh couldn't have imagined anything worse than the car accident he'd been through, but this...

"Cade has used his source of power to kill others too. All to gain more. Certain spells and rituals can increase his magick. He was performing one of those spells with the fire. Your aunt saw him and put a stop to it. When he witnessed her bringing me back, he knew she had magick, and it cost Melinda her life."

"Wait a minute, my aunt died in a home invasion," Josh said. "It was a robbery gone wrong." That's what the police told him and Grace when they'd tried to find his next of kin.

"Cade killed her. The robbery was what the police thought happened."

Josh's parents murder had been an assumed accident too, believed even by him until he remembered the truth. "You said Melinda brought you back to life. Did she use the Beginning to save you?" Almost everything else in their origin stories had lined up.

"No, she used an amulet." Kallie's eyes swept his features. "The Beginning is a difficult spell. It takes an enormous amount of power to invoke. I've never heard of anyone successfully casting it."

Josh exchanged a knowing look with Sarah. "It was the spell my mom cast to save my life."

Kallie gasped, her palm cupping his cheek again. It was still as warm as it'd been in the alley and tingled with the crackling of her energy. *What is she doing?*

A rush of images invaded Josh's mind, blinding his vision. He blinked back the glare of the streetlight and the sparks thrown around him as the metal box of a car he was trapped in slid across the black asphalt. He jolted against the couch, the soft material replaced with leather seats, sticky with blood and soaked in rainwater as his mom's hand pressed into his ripped flesh and her magick lit the surrounding air. *No. No. No!*

He violently summoned his energy to his fingertips, allowing the red power to destroy the memories tearing at the hole in his soul. His hands pulsed with heat as he grasped Kallie's wrist and pushed her away.

The strength of his magick rocked her, and he experienced it just as physically, wiping at his forehead and mopping up beads of sweat while Kallie's pink lips quivered.

Sarah, who'd jumped to her feet in the commotion, hovered to his left. He signaled that he was okay and concentrated on her lowering back into the armchair.

"What did you just do to me?" He turned to Kallie.

"I needed to see if it was true."

"You looked inside my mind?" His fingertips trembled against his forehead. Why would she do that? *How* could she do that?

She swallowed thickly. "It's called glimpsing. It's a spell I use in combination with my natural ability."

"What ability?"

"Before I learned about witchcraft from Melinda, I could see... things... visions of the future."

Her voice lowered as she spoke the last few words, her hands tangling as she weaved her shaking fingers together. Did she think he wouldn't believe her? He glanced at Sarah. They'd both seen enough strangeness to consider anything. If Kallie said she could see the future and inside people's heads, he trusted that she could. He just wished she hadn't looked into his.

"What you saw was private."

Kallie hands parted. "I'm sorry. I... didn't think. I won't do that to you again."

Her promise was genuine, but it didn't erase what she'd done. Silence settled between them and he wondered what he was supposed to ask her now. Could he get an answer without being forced to relive the most horrible thing that had ever happened to him?

"So, um," Sarah spoke, rearranging herself to face Kallie. "If you can see the future, didn't you know your own death was coming? To me that seems like one benefit of such a... talent."

Kallie briefly scowled, before shifting her features into a more relaxed expression.

"I don't control what I see," she explained. "I also didn't believe what I'd been seeing was real."

"Okay." Sarah glanced at Josh, gesturing for him to ask another question.

He stilled the shake in his hands. Answers were important right now, and he needed to concentrate on something other than the memories Kallie's glimpse had stirred up. "You said Melinda used an amulet to bring you back. Can you explain more about that?"

Kallie nodded; her smile no longer forced. "The amulet has two sources of magick in it. One that brings death and another that brings life. Melinda used the life power to revive me."

"Is that how you got your magick? I didn't become gifted until my mom brought me back."

"So I saw." Kallie shook her head. "Sorry." She returned her attention to the floorboards. "To answer your question, I became gifted the night Melinda died. Instead of letting Cade steal her power, she passed it to me."

Josh grimaced. His aunt gave Kallie her power? Did his mom do the same? She can't have. Not after the lengths she'd gone to to hide it from him.

"Did my answer confuse you?" Kallie asked, her eyes darting to his face and studying it.

"No." He sighed, annoyed his expression had betrayed his thoughts again. "I'm just trying to get my head around how it works. You said Melinda purposely gave you her power, but I don't think my mom did that. She cast a spell erasing my memory, which suppressed my energy. She didn't want me to know about the existence of magick."

"If that's true then you receiving her power was probably a side effect of the Beginning. She gave every part of herself to you by casting that spell. It makes sense her magick went to you too."

"What happened to the amulet?" Sarah asked. "Life and death power doesn't sound like something you'd want falling into the wrong hands."

"It has a spell on it. One that moves it around to avoid exactly that. I've been trying to track it and believe there's a strong chance it's here in Blackbirch, where Melinda grew up."

Is that something Josh should have known? He examined the green-tinged veins on the back of his hands; the energy inside them silent. "My aunt sent the amulet here?"

"The spell was cast by someone with the future knowledge to know where the amulet is needed next. Melinda didn't have that."

"So a person like you sent it?"

Kallie laughed. Was his question funny?

"I don't have enough power to pull off such a spell."

"What about Cade?" Sarah asked, her forehead wrinkling. "Will he be coming to Blackbirch?"

"He can't sense energy. He has no way to find Josh or the amulet. Cade is persistent, though. He held onto me after killing Melinda, and now I've escaped, he'll be looking for me."

"Then how can you say for sure he's not in town already?" Sarah's voice pitched up a notch.

"I would know if he was here," Kallie assured her.

A jingle of bells sounded from Sarah's lap and she sprung out of her chair, pacing out of the room with her phone pressed to her ear. "Max, I'm so, so sorry."

Josh followed her with his eyes until she disappeared into the kitchen. Kallie was already looking at him when his attention returned to the couch. She really was there. Sitting next to him.

"This is a lot to take in, especially so much at once." She stretched her hand out gingerly, giving his knee a gentle tap. Even through his jeans, her touch made his skin tingle.

"It is a little overwhelming," he admitted.

"I'm happy to tell you everything," Kallie offered again. "But maybe tomorrow would be better? When you've had time to deal with what I've said so far."

"Sounds good." He nodded. "I have just one more question tonight."

"Anything." Kallie patted his knee again.

"My aunt. What was she like?"

A twinkle sparked in Kallie's eyes. Josh wasn't sure if it was at the memory of his aunt or his question, but it stayed as she answered.

"Melinda was a witch."

TWO

Kallie's key slid into the door and clicked, letting her into the sparse motel room. Once inside, the chill gathered from the night air evaporated from her bones and she drifted wearily toward the bed.

Settling on the end, Kallie put ripples in the thick quilt lining as she spread her hands to smooth it. With little money, the best she could afford housed a headboard with a mattress and a cream-colored chair in the far corner. There was no TV, and the bathtub was spider-webbed with so many cracks it'd be a surprise if it held water, but at least it was some place warm.

She mustered the last of her strength to slip off her boots and crawled onto the bed. *Just one night, please. No dreams.* She didn't know why she asked. It changed nothing. Her sleep would always be tainted with memories of the past. The images were ever present, crafted into nightmares designed to never let Kallie forget her mistakes, or that night six months ago in Landport that started it all...

Kallie stared so hard at the flame the orange glow lost its pointed shape, turning into a formless blur against the wax melting into the wooden porch.

"You'll burn the house down."

Her mother's voice floated from behind, breaking Kallie's concentration.

"Sorry." She turned, eyeing the youthful woman the scolding words contrasted with.

Even on a bad day, thirty-two-year-old Julia Jacobs didn't look older than twenty. Her tiny frame and five-foot-two height helped; traits she shared with Kallie, but that was where their physical similarities ended.

Kallie's locks were more chocolate than auburn, her skin a deeper olive, and her brown eyes absent of the green flecks coloring her mother's irises. She assumed her differences were the features she'd inherited from her father, but it was hard to know when she'd never seen a picture. Her mom raised her alone, and from an age young enough most out-of-towners mistook them for sisters; a mistake Julia never corrected.

"I didn't know the candle had melted so much," Kallie apologized, attempting to scrape away the hardening wax with her fingernails.

"You've been out here for hours. What have you been doing?"

"Thinking."

"Well, it's time to come in. Dinner's ready."

Kallie gathered the candle's remains and walked the weathered boards of the wrap-around porch to the trash can under the kitchen window.

Their house was surrounded by a wheat field, and her mom was right, if anything caught fire out here it would spread quickly. Maybe even reach the forest that sat opposite, separated from their property by nothing more than a thin dirt road.

Kallie eyed the golden stalks before settling her stare on the only other house nearby, a small cottage just inside the tree line. At night, she could see the lights from her bedroom, but she was forbidden to go near it. As were the other children. It was the local legend that a witch lived there.

"Your dinner's getting cold."

Kallie flinched at her mom's appearance in the kitchen window, and the single plate on the wooden dinner table behind her. "You aren't eating?"

"I have to work. Landport's biggest restaurant doesn't run itself." Julia straightened the gold name tag pinned to her stiff black shirt.

"But it'd run fine without you," Kallie mumbled.

"What?"

"Nothing."

"The Char-Grill is open twenty-four hours a day. Someone has to supervise the night shift." Julia straightened her name tag again.

Did she think it was important? It wasn't a police badge. She wasn't protecting anyone from harm by bossing around overworked waiters. "I know. God forbid the truckers pulling up at 2am miss out on the best cuts of meat this side of the highway." Kallie mocked the Char-Grill's slogan.

"Yes, it would be a shame if they missed out on their steak."

Her mom missed the sarcasm, along with seeing her off to school and being home every weeknight.

"I want you to go to bed early tonight," Julia said as Kallie slipped into the kitchen through the back door. "No watching those horror movies before you sleep. I won't be here if you have any more nightmares."

"The movie didn't give me nightmares." She wasn't twelve.

Her mother paused mid-reach, abandoning her bag on the counter. *Damn.* Kallie shut her eyes and counted to three. When she opened them, her mom's hand was still raised, her glossy peach lips twisted downward. They'd had the same fight last week and here was Kallie bringing it up again. *Moron.*

"I can't keep going through this with you." Julia's quiet voice didn't hide the sternness at its edges.

Kallie slipped into her chair and focused on her plate. She'd been given the only chipped one again. It ruined the blue grapevine pattern stamped along the white rim. Maybe if she avoided her mother's gaze long enough, she'd escape her familiar lecture.

"Look at me, Kallie."

No such luck.

Julia strode to the table, hovering at the edge, her hands on her hips. "You need to get the notion out of your head. The images you see are not real. They mean nothing."

Kallie nodded. *Pretend to agree. She'll leave you alone.*

Julia huffed, pulling her hand off her hip long enough to twist her delicate wrist around and eye her silver watch. "I've got to go." .

Of course you do. Kallie picked up her fork and poked the piece of chicken on her plate while her mom reached back to the counter and snatched up her purse.

"I'll see you in the morning."

Kallie stifled a laugh, knowing her mother wouldn't drag herself out of bed until after noon.

Julia let out an annoyed sigh and marched to the front door. A few minutes later, her car rumbled to life, its tires crunching over the dirt road as she drove off their property and into town, honking as she went.

A honk instead of a hug. *Thanks, Mom.* Kallie picked up her plate and walked toward the refrigerator. Fighting with her mother didn't do much for her appetite. She placed the plate on the shelf in the fridge and moved into the living room, relaxing into the couch stretched across the small space. Amongst the plush cushions, she shut her eyes, trying to clear her mind.

For as long as she could remember, cryptic images had haunted her. Ones that had gotten clearer in the last few months. Most she saw while asleep, which led to her mother's conclusion it was nightmares. The stronger visions, however, Kallie experienced during the day.

They'd become so vivid, sometimes she didn't know they weren't real. Like the one from three weeks ago when she was walking home from school. Because her house was so isolated, it was unusual to see anyone other than her mother roaring down the dirt, sending brown dust into the air. That's why the appearance of the black car was so surprising.

She'd watched it approach, wondering where it'd come from and where it was going. The driver must have taken a wrong turn off the highway and gotten lost. As the car came toward her, it jerked across the single lane, turning on an angle and skidding past at full speed, as if it hit water.

She closed her eyes when it crashed on its side, and covered her ears, waiting for the strange screeching sound to stop. She didn't understand at the time why the vehicle sounded like it was dragging across asphalt instead of through the crumbly, dry earth.

When she reached the mangled car, the woman behind the steering wheel wasn't hurt, but the same couldn't be said for the poor man in the front passenger seat.

Frantically unstrapping herself from her tangled seat belt, the driver scrambled into the back of the car. The entire passenger side of the vehicle was smashed against the ground, the front windshield pierced by a steel beam. Kallie remembered wondering if it'd come off the car, and why it looked like the remains of a streetlight. Whatever it was, it pinned the back passenger right through their shoulder.

The driver was hunched over them, blocking Kallie's view. It didn't matter. She knew it was too late for the passenger. There was too much blood.

She'd kneeled beside the wreck and called out to the woman. When she didn't get a response, she raised her voice, but all it did was echoed through the car as it vanished before her eyes. Just like that. Gone.

Back on the couch, Kallie sat up, shaking off the memory. It was still so clear. Why had she seen that accident? It hadn't occurred in the following weeks. She'd checked every local newspaper. Maybe her mom was right and everything she saw was a nightmare.

"Or your 'overactive imagination'," she mumbled her mom's favorite line, moving to the kitchen and raiding the fruit bowl below the window for an apple. The crunchy green flesh was tart, and she wiped at the sticky juice that rolled down her chin. *Much better than cold chicken.*

As she stood eating her apple, a breeze ruffled the curtains. It wasn't exactly a summer night, yet the wind was warm. Kallie dropped her apple into the sink and pulled open the curtains. Heated air swirled through the window gap at the edge of the sill, the dusty clear glass reflecting a flickering orange light.

"Shit!"

The wheat was on fire.

Tall flames rippled in the dark sky, eating its way through Kallie's front yard. She ran through the back door and bolted toward the garden hose.

"Where are you?" Her hands smashed against the cladding of the house, feeling in the dark for the spongy softness of the hose. She turned the tap full blast once she had it, dragging what felt like a slippery snake to the front of the house and pointing it at the wheat.

The water blasted from the nozzle, soaking the tall stalks, but it was precious seconds before she realized the water was feeding and not saving them. Where were the flames and the burned field?

She dropped the hose to one hand. She'd *seen* the orange glow. She'd *felt* the heat.

Kallie clenched the hose, cutting off the stream drowning her sneakers, and checked the wheat again, blinking until the golden stalks blurred.

She sniffed the air, searching for a smoky note amongst the malty, earthy scent. Perhaps she'd gotten the location wrong? She tugged on the hose, dragging it to the left. Even in the dark she could see no damage. Had she imagined it? Maybe she was going crazy and her mother could gloat that she was right.

Kallie shivered in the night air and remembered how warm the breeze through the window was. It wasn't a hallucination or a nightmare, she'd experienced the heat of those flames. To her, they were real. *Isn't that what a crazy person would think?* No, a crazy person would say it out loud, and she hadn't done that. Kallie scanned her yard. It was just her, the hose, and the wheat. "A typical Wednesday night." *Okay, now you're talking to yourself.*

She opened her mouth to laugh, but it caught in her throat, stopped short by what her eyes could see.

A figure stood across the road, their silhouette sticking out against the clear night sky. They could have slipped into the nearby woods as soon as Kallie spotted them, but they didn't. The person sauntered down the dirt track leading to the witch's house, disappearing behind the shrubbery that kept it hidden from prying eyes. No one in town went near that strange shack. No matter the situation.

Kallie dropped the hose, her hands going to her sinking stomach. The woman Landport warned its kids about, the lady who chose to live in the darkest part of the woods, the person everyone said was a witch, had been watching her.

THREE

Josh slipped his gray t-shirt on, pulling down the hem as his cell pinged. He glanced at his bedside table, grinning at the text message lighting the phone screen.

He'd exchanged numbers with Kallie before she left last night, and now he had her room at The Blackbirch Motel and a time to meet up. He wanted to show her his mom's mysterious notebook and pulled open the drawer of the bedside to retrieve it.

Inside with the black cloth-bound book was the photo of himself and his parents standing outside their old greenhouse. He'd re-framed it after breaking the glass and then squirreled it away. It was a step up from where the photo once sat, sealed in a cardboard box along the far wall. He glanced there now at the empty space. He'd finally unpacked his old life into his new one, but exchanging the photo's cardboard prison for a wooden one wasn't what the memory deserved.

He pulled the silver frame out and arranged it on the bedside, angling it so the light streaming from the window didn't glare across the smiling faces of his parents. *Perfect.*

Snatching up his cell, he re-read Kallie's text and then fished out the book, tucking it under his arm. To anyone else it looked like a plain notebook, the only feature on it a witches' pentacle etched into the cover. The pages inside were blank, the faint blue lines on the white paper void of words or pictures. That was until Josh let his power sink into the paper. The red energy forced hundreds of hidden letters to the surface, all crafted in his mom's loopy, big curved handwriting.

Much like everything connected to her and magick, the words were a secret, written in a language he didn't recognize and no one else had been able to see. Hopefully Kallie could help him make sense of it. Unlike Sarah.

She was at the bookstore working a shift, something she'd complained about at breakfast. She wanted to go with him, and he was secretly glad she couldn't. He was looking forward to seeing Kallie alone.

"House keys?" he muttered, patting down his jeans and finding them stashed in his back pocket as he made his way downstairs.

Grace had the van, so he walked, enjoying the green streets of Blackbirch bathed in the warmth of what felt like a spring day, despite it being the last weeks of winter.

It took fifteen minutes to reach The Blackbirch Motel. Its cobblestone exterior matched the storefronts on Main Street, and like all other businesses in town, had a black birch tree growing from every spare patch of dirt. There was even one outside of Kallie's room. She opened the door seconds after he knocked, giving him a wide smile. He wasn't used to seeing her happy. It was welcome and infectious, doubling the strength of his good mood.

Kallie was wearing a black T-shirt with her jeans today, just as fitted as the shirt from the night before, and her boots were already on her feet.

"Are we going somewhere?" He readjusted the book under his arm, his eyes sweeping the neat room for a place to put it. There wasn't even a table.

"I was hoping we could go into the woods." Kallie tucked her wavy strands behind her ear with one hand while the other slid her motel key into her pocket. "I'd like to know more about what happened to you the other night."

Josh had only briefly told her about the clearing they'd found in the middle of the forest and Arden's attack. As they moved from the motel toward the trees, he went into detail, Kallie listening intently.

"So, how did it feel when the book gave you that image of the house in the clearing?" she asked.

"Like a haunting," he admitted. "It was burned into my brain and I couldn't stop thinking about it until I went there."

"And then?"

"I never thought about it again."

"Interesting."

"Why?" It wasn't what he expected her to focus on, given the rest of his tale was about a dead man covered in hidden scars only Josh could see.

"I was just wondering if it was similar to what I experience."

"You think I saw a vision?"

"No. But it sounds like your notebook had a spell on it. One to lead whoever unlocked it to a certain object or place. What was in the house?"

"I never went inside."

"Do you want to go there now?"

He glanced at the book cradled in his hands. He'd brought it along because he thought it'd be enough to keep them in this area of the forest, where the trees weren't dead. "I've got the book right here." He held it up.

Kallie paused and held out her hand, taking the book and flicking through it. Could she see what he did? Her stare fluttered over the blue lines, but there was no confused wrinkle to her brow, and her chin didn't drop like his had when Josh realized what his magick had done to the pages.

"When I fed my power into it, I could see the writing."

Energy ignited across Kallie's hand and she passed her blue-glowing fingertips lightly along a page. Nothing happened.

She handed the book back to him. "Maybe you should try?"

He nodded and pulled the book into his chest, concentrating on lowering his veil. Kallie's hand clamped over his.

"For something so simple you don't need to remove your veil." She pulled away her touch. "I would keep it up if I were you."

"Why?" It was just the two of them.

"For your own protection. Your energy is strong. If the wrong person knows how to track it, not having the shelter of the veil makes you easy to find."

"Like how you found me."

"Exactly."

Josh wondered if that was how Arden found him too. He'd said Josh's power had called to him. Shivering at the thought, he left the veil where it was and allowed a thin layer of red energy to filter out of its edges instead. The book reacted instantly, a white glow rolling across the lined paper and leaving a trail of handwritten sentences in its wake.

Kallie reached for the notebook, her wide eyes tracing the glowing pages. She put her own power-infused fingers to the paper, and the blue melded with the white.

"I guess it's my power that activates it." Josh shrugged.

Kallie's hand withdrew, and she examined the tendrils of power clinging to her skin. "This isn't your magick." She closed her eyes, flinging them open again a second later and pushing the book into his hands.

"What's wrong?"

"It's... so strange."

"Did you see something when you touched the white power?"

She nodded; her gaze darting to the book again. "The spell, the one showing the hidden writing, can only be revealed by the person who cast it."

"This is my mother's notebook. It's her handwriting."

"It's her spell," Kallie confirmed. "Only her power can activate it."

"But my power activated it." He tightened his grip on the book.

"I know."

Why did Kallie look so worried? "Couldn't this be another side effect of the Beginning? Like me having kept some of my mom's memories?"

"You might have gotten her power through the Beginning, but once it was in you, it became yours. It gives you your own color, your own unique ability. Just like I gained a different color and ability when Melinda's power was given to me."

"But my mom's power must still be a part of me then. If I could unlock her spell."

"I'm not disagreeing with you."

But she had a problem with something. "Is this just magick you've never heard of?"

Kallie shook her head. "It's magick that's not even possible."

"But we both just saw it happen." She had to be wrong.

Kallie's lips pursed, her head cocking to one side as she scanned the pages again. "Maybe we'll find something in the house? The book wanted you to go there, right?"

The house didn't want him there. Or at least something in that dead place didn't. His stomach sank at the thought of how the clearing made him feel wrong for setting foot on its tainted soil. *Maybe it'll be different now Arden's gone?* He tucked the book under his arm. It was his mom's. Her power. Her spell. It couldn't be dangerous for him to follow the message and check the house, could it?

They weren't far from the clearing now. He pointed toward a gap in between a cluster of large black birches and gestured for Kallie to slip through first.

The sun was above them and he basked in it for a second, willing the warm rays to sink into his skin and stick to his bones. Once he followed Kallie through the trees, they would be in the heart of the woods, surrounded by full bloom black birches. Their dark branches would be flush with leaves and flowers, canopying high above them and blocking out the light and warmth. Then they would be in the clearing, an area where even cold shadows were blocked by twisted, dead, bare branches that shouldn't be capable of such a thing.

"Are you coming?" Kallie's voice called through the trees.

Josh paused before answering, needing a second to prepare. He was, after all, about to visit the one place he swore he'd never go back to.

FOUR

Sarah sat at the bookstore counter, cursing the voicemail echoing from her cell phone's earpiece.

"Come on, Josh. Pick up!"

It'd been hours since he'd gone to meet Kallie. Sarah twisted her bottom lip with her free hand, her gaze flickering between the grandfather clock in the reading area of the store and the bay window. Each ray of orange sunlight imprinting in the pink sunset sky added to her paranoia.

If her mom hadn't left while Sarah was on shift, she would have been out there already looking for him. Instead, she had to be content with trying Josh's cell in between customers. Right now, there was no one else around so she cursed louder when her phone went straight to his voicemail again. "Son-of-a-bitch!"

"Such shocking language!" Max's mocking voice broke in from behind.

She turned to find him striding up the hall from the back door, two tote bags bearing The Playhouse logo in his left hand.

"Mmm, what treats have you brought?" Her mouth watered as the scent of hot fries reached her. Max must have raided the kitchen after finishing his shift. Thank god he'd forgiven her for abandoning him the night before.

"Not sure if you deserve them with that potty mouth."

"I thought I was alone." She ended her call and grabbed one of the bags dangling from his long fingers.

"Who were you swearing at?"

"No one." Sarah threw the tote on the counter and dug in, pulling out a tightly wrapped burger and a paper bag of fries. The hamburger was still steaming when she closed her hands around the toasted bun.

"Josh here?" Max asked as he settled on the other side of the counter, arranging two burgers in front of himself on a bed of napkins.

"That's who I was trying to call. He's not answering his phone."

Max's brow furrowed, softening slightly as he took a bite of his first burger and melted cheese oozed out its side. "You sound overly concerned," he mumbled through his mouthful. "Should I be jealous you're so worried about Josh? You'll make me think you don't like me."

"I don't like you," Sarah said, throwing a napkin at his cheesy stained chin. There was no way she was being too cautious. Max simply didn't know what had happened the last time Josh came across another person with power. He wasn't there when Arden tried to steal Josh's magick and set him alight. "Hey!" She swatted at Max's hand. After reaching for a fry, he'd snatched up her phone. "Give that back!"

"You're just in denial about how much you like me." He winked, mashing his greasy thumb on her cell's call button.

"What are you doing?" Sarah launched herself against the counter edge, grabbing for her phone but only succeeding in dropping her burger filling everywhere. She glared at Max as she scooped up her lettuce and tried to push it back in between the buns.

"It's going to voicemail." Max swapped the phone for the bag of fries.

"I know that," Sarah said. "I've been listening to Josh's 'leave a message' speech since lunch."

"Do you think he's seeing your calls and just hitting the ignore button?" Max asked.

"No, I *do not* think that." Would Josh ignore her calls?

"Maybe wherever Josh is, he's got no reception then." Max shrugged.

No reception? Of course! He must have taken Kallie out to the clearing. There wouldn't be any service in that dank place.

"Why do you care where he is?" Max asked. "I thought the hospital cleared him and everything was fine now. Can the guy not be alone if he wants to be?"

"He's not alone. He's out with his new friend."

"Oh, so you *are* jealous," Max teased, pushing the half-empty bag of fries to her side of the counter.

"I'm not jealous," Sarah snapped, curving her hand around the fries protectively so Max couldn't take any more. "I'm just looking out for Josh."

"Is his 'new friend' the hot brunette from The Playhouse?"

Max knew about Kallie? She raised onto her toes and leaned across the counter. "What do you know about her?"

"Calm down." Max laughed. "You know I prefer blonds." He winked again.

Sarah lowered back down to her heels and eyed her messy burger. Her fingertips edged toward it, but since she couldn't decide if she would eat it or throw it at Max, she left it alone. "Do you know anything about her or are you just doing your best to annoy me?"

"I'm always doing my best for you, Sar."

Ding.

Sarah's attention swung to her phone, but the grease-smeared screen remained dim.

"It's the door, genius." Max chuckled, twisting his head toward the brass bell knocked astray by the corner of the front door.

Shit! Her mom would kill her for eating at the counter where customers could see. She shoved her half-eaten burger into its wrapper and flicked the last few fries into the tote bag at her feet.

"Don't worry, it's just Eve." Max shrugged before taking the final bite of his first burger.

Sarah froze, her hand losing its grip on her hastily wrapped burger. The top bun fell onto the counter, the lettuce and sauce staining it once again. She hadn't spoken to Eve since watching her knife their former guidance counselor slash zombie-gifted-witch in the back. Sarah leaned to the left to see around Max's tall frame. *What do I even say?*

Eve was carrying a polo shirt dangling off a coat hanger. The familiar shape of a black birch tree silhouette surrounded by the circular font of 'The Blackbirch Bookstore' was stitched over the pocket.

Was Eve supposed to be working tonight? Sarah racked her brain for the shift details. She should know, she was the one who put them together.

"Can you take this mess up to the stacks?" She shoved her dinner at Max.

His second burger was unwrapped in his hand, but he put it down and collected hers, before he disappeared up the nearby stairs. With Max out of earshot, Eve strode to the counter.

"I'm here to return this." She dangled the shirt in Sarah's face. "I quit."

Sarah scanned Eve from head to toe, looking for signs she was an impostor. If it wasn't Eve, it was a great copy, wrapped in a long black cotton dress and lashings of midnight hued eyeliner smudged around judging eyes. "You're quitting?"

Eve nodded, shaking loose her black shoulder-length hair. "I think it would be better for all involved if I no longer worked here."

Sarah's mouth dropped open. Eve wasn't one for emotion, but this was robotic, even for her. "You love working here. You *begged* to work here. You work here even when you have to take orders from me, even though we—"

"Hate each other?"

"I was going to say even though we're no longer friends."

"Are you accepting my resignation or not?" Eve threw the coat hanger onto the counter.

Sarah stared at the shirt and ran her hand along her stomach. It felt as if her gut was lined with lead. She should be happy Eve was quitting. And Eve should be sad that she was leaving a job she'd stuck with, even with all the bullying at school, but she wasn't. Eve was just standing there, her pale face blank and those smoky, Kohl-rimmed eyes glaring at Sarah like they always did.

The lead gave up its grip on her stomach, replaced by the hot flush of anger. "You know if you don't work here you can't have access to the rare book collections anymore." She'd seen the darkest side of Eve the night Arden died. Someone with a willingness to kill, no matter how much Eve tried to insist it was self-defense, couldn't be trusted with such powerful texts.

Eve smirked and finally gave away an emotion.

"I don't need the books in the stacks." She sighed. "You and Josh can comb through such useless fluff if you must."

Useless? The heat switched to Sarah's cheeks, and she pulled on the collar of her work polo, tugging open the top button. How *dare* she. "We won't need the books either!" Sarah spat, glaring at Eve's back as she turned away. "We've met a *real* witch."

Eve spun, the long hem of her dress flaring out as she slammed her fist on the counter edge. "What other witch?"

Sarah tilted her head to the side, her mouth stretching into a smile. "She has *actual* power. I've seen it with my own eyes. You couldn't even fathom it."

"What is she doing here?"

"She's here to help Josh. You know, *not* here to murder people."

"And how do you know that for sure? You don't find it highly suspicious she's here? Right after someone with power tried to kill him and failed. How do you know she wasn't sent to finish the job?"

Sarah's hand returned to cradling her stomach.

"That's what I thought. You're so pathetic, Sarah."

She closed her eyes. If she couldn't see Eve, Eve couldn't see her. *Keep your face blank. Don't give her more ammunition.* "You're wrong," she croaked, her eyes opening and darting to her dark phone screen. What if bad reception wasn't the reason she couldn't reach Josh?

"I would offer to help you look into this so-called witch," Eve said. "But I know how much you *don't* need *my* help." She slammed the door behind her, the thud making Sarah jump.

Immediately wrapping her trembling hands around her cell, Sarah hit the call button again. Eve was the last person in the world she trusted, but she at least knew her. Kallie, despite Josh's glowing recommendation, was a stranger. One he was with this very minute.

"Pick up the phone!" she growled when the voicemail clicked on again.

"Are you finishing dinner or what?" Max called from the top of the stairs.

Sarah shut her eyes, her hand going to her heart. "Sorry." She tried to get her thoughts straight. "Eve quit, I've got to do some damage control, roster-wise."

"Eve quit?"

She could hear Max's delight in his question, but Sarah didn't have the time for it or to feel the same way. She hit the cancel button, her thumb immediately hovering over the call button again. The lead was back, only now it had crept into her throat. *Stupid Eve, making me paranoid.*

She contemplated leaving the store. Her mother was out picking up stock and wouldn't return for at least another hour and it was still two hours from closing. It was dinnertime. Her potential customers were more concerned with visiting the cafés across the road than the bookstore. Would Max cover for her? He'd done it before in a pinch and all she'd have to do is ask. *Mom will kill you.*

Her thumb lowered toward the call button again. Maybe Max could go looking for Josh? How would she explain it though? Max didn't believe in magick. If she sent him to the clearing, he wouldn't even be able to see the dead trees, let alone enter them to find Josh. If Eve was right and Kallie was there to hurt Josh, Max couldn't help, anyway. *And neither can you.*

She scrolled her contacts until she found the right number. The call was answered within seconds.

"He's probably out at the clearing." Sarah cleared her throat. "Can you go and at least check the woods?" That's the best any of them could do.

"Of course I can."

Sarah let out a breath. It didn't shift the lead. "Thanks, Eve."

FIVE

Eve slid her phone into her satchel and increased her pace as she hurried along the sidewalk. Even before the call she'd planned to locate Josh and the witch, now the job had been made easier. *You're not as smart as you think you are, Sarah.*

Unbeknownst to her former friend, Eve didn't need to go to the clearing directly. She had a connection to it now. As she had watched Arden fail to kill Josh, the black birch stump she leaned against gave her power. All it wanted in return was for her to throw a knife. One flick of her wrist and a man who was already dead was done away with. Now she could see what was happening in the darkest part of the woods from the safety of her bedroom. And she needed that distance.

Josh didn't know she had power like him, but she couldn't assume the other witch wouldn't sense it. Eve had to avoid her at all costs if she wanted to keep working undetected. She wasn't ready for anyone to know she'd been blessed with her own magick, especially when her reward would be more if she did what she was asked.

Arriving home, she rushed past her mom in the kitchen.

"Eve, I need your help with dinner!"

"Not tonight!" *Or any other night.* She went straight to her bedroom, locking the door behind her. She pulled off her satchel and threw it on the floor, making a beeline for her bed and kneeling beside it. Her box of candles wasn't far from reach, and it only took a few seconds to set them up in a circle on the bare floorboards.

This had been her ritual since she first visited the clearing by herself. She'd gone there not long after killing Arden, doubling back as soon as Josh and Sarah dropped her home. She couldn't stay away, not while the energy in the ancient, broken black birch stump called to her. It gave her what she desperately wanted—a share of its power, her *own* power.

Eve's energy wasn't as strong as Josh's. She couldn't call it at will and it didn't flicker along her skin, defined by its own unique hue. She didn't even have enough to manifest her own gift, but she could connect to the clearing and carry out the one thing requested of her. The power wanted her to monitor Josh. It had shown her how to find his magick, to sense it within the world.

After Josh became empowered, it was easy for her to track him. His red power burned bright—too bright. She rubbed her temple in anticipation of the headache to come. It was a small price to pay for what she'd receive. Eve flexed her hands and turned them over, studying the blue veins pulsing against her pale wrists. Soon they'd be pulsing with energy. Every time she located Josh and fed the information back to the power, it gave her more of her own.

Eve got herself ready, lighting the candles and sitting cross-legged amongst them with her hands resting in her lap. Her eyes closed on her last exhale, shutting away the glare of the flame-ravished wicks, but not the heat prickling along her bare arms.

"Where are you, Josh?" She focused, pushing her consciousness into the void, looking for the now-familiar flare of his energy. Usually it showed itself as soon as she even thought about it. Today was different. It was buried, weak, like something was blocking it. "The clearing." She switched tactics, narrowing in on the call of the dead trees.

As instantly as her thoughts touched on the desolate trunks, the power haunting the clearing made itself known to her. Blackness suffocated her senses, pushing a weight onto her chest and deepening the inky darkness behind her closed eyelids. Intuitively, her hands found the floor, her palms pressing into the wooden boards to keep herself upright. Josh was definitely in the clearing; the power wouldn't be this overwhelming if he wasn't.

Eve sparked her energy, flooding her veins with an icy coolness so comforting it was like wrapping herself in a warm blanket. She was whole when the energy was a part of her, and she used it to let the power know she was there. It answered her call, funneling more magick into her body. The chill was now a flood of ice-water, soaking her bones and drowning her.

Her lips parted into a smile, her eyes opening in time to see a shimmer of green erupt from her skin. *Yes!* The surge extinguished half of her candles, but she didn't need their light—or their protection. Her vision shifted, the small walls of her bedroom falling away and replaced by the dark, twisted limbs of the dead black birch trees.

The clearing was empty. No sign of Josh or his new friend. The power redirected her sight to the abandoned wooden house and Eve searched for Josh's energy again, this time locking onto its faint trace. It was still blocked, but that was the least of her problems. The other witch. Her magick was so strong.

"Who *are* you?"

The power wanted to know, too. Eve's limbs froze and then thawed; her skin so thickly coated in green energy she never wanted it to go away. She was all magick. All powerful. And she was more than ready to zero in on the witch.

Josh brushed the back of his neck with his fingers, flattening the tiny hairs that rose as they drew closer to the clearing. His stride shortened as the two large bare trees marking the entry came into view, and he prepared to drop his veil.

"I can't feel anything." Kallie's hand edged his shoulder. "There's no danger."

"Are all my moves obvious to you?"

"You don't know how to mask your power yet or what you're doing with it," she said. "It's okay, I can teach you."

He eyed the rough bark clinging to the tree's edges. Kallie hadn't been inside the clearing before. She didn't know how stifling it was or how its staleness tried to pull the fresh air from your lungs. If she did, she mightn't be so confident there was no hazard beyond the trees.

"It's not a nice place," he said, staring at the space between the tree trunks and trying to see through the darkened, translucent haze. He wanted to pull his veil down and bring the full light of his power to his hands, anything to chase away the unpleasantness that would try to seep into them both, but Kallie was right. He wasn't as experienced as she was. If she couldn't sense any trouble, who was he to question her advice?

"The space grows wider when you go through." He told her about the trees.

She gave his hand a squeeze, encouraging him forward.

The width of the trunks shifted, their dead bark clinging in place as they contorted to let them pass. His stomach flipped as they shrank back, closing them in once they were on the other side.

He glanced at Kallie, looking for her reaction and studying her mannerisms as she surveyed their surroundings. Could she sense the power in the circle of dead trees? Even under the protection of the veil, he could feel their rotten buzz radiating from the clawed branches.

They strode to the center, and he pointed to a soiled patch of earth imprinted on the blackened dirt floor. It was the place Arden had fallen when Eve threw his own knife into his back. His body had burned there, thanks in part to his own flames and a special powder Sarah had thrown on him. Kallie's features darkened when she saw it.

"This was the gifted man who attacked you?" She kneeled on the ground, running her hands through the air just above the outline. Her palms quivered as she passed over a white residue scattered across the ash. "Someone's been here. They've sealed the earth."

"Is that a good thing or a bad thing?"

Kallie climbed to her feet. "Arden can never be resurrected."

"So, good, right?" Josh pushed aside the part of himself that mourned Arden. His grief was for the man he'd been, not the monster.

"Not if Arden was sealed so someone else could take his place." Kallie's gaze shifted from the stain to the broken tree trunk.

Take Arden's place? Josh studied the powder mixed with the finer ash. He could almost taste it in the back of his throat, the smoky dirt cut with whatever the white stuff was. His taste buds seemed to have decided it was salt, the way his mouth suddenly filled with tart saliva. "Who would want to take his place?" He joined Kallie beside the massive stump.

"Anyone who wants power."

Her reply hung in the air as she examined the stump. Josh hadn't been this close to it before. He squinted at the cracks splitting its craggy surface, trying to see through the light bathing the clearing in a gray-tinged haze. Was it still daylight? It must be. The sun had been high in the sky when they entered the woods, but now as they settled into the clearing, he was certain it was early evening and the rest of the forest was as dark as the black trunk before them.

The old tree was as thick as it was wide, the height reaching over him, yet not so tall he couldn't see the top half had been ripped clean off. The edges of the stump had been left torn and jagged. The damage ran all the way to the base, tearing at the fat crusts of bark that stayed attached. Knife marks, which Kallie bent down to examine, marred some sections.

"Your friend, the one who killed Arden."

"Eve."

"Do you trust her?"

"She saved my life."

Kallie lifted her fingers from the grooves and gestured back to the ash and salt. "Do you think it's possible she did that?"

"I don't see how she could have. I'm sure you've realized you need our level of power to gain entry here. She doesn't have that."

"What if she talks about you and your magick, or what happened?"

"She has more to lose if she talks than I do. She won't tell anyone."

His answer seemed to satisfy Kallie. She didn't ask anything else as she continued to examine the trunk. Josh watched her, noting how her forehead crinkled when she saw something she didn't like.

"What is it?" he asked.

"Do you see anything there?" She pointed to the place where the stump met the dirt, at a section where the roots were visible above the ground.

He followed a large root to the distinct edge of a solid object and bent to get a closer look. "It's a slab of rock." He pressed the tips of his fingers into the narrow space between two roots to confirm. The earth covered most of it, but underneath the grainy surface was a hard, square base. "Do you think this tree was planted on top of something?" Why would someone do that?

"Maybe we'll find an answer in the house?" Kallie strode toward the worn structure.

Josh rose to his feet, wiping the dirt on his fingers across his jeans. The door to the house looked older up close, the black birch panels cracked, faded, and as rotten as the trees. He wondered how long it'd been out here, exposed to the strange elements of the clearing.

"Should you be doing that?" He tensed as Kallie pushed against the front door.

He raised his hands to his ears, expecting a creak as loose dirt and chips of wood fell from the doorframe, but the door swung in soundlessly.

"It looks brand new." The four walls inside were built from healthy black birch panels that could have been nailed in place that day.

Kallie stepped inside the doorway and drifted along the left wall, dragging the tips of her fingers across the planks. If she was sensing for something, she didn't appear to find it. Another forehead wrinkle marred her features as she removed her touch from the house and scanned the rest of the small, empty room. "It's such a strange little place."

Josh stayed at the doorframe and gingerly reached a hand to the closest wall and pressed his palm into it. It was ice cold, like the room had frozen in time on the inside, while the outside aged and rotted.

"Is it icy?" he asked Kallie, reluctant to step over the threshold. The floorboards looked slick, yet she walked on them with ease. He raised his head, waiting for her answer and found her slumped against the wall, both palms pressed into either side of her forehead.

"What's wrong?" He rushed forward, sliding across the floor to catch her before she crashed into the boards.

Kallie's eyelids fluttered, her entire face scrunching in pain as he wrapped his arms around her waist to keep her still. She bucked against him, slamming backward and making something outside thump. It sounded like shards of wood peeling off the damaged exterior. *Please don't collapse*, he silently begged the house. He tightened his grip on Kallie, pulling her away from the wall. This time she didn't struggle.

"Are you alright?"

He felt her head nod against his chest and loosened his hold.

"I need some air." She straightened and stumbled toward the doorway.

Josh followed her away from the house and the stump, helplessly watching as she wearily massaged her forehead. There was a flatness in her gaze, the natural flush of her cheeks faded out against her matted dark waves. She looked tired. Scared. Like in the nightmare they'd shared where she showed him the tiny room she dreamed in.

At the time she said she was bound there, and he hadn't understood what that meant. Now he knew her history, it must have been when Cade held her captive. Josh glanced back at the house. The door was open, but it was too dim to see inside. The opening looked like a dark cage that couldn't be climbed out of.

"The house, did it remind—"

"I don't know what happened," she interrupted. "It was like someone was trying to get into my mind."

"It wasn't the house that triggered you?"

"No." She moved her massage to her temples.

It was hard to feel relieved by her answer when it raised more questions. "Take a deep breath," he advised, regretting it immediately. Breathing in the clearing was like swallowing exhaust fumes.

"Maybe we should leave instead," Kallie suggested.

He scrambled to his feet, reaching down to help her up. He kept hold of her as he guided them back to the entrance, confident the forest would make her feel better. She just needed the living trees and the fresh air.

At the entrance, Kallie's hand slipped from his, as she turned to face the middle of the clearing.

"What are you looking for?"

"Nothing. Just taking it in. The energy is so strange in this place."

"I think it's better to keep away," he said. There was no reason to come back, especially now that he knew for sure there was nothing in the house.

"You're right," Kallie agreed. "It's just death and decay. Besides, it's not the clearing we have to worry about. It's the person who didn't like us being here."

"You think what happened to you was someone's not-so-subtle way of getting us to leave?"

Kallie nodded. "And I think whoever it was didn't know who they were messing with."

SIX

Eve threw herself forward as the room tilted, lifting her hands to her cheeks to keep her head in place so it wouldn't feel like it was rolling off her shoulders.

Her palms dampened at the touch of her skin, the cold sweat soaking her entire body. No wonder she was chilly, all her candles had blown out.

Wax vapor wafted from the wicks, dancing their way across her face and clouding her already altered vision. She violently swatted at the mist as if it cared that it was bothering her and scolded herself for the misplaced anger. She should direct it at the power. When it encouraged her to zero in on the witch, she assumed it would be the same as tracking Josh and only give her a sense of presence and energy. But the power wanted more. It pushed Eve further—right into a stranger's head.

She massaged her tender forehead. The headache brewing beneath the surface was shaping up to be a big one, and it wasn't even worth it. Eve was no closer to knowing anything other than the witch was powerful.

"Too damn powerful," she muttered. The witch kept Eve stuck behind a wall of hidden energy bigger than either she, or the power, had expected. "And I didn't even get to see her face."

Eve's fingers spasmed against her damp skin, a heat rushing to them that warmed the coolness of the sweaty chill. The green glow was back, reminding her of when she once experienced the thrill of magick in her veins. A crystal shard had given her a taste of Josh's power—

although she didn't know it was his at the time. The memory strengthened her will, begging her not to forget that being gifted was her right, and would be hers if she did what she was asked.

"What's next?"

The green glow surged, flooding her body with her reward. Along with the increased level of magick was one thought, uttered in an inner voice that was nothing like her own.

Discover the witch's ability.

Her ability? *Of course!* Eve's mind swirled with spell ideas and how well they'd work with her newly rewarded magick. If she was powerful enough now to track the witch *and* affect her from a distance, Eve could use that to her advantage. All she needed to do was watch and wait for the perfect opportunity.

Josh stepped aside, allowing Kallie to move ahead of him into the lamp-lit living room.

"Sarah must be home." He pointed to the brighter lights of the kitchen.

As they got closer to the wide doorway, a murmur of voices floated toward them, carried on the scent of herbs and a burst of hot steam.

Josh felt the temperature shift as soon as they stepped into the room and sighed. Finally, the chill of the clearing left his bones.

Grace stood at the stove, dropping pasta into a pot of bubbling water, and it made him question what time it was. She was rarely home early enough to cook.

It was dark when they left the clearing, confirming his suspicion that minutes and hours moved differently in that place, but surely it was still early evening? *Nope.* He glanced at the kitchen clock. It was after 8pm.

"Ah, here you are." Grace spotted him, waving a sauce splattered spoon. "And you've brought someone home for dinner!"

"Yeah. Grace, this is Kallie."

"Hello, nice to meet you." Grace waved the spoon again.

"Hi." Kallie nodded politely. "If there's not enough to go around, I can leave."

"Don't be silly." Grace dipped the spoon into her pot of sauce. "Are you from Blackbirch? I can't place your face."

"Landport."

Behind them came a thump, drawing Josh's attention to the dining table. Sarah was sitting in a chair, her arms crossed while a scowl deepened across her face.

"You look like you had a great day too, Sarah." He directed Kallie to the table and pulled out the chair next to him, gesturing for her to take a seat.

"You guys were gone, no word." Sarah glared. "I've been calling you *all* afternoon."

He dragged his cell from his back pocket. Thirty missed calls. He didn't hear his phone ring once. "I guess there's no reception out in the forest. Sorry."

"You were out in the woods?" Grace called from the kitchen sink, where she was draining the pasta.

"Yeah, we were hiking all day." Josh eyed the glasses and water jug at the center of the table and licked his parched lips. When was the last time he'd had a drink? Orange juice this morning with Sarah, sitting right where they were now. Only then she wasn't giving him death stares.

"Thirsty?" he asked Kallie, raising the jug when she nodded. "I wanted to show my friend the woods." His answer was for Grace, but he kept his gaze on Sarah, hoping she would understand.

"What did you think, Kallie?" Grace called out. "Bet Landport doesn't have a forest like ours."

"Blackbirch is very impressive."

"Well, you don't win *Best Small Forested Town* three years in a row without impressive trees." Grace began listing Blackbirch's accomplishments, the pride and joy evidence in her voice.

Sarah was not in a joyful mood.

"I waited all morning for you to come to the bookshop," she hissed at Josh. "Then I spent the whole afternoon wondering where you were!"

Josh drained his glass, putting it down after glancing at Kallie. She squeezed his shoulder and stood.

"No, I haven't heard of the *Highway Awards*, Grace, but it sounds so interesting."

Thank you, Kallie. Trust Sarah to make this awkward.

"Look." He brushed his hands through his hair, tucking the straight ends behind his ears. "I'm sorry, okay? I honestly didn't know you called."

"I was freaking out all day!"

"Well you didn't need to. We're fine."

"And how was I supposed to know that? Do you not remember what happened the last time you were out in the woods?"

"Of course, I do." Josh glanced over his shoulder. Kallie was gathering dinner plates while Grace listed the awards her bookstore had won. He refilled the glasses, wiping at stray water droplets until Grace bustled over with the saucepan, her pasta and red sauce mixed into a gooey swirl.

"So, you and Josh are old friends?" Grace asked, as Kallie set a plate in front of him.

Should he correct her and tell her they just met?

"It's so obvious." Grace beamed, slapping a huge spoonful of spaghetti bolognese on his plate.

Flecks of red sauce hit his t-shirt, joining the residue of clearing dust.

"And it's lovely to meet one of Josh's friends from before he moved here. I didn't even realize he knew anyone in Landport."

Kallie nodded along as she placed a plate in front of Sarah.

"Why does Landport sound so familiar?" Grace pursed her lips as her serving spoon hovered over Sarah's lap.

Grace was probably one thought away from remembering that Melinda lived there, and he didn't want her to make that connection.

"Didn't you go there for a pickup?" He gave Grace's elbow a slight nudge, so the spaghetti strands hung above Sarah's plate. "I'm sure I saw that town listed on an invoice from the store."

"Yeah, I think you're right." Grace tipped the spoon, splashing Sarah's bookstore polo shirt with red sauce before moving to fill Kallie's plate. "I'm glad you've come to visit. Where are you staying?"

"The Blackbirch Motel."

Grace slid into her seat at the head of the table, serving up her own food, yet keeping her clothes clean. "With your parents?"

"Yes."

"I hope they won't mind me feeding you."

"It's not an issue," Kallie replied, her attention not leaving the mountain of spaghetti in front of her. "Thank you for the invitation."

"No problem at all. Sarah, can you please get some napkins for everyone? Hiking today did you some good, Josh, you look famished."

He nodded, ignoring Sarah's audible sigh. She rolled her eyes before getting up from the table, mumbling a reply he couldn't understand.

"I hope it's okay that I'm staying," Kallie whispered, her head following Sarah as she stomped into the kitchen.

"Of course. Just avoid mentioning Melinda. Grace knew her."

Kallie's complexion lost a shade. "I wouldn't have mentioned Landport if I'd known that."

"Don't worry." The topic was forgotten now, and if Sarah didn't sabotage them as payback and bring it up again, they could get away with Grace not knowing anything.

As they ate, Grace talked about the books she'd picked up in a neighboring town, sparking Kallie's interest, and the two of them started discussing specific volumes. Kallie must have learned about them from Melinda, which made him wonder where such tomes were now. He made a mental note to ask her later, not wanting to interrupt the conversation.

Sarah kept quiet, picking at her spaghetti. He was only out of contact for a few hours. Why was she so annoyed about it? "Not hungry?"

"I ate earlier with Max."

"If it makes you feel any better, I didn't get to eat lunch."

"Why would that make me feel better?"

Josh shrugged. "Seems like you hate me right now."

Sarah put down her fork, flicking more sauce his way. He was going to have to throw his shirt out.

"It's not you." Her blue eyes drifted next to him and her whole face hardened.

She has a problem with Kallie?

Kallie had finished eating, her plate pushed to the side, elbows up on the table with her chin in her hands as she listened to Grace.

"And I said there was no way anyone had a genuine copy. I mean really, who did he take me for?" Grace laughed.

"People have tried the same thing with my mom when they hear about her collection of Crystalpedia hardcovers," Kallie said.

"Her mom?" Sarah mouthed at Josh, rolling her eyes again.

"How about we clean up?" He nudged Sarah, standing up and stacking the dirty plates together.

He didn't understand Sarah's issue. "What's Kallie going to say?" he whispered when he and Sarah were at the kitchen sink. "'The books we're talking about belong to Josh's dead aunt. You might know her? You grew up together. She was the older sister of your best friend.'"

Come on, Sarah.

"Why does she need to talk at all?" Sarah's voice raised in volume before she grimaced and lowered it. "It's all lies."

Ah, so that was Sarah's problem: the lies. She was honest to a fault. No wonder everything out of Kallie's mouth was bugging her. He should count himself lucky Sarah had kept his secrets. But if anything was stronger than her honesty, it was her loyalty. And Kallie didn't have that yet.

"It's all necessary," he said. "She can't exactly tell your mom about how we really know each other."

Sarah glanced back at the table, holding Kallie in her sights. "Fine, that makes sense, but that's not what's bothering me."

It wasn't? "What's the problem then?"

Sarah's eyes found him, softening under his stare. "I couldn't get a hold of you today."

This again? Couldn't he go places without her?

"The last time you were in the clearing with another witch, they tried to murder you."

"Kallie's not trying to kill me."

"I know you trust her—"

"I do," he whispered. "She's the only one who knows what I'm going through and is going through it too."

"I'm just trying to look out for you."

Josh sighed. "I know, but I don't need you to. I'm not sick anymore. I can look after myself and I have Kallie if I need help."

"And I can't help you because I'm not gifted, right?"

"Arden hurt you, Sarah," Josh reminded her. "And I didn't know enough about my power to stop him. If something happened to you again... it's just safer for you to not be in that situation."

Sarah's head dropped, hiding her expression. Was she frowning? He steeled himself for an argument. As well as being honest and loyal, Sarah didn't like to let things go.

"Eve quit her job today."

He didn't expect her to say that. "Did you speak to her?"

"Yeah, she came into the store."

"Did she talk about anything else?" He twisted his neck to check on Kallie. She was safe at the dining table. What if Eve found out she was here and did to Kallie what she did to Arden?

"No... she just handed back her work shirt."

"That's all?"

Sarah nodded, her blue eyes fixing to the sink.

Was she lying to him? "It's probably a good thing Eve won't be in the store anymore," Josh said. Without access to the books, how much harm could she really do? He glanced at Kallie again. Maybe she could use her magick to get a sense of Blackbirch's wannabe witch? Find out once and for all if she was a threat. "I guess that's one less thing we need to worry about."

Sarah cleared her throat. "Yeah."

That was all she had to say? Josh's gaze crossed to the window above the sink and the thicket of trees surrounding the house. In between the black birch branches, he could just make out the shape of Max's lit bedroom window in the distance.

"I'm surprised Max is home and not here."

Sarah's shoulders shrugged. "He ate already."

"Yeah, but when has he ever not had seconds?"

"Or thirds."

"Or fourths." He chuckled.

"And fifths and sixths!"

Was that almost a laugh? He'd have to remember that for the next time he pissed Sarah off; Max cheers her up.

Sarah's untouched plate sat on the bench and Josh watched her reach into the lower cupboard for an empty container to pour the spaghetti into.

"I'm going to run this over to Max's," she said. "Text me if those two start talking about anything else."

"Sure." Josh nodded, looking at the table again. He must have kept his eyes on Kallie longer than he thought, because when he turned back to the sink, Sarah had left.

SEVEN

Sarah stomped her feet along the path to Max's, cursing Josh for dismissing her concerns so easily. He was so eager to finally have answers, he wouldn't even entertain the idea Kallie might not be there just to help him. But could Sarah really say she wasn't? Josh had come out of the clearing unscathed. Kallie didn't try to murder him.

"Damn, Eve," she growled, a puff of cool air escaping her curled lips. Her former friend had made her so paranoid. Eve would probably laugh at the way Sarah had been acting tonight.

Unless she's right?

Kallie had mentioned she lived in Landport, only a few hours' drive from Blackbirch. Assuming she hadn't lied about the house fire that killed her and her mother, there ought to be something in Landport's local paper. Maybe Sarah could use Max's computer to look it up and try to soothe her racing mind.

Approaching the front door, she glanced in the lit window. The sheer curtains didn't hide Mr. and Mrs. Ryan sitting tensely across from each other at the empty dinner table.

Whenever Max was eating with her and on his third helping, she often joked his parents didn't feed him. He always said they were too busy ignoring him. Looking at them now, perched in their chairs the way they were, she could see why he said that. His folks were too caught up in their own issues to be thinking about him.

Maybe this wasn't the best time to drop by? Sarah stepped back, inching her raised hand away from the doorbell. Unfortunately, in her bid to avoid looking at her husband, Mrs. Ryan saw her through the window and waved her to the front door.

This won't be weird at all, Sarah grimaced as the door peeled away from the frame. "Mrs. Ryan, how are you?"

"Hi, Sarah. Come on in." The friendly greeting sounded strained.

Mr. Ryan gave her a quick nod, the gesture a far cry from his usual smile-filled greetings.

"Um, we had some extra food I thought Max might want." She raised the container of spaghetti.

Mrs. Ryan's face lit up as she collected the leftovers. "Thank you. You know where to find him."

Sarah sure did. She climbed the nearby stairs, quickly reaching Max's room. The distinctive beat of dance music vibrated through the closed wooden door, and she timed her knock to the pumping bass, struggling to hold in a laugh. Max would find it hilarious.

He was scowling when the door cracked open, the odd expression taking a few seconds to melt once he recognized her.

"What's wrong?" When was the last time she'd seen him in a bad mood? She couldn't even remember.

"Nothing." He leaned sideways, glancing past her. "Did my parents let you in?"

"Yeah, your mom did."

His face twisted again, his lips pursing together.

"Is something the matter?"

"No."

"Can I come in then?"

Max moved aside, pushing the door wide enough for her to slip through. His bedroom was the literal manifestation of mess, with every surface covered in misplaced junk. Even the sound system blasting the music was draped in t-shirts and jackets.

Max switched the speakers off, clearing a bunch of magazines and loose papers from his bed so she could sit. She didn't want to crash on the end of his mattress like she normally did, so she moved to the far wall, hovering around the space where his desk sat. Max's computer was buried somewhere beneath his work uniform and a math textbook.

"I have no idea how you find anything in here?" She pinched the sleeve of his monogrammed 'Playhouse' shirt between her index finger and thumb and threw it toward the bed. Now she had a clear view of his chair and pulled it out, sitting down while she tried to spot his keyboard.

Max came up behind her, snatching at bits and pieces until he revealed the monitor.

"I have a system," he explained as he balled the navy button-up she'd seen him wearing at school last week and threw it toward the hamper. His aim was off. The shirt hit the basket before joining a pair of dirty jeans on the floor.

"I brought you bolognese." She brushed aside a scuffled sneaker and found the computer mouse.

"Thanks." Max cleared a stack of notebooks directly in front of her.

"I need to borrow your computer for something." She leaned forward and tugged the keyboard toward her. It was cleaner than the bottom of the dark wooden desk, which had a thin film of dust on it. No surprise there. Max looked after his tech. She counted three computer towers stacked next to each other, and Max revealed another monitor as he finished clearing the rest of his clothes.

"Which one am I looking at here?" Her eyes shifted back and forth between the identical lit screens featuring a picture of them together at The Playhouse as the wallpaper. Max really loved his job.

"You can use either," he replied, before pointing to the closest monitor when she stared at him blankly. "Is your Internet down or something?"

"No." Sarah clicked on the browser. "I just couldn't look this stuff up at home."

Max snorted, his mouth opening wide to make what she knew would be a dirty remark. She cut him off. "Your parents are fighting again. You okay?"

Max's merry mood instantly evaporated. "They can't even talk to each other without arguing."

He added a shrug like it wasn't a big deal, but she knew him too well. "Are you okay?" she repeated.

Max snorted again. "Of course."

She listened to him force a laugh after flopping into the middle of the mattress and pulling out his phone. She regarded his sudden interest in scrolling the screen as a sign he didn't want to talk. That was fine. She had other things to do.

Sarah typed 'Kallie Jacobs' into the search and waited for the results to load. It gave her two. She clicked on the first link, which led to a three-paragraph news item about a sixteen-year-old named Jerry Miller. He'd drowned in Landport earlier that year. *And this has come up because?* She sighed and scrolled to the final section. The last sentence caught her eye: '*Kallie Jacobs, the only witness, was not available for comment*'.

Hmm. So, she'd witnessed a guy drowning... Sarah clicked back to her results and read the next listing. This news piece was about the house fire and it surprised her how she was both annoyed and relieved that Kallie hadn't lied about it.

"What are you doing, anyway?" Max's voice broke through Sarah's thoughts. She turned to see him stomach down on his bed, eying the computer screen over her shoulder.

"Just some research." She tried to make it sound boring, but he got up and settled behind her, leaning in to read the piece. She could feel his warm breath on her ear and her nose twitched at its salty scent. "You still smell like fries."

"And you reek of boredom. What's so interesting about a house fire?" He flopped back on his bed, picking up a discarded tennis ball and throwing it in the air before catching it.

"You're the boring one," she muttered under her breath, focusing on the article. It covered what Kallie told them: the fire department put out a blaze, the owner perished, and her teenage daughter was rescued with non-life-threatening injuries. Sarah hovered the mouse over the back button before she noticed a related link. This one was about a home invasion the same night. Another local woman in the street died. She recognized the name instantly. Melinda Tucker. Josh's aunt.

Sarah clicked on an email icon and sent the link to herself. As she prepared to shut down the browser, another name caught her eye—Detective Brewer. He was mentioned in the house fire article. She clicked the link highlighting his name, and the site refreshed with a listing for everything featuring him. The oldest article named him as an entity to be reckoned with on Landport's force. He had a high close rate for cases and had risen quickly through the ranks.

Sarah thought that was notable until she remembered that Landport wasn't much bigger than Blackbirch. Detective Brewer's work as an officer was impressive, but it was a small pool of talent. Blackbirch's own sheriff was the sheriff because his father had been and his grandfather and so on. Yes, he still had to train and pass all the requirements, but those were formalities in the eyes of the town. Sheriff Stevens was always going to be the lawman in Blackbirch, the same way Sarah knew she'd one day run her mom's bookstore. It seemed to be a similar case for this guy. In Landport, he was a third-generation cop, and the best candidate a small town had to offer.

One article Sarah skimmed showed a picture of the detective. *Don't you look smug.* Even from the black-and-white image, she could tell. She glanced at the latest piece under Brewer's name. This one also contained a photo, but it was like a terrible before-and-after.

Gone was the smugness, replaced with a sneer. Sarah didn't need to read past the first section of the headline to know something was amiss. '*Disgraced Former Detective...*' it began, listing the downfall of Brewer. A spate of deaths and his mishandling of the cases had led to him being dropped from the force. She looked up his case history. The last three he'd investigated had been about Josh's Aunt, Kallie's mother, and Jerry Miller. They all involved Kallie. *That can't be a coincidence.*

Sarah clicked on the next link, her mind swirling. The news article confirmed some of her suspicions. Kallie was the key witness in all the cases, and if Brewer was to be believed, a suspect.

He'd named her as the person of interest in all the deaths, a view that had him suspended from the force. They removed him when Kallie vanished. He then became a key figure in *her* disappearance. That case was still ongoing. Sarah read the date of the article. *Four months ago.* Kallie had already been missing for a few weeks by then.

It was definitely time to check out her other claims. Sarah decided to start with Cade. It wasn't a common name, which would hopefully mean some results. When the search refreshed, Sarah's breath caught in her throat.

Cade was the surname of Julian Cade, a professor who'd made headlines a few years earlier after convincing two of his students to go to a national park with him. Neither of them survived.

Sarah knew the story. She'd even spoken to Josh about it once. Cade claimed he'd found a crystal containing magick, and in his bid to prove it was genuine, he buried one student alive and pushed the other off a cliff. He then disappeared. If what Kallie was saying was true, he resurfaced, set the fire at her house, killed Melinda, and kept Kallie captive.

Sarah sat back from the screen, not realizing she'd moved so close to it. Now she had a lot of questions, but would Kallie answer them if she asked? *Go to Josh.* If Sarah showed him the articles, he'd find out the truth.

She emailed more links to herself, cleared the browser history, and shut it down. Max was still lying across his bed, abandoning the tennis ball for his phone.

"I'm done!" She pitched up her voice, not wanting to raise Max's curiosity. If he asked her more about what she'd been looking at, she might just tell him everything—and she promised Josh she wouldn't do that.

Max lowered his screen. "Wanna get out of here and grab something sweet at The Playhouse? The specialty tonight is your favorite, Chocolate Mousse."

"And you didn't bring me any of that earlier?" She kicked a leg up and tapped the side of his bed with her ballet flat.

"We can get some now."

She wanted to say yes, but hesitated. The best dessert in the world wouldn't distract her from everything she'd found out about Kallie. She needed to talk to Josh, now.

"Uh, rain-check? I've got a heap of homework to do."

"You're picking schoolwork over me? Over fluffy chocolate heaven?"

"Afraid so. Tomorrow night, I promise." Sarah stood from the chair. Her offer seemed to pacify Max, his good mood returning as she left the room.

Maybe she should have gone with him to The Playhouse and told him everything while they devoured a mousse or two. It was strange not sharing any of this with her best friend. *He won't believe you.* Max would want proof, and Josh had already refused to show anyone else his magick. She wondered if that stubbornness would extend to questioning Kallie, and how partial Josh could be when it came to her.

"Leaving already, Sarah? Usually you're here until midnight."

Mrs. Ryan caught her at the bottom of the stairs. "Yeah, I've got studying to do. Goodnight." She waved as she passed Max's mom, letting herself out.

The chill of the Ryan's dining room extended to the night air, and she hugged herself to keep warm, missing the cardigan she'd left at work.

As she reached her front yard, a figure strode toward her in the dark.

"Josh?"

"Hi, I just walked Kallie back to her motel. Her and your mom finally stopped talking about books."

"Oh, yeah?" Did Kallie talk to him about how many dead bodies she's seen. Sarah pulled her phone from her pocket and brought up the emailed links.

"Kallie's probably read as many books as you. I think you guys would get along."

Maybe. If she really could be trusted.

"Looks like Kallie will stick around a while, at least I hope she does. It's nice, you know. Having someone here who… understands."

He looked so happy. *Damn you, Josh.* Sarah glanced at her phone. She couldn't be the one to destroy that, not when she'd seen the alternative. She didn't want mopey Josh back.

"I'm glad you're... happy." She hoped it didn't sound as bitter out loud as it did in her head. It mustn't have, given the way Josh smiled at her again. "So, did Kallie happen to mention anything more about what she's been doing the last few months?" She tried to make the question sound casual, but she knew she hadn't as soon as she finished asking.

"What do you mean?" A clipped tone entered Josh's voice.

"I was just wondering what she's been doing since escaping Cade. I know she was trying to find you, but that can't have been all she was doing."

"Kallie was running for her life. She told us both Cade was, and still is, looking for her."

"But that's all?"

"Is that not enough for you? She lost her family and was kept in a small, dark room by a murderer. Would you be doing anything other than just trying to survive?"

Okay. He was not ready to read the articles she'd found. Sarah nodded at the front door, hoping to gracefully change the subject. "Do you have keys? I forgot mine."

Her question seemed to calm Josh. "Like it won't be open." He chuckled. "This is Blackbirch, no one locks their doors."

With his back to her, she linked the articles to a new text, and as Josh disappeared inside the house, Sarah sighed and pressed send.

EIGHT

Landport. Five months ago.

Kallie peered over her book stack, eyeing Jerry Miller. He was leaning back in his chair, his legs propped on the library table next to a pile of books—head swaying to whatever was playing through his headphones.

If he opened his eyes, he'd see how close his dirty shoes were to knocking down the books. Maybe if they fell, the librarian would ask him to leave. Then she would have the research room to herself. She should anyway. She was a senior on a study period, and he was a sophomore, most likely ditching class. Although who ditches class and goes to the library? *People like you who choose researching over hanging out with friends.*

She wondered if her few friends remembered her. It'd been so long since she'd seen them. She could probably disappear, and they wouldn't notice. All because she was too caught up in visions of fire.

That's why she was really in the library. She needed to find something—anything—to explain why she was seeing such things. Even now, as she watched Jerry and his bouncing jet-black hair, images of flowing water forced their way through her mind.

"It's great, isn't it?" Jerry caught her staring.

"What?"

He pulled his sneakers from the table, narrowly missing the books, and walked over. She didn't want to chat, but if she stayed silent, she would have gone the whole day without talking to another soul, and she couldn't do that again. Not for the third day in a row and with another night in an empty house ahead of her. *Mom and her shitty night shifts.*

"Here." Jerry held out his headphones, shaking them side-to-side.

She slipped them on, mentally preparing to be blasted with something awful like heavy metal music. The only beat was the steady thump of running water. She snatched the headphones from her ears and handed them back.

"It's the stream in the forest." Jerry beamed. "Do you know it?"

Kallie nodded. The small body of water was just inside the stretch of woodland across from her house.

"I get some great recordings out there." He held a headphone to one ear like he couldn't be without the sound, even for a second.

"It is a nice place." At least it used to be. She rarely went into the trees anymore. Not since the witch who lived at the tree line started watching her.

Jerry switched the water sounds off, glancing around as he lowered his headphones. "I've found something out there," he whispered, leaning toward her. The smile on his face was so big, she envied he had something in his life that made him so happy.

"What do you mean?"

Jerry's green eyes scanned the room, settling on her. "There's an underground cavern the stream runs from... and it has things in it."

She wrinkled her forehead. "What type of things?"

"Well, you know how everyone says the lady who lives in the woods is a witch."

Kallie swallowed thickly, nodding.

"I think it's stuff that belongs to her."

"Why?"

"Because." Jerry raised his eyebrows. "It's weird things."

Weird things? *Says the guy listening to recordings of water.* She glanced at her book stack. She had bigger things to worry about.

"I can show it to you if you don't believe me."

"It's not that I don't, I'm just busy."

Jerry eyed her books. "You interested in fires?"

Kallie shifted in her seat. "It's for a science assignment."

"I've got all the volumes on water." Jerry gestured back at his table. Now the pile of blue books made sense, and the images. What didn't make sense was why the books about water were making her feel sick. She swallowed again, trying to push down the bile coating her throat.

"We'd make a great team; Fire and Water." Jerry laughed before putting his headphones on and dropping into his chair.

He didn't put his feet back on the table, but he started thumbing through his books. As Kallie watched his head sway again, the images of water returned, bombarding her until a headache worked its way in from her temples.

She placed a hand on her stomach. An ache in the pit of her belly joined her nausea and throbbing head. It wasn't a cold or a bad reaction to the cheese sandwich she'd eaten for lunch; it was this boy and his water.

"Dammit," she muttered, closing the open book on her table before moving over to Jerry's. He looked up from his page when her chair legs screeched along the tiled floor, the big smile returning to his face.

"The stream," Kallie said as he slipped off his headphones. "When did you say you wanted to go back?"

Sarah knocked on Eve's bedroom door, hoping she wasn't about to regret how she'd chosen to spend her morning. When she texted the links to Eve the night before, it was to get a second opinion, not join her in some crazy casting, yet here she was.

Sarah wasn't even sure the articles were proof of anything anymore. Hindsight and sleep had given her a new perspective. They made her realize that while the articles may be full of the facts about each event, it didn't mean it was the truth.

If a factual article had been written about Arden's death, it would state a seventeen-year-old girl stabbed a hero firefighter to death; the revenge of a troubled student against the only teacher who tried to help her. It would be a major headline, not just swirling gossip like the current rumors of Arden skipping town. But none of it would come close to the truth of what happened that night.

Sarah hadn't accounted for that when she found those articles. She'd forgotten that Kallie said magick caused her house fire, wielded by Melinda's murderer—a crime reported as a home invasion gone wrong. There was more to those stories. The same way there was more to what happened to Arden. Sarah had been foolish for getting so suspicious and wished she could take it back, even more so after accepting Eve's invite to come over.

If Sarah was wary of Kallie, Eve was downright paranoid about her. Her texts demanding Sarah come over still pinged her phone even as she'd walked up Eve's driveway.

"Finally, you're here!" Eve said after flinging her bedroom door open.

Sarah took in the attic space Eve's mom had directed her to. It was a far cry from the childhood room she remembered Eve having. That had been in the main part of the house and decorated with over-sized purple pillows and posters of Unicorns. Eve's new space was bare of anything except a simple framed bed, a wooden bookshelf, and a collection of candles and crystals rivaling the stock at the bookstore.

"It sounds like the girl who's come to visit Josh has a shady past." Eve pulled Sarah in, shutting the door so loudly behind her it made Sarah flinch.

She'd had only given Eve three news articles. Eve didn't know Kallie had also been killed in the house fire, that she had power because Melinda gave it to her before being murdered, or of Kallie's link to Cade.

Eve knew as much about the dark history of Professor Cade as Sarah did. Given the way Eve was acting based on the small snapshot of info she had, Sarah was glad she hadn't revealed the true extent of Kallie's life. She wasn't sure Eve could handle it. It was hard to miss Eve's signature midnight eyeliner smudged on thicker and darker than usual but still failing to distract from the shadows under her eyes.

Was guilt over Arden keeping Eve up? The whole night was never far from Sarah's thoughts and she assumed it was plaguing Eve too. Until she remembered who Eve was and that her soul was as black as her dyed hair.

"We've all got history we're not proud of," Sarah said, hoping Eve would ignore the importance of the articles. Just like she did everything else.

"You said yesterday this girl was a witch like Josh."

Sarah nodded, curious to see where Eve was going with her question.

"What's her ability?"

"Her ability?"

"With the magick comes a gift," Eve said sharply. "Josh has strength, Arden had fire. What is this witch's gift?"

Sarah drew a blank. Had Kallie mentioned it? "It hasn't come up."

Eve glared at her. "Of course you don't know, that would make it too easy," she muttered.

"Make what too easy?"

"Nothing. You really don't have a clue?"

"I remember that she told us her magick helps with her natural ability," Sarah said.

"What natural ability?"

"She sees things. Visions."

"She's a psychic with supernatural power?"

"Yes."

Eve's mouth dropped open. "That's just great," she muttered. "Are you sure?"

"I saw her have a vision. She used a spell called glimpsing to look into Josh's past."

"Glimpsing? Glimpsing? Are you positive?" Eve strode to her bookshelf, pulling the notebook she always had with her from the end of the second shelf.

"Pretty sure. Why?"

"Here!" Eve squealed like Max did when it was tater-tot day in the cafeteria, the show of emotion surprising Sarah. "I have the details of that spell. We could try it ourselves. See what we can find out about her."

"*We're* going to cast it?" Eve had officially lost it, and Sarah had voluntarily come over to see it happen in real time. "We can't do that, Eve."

"Yes, we can." She dismissed Sarah's concerns with a wave of her hand. "We're not gifted like them so it won't be as strong, but we can do it." Eve raided her bookshelf, pulling down a glass jar of yellow sand and handing it to Sarah. "Make a circle."

"Fine." Sarah took the jar and began pouring it out on the bare floorboards. "But as soon as this doesn't work, I am out of here."

"Hold this too." Eve ignored Sarah's promise and passed her another glass jar. This one was full of dead spiders.

"Ew!" Sarah gagged. "Can't we just cast another love spell on Ashton Jones like we did when we were twelve?"

"Take a seat." Eve directed Sarah to one of two satin pillows she threw on the floor before she finished dressing the circle with black candles.

Sarah lowered herself slowly, trying not to drop her jar of spider bodies.

Eve sat opposite her, two items in her hands. One was her own jar, filled with blood-colored sand, the other was Arden's knife.

Sarah stiffened when she saw the long silver blade. "I can't believe you still have that."

"It's only a knife." Eve put it in her lap before leaning forward and unscrewing the lid of Sarah's jar.

Thank god the spiders were dead, Sarah's skin crawled just looking at them. She watched Eve close her eyes and wondered if she was supposed to do the same before deciding she'd rather keep them open. She eyed the knife again, then watched Eve's lips move as hushed words escaped them in a language she didn't recognize.

"Pour the dirt in the jar," Eve said.

Now she's understandable. Sarah rolled her eyes.

"Picture the witch in your mind. Since you've met her, I need you to make her the focus of the spell."

"Her name is Kallie. She's a human, Eve, just like us." Sarah eyed the knife again. *Just like Arden was... or had been.*

"The jar." Eve jutted her chin.

Sarah placed the jar between them and leaned back as Eve threw in the red dirt. It sank to the bottom of the glass, filtering through the dead spiders. Long stick legs straightened and curled as the arachnids thrashed through the sand.

"What the f—"

"Sarah!" Eve latched onto her wrists, holding her down.

Their eyes met, Eve's stare burning into Sarah's brain.

"Picture the witch," Eve demanded.

Sarah squirmed, trying to weasel out of Eve's iron grip.

A chill settled over the room, icy air prickling along Sarah's neck. She wiggled her head to pull her long hair loose, but the strands stuck to her skin as the temperature burst into a suffocating heat.

Cracks popped like the air was creating a spark, and a haze rose around them, borne from the candle flame vapors.

Sarah blinked, trying to force her eyes to focus. The vapor looked green. How was that possible? As the strange haze clouded her vision, Sarah's eyelids grew heavy, closing against her will and plunging her into darkness.

A field of flames broke the sudden black, its orange glow playing behind her closed eyes clearer than if she was staring at a TV screen. *Eve's spell worked?*

The glimpse shifted, framing a two-story wooden house ravaged in flames. A blond woman, around the same age as Sarah's mom, stood in the middle of wheat stalks, with her outstretched hands formed into fists. Energy lit her skin—purple sparks of magick flicking across her knuckles the same way Josh manifested his power.

This witch's power was strong and so abundant it blotted out the color of her alabaster skin. It was especially rich in her right hand, which she opened to reveal a circular object. The amulet was made from a thin ring of silver, the center an outline of a tree.

Sarah memorized its details, from the roots lining the base, the branches stretching across the side and top, to the delicate leaves adorned with tiny crystals. It looked so familiar she tried to place where she'd seen it, before realizing it was the tree that sparked her memory. It was a black birch.

The woman closed her fingers around the amulet, dropping to her knees next to the body of a girl.

"Kallie." The whispered name escaped Sarah's lips when she recognized who she was staring at, and it was met with what sounded like a knowing gasp from Eve. Why? Eve didn't know Kallie.

The vision Kallie lay covered in ash, her white T-shirt and jeans already streaked with dirt. Her lips were blue, the smoke having choked the life out of her. Sarah sniffed, her head swimming with the woody scent of soot. It traveled to her throat, a thick coating clinging to the back of her mouth. She wanted to gag and cough it up. *It's not real.*

The blond woman kneeled at Kallie's body and placed the amulet over her heart. This had to be Josh's Aunt Melinda. Her purple energy flared, soaking into it like rain feeding the tree.

The power filtered toward a crystal engraved in the end of a branch. There were seven crystals in total: three clear, three that sparkled, and one with a dark tint. The purple energy funneled through a sparkling crystal before coating Kallie's body, soaking through her ash stained shirt, flooding her skin, and seeking the damage from the fire.

As Melinda sat back, pulling her magick with her, Kallie's chest rose, inflated by a ragged breath. Another followed until a cry escaped her throat and her eyes flung open. The amulet continued to glimmer; the energy retreating through the crystal that had been used and turning it clear.

Kallie bolted upright, tearing the ornament from her skin. Her wide stare fixed on Melinda and narrowed in recognition.

Melinda summoned her energy again, throwing it into the surrounding flames. The purple power covered the raging fire and attached to a shimmering ripple at its heart. The ferocity died, and the flames smoldered before the vision shifted.

This time, Melinda was dying, sprawled on the floor of a house so darkly lit it was impossible to see its surroundings. A gash, deep enough that bone appeared at its core, ran across her chest. Blood dripped freely from the wound, coloring the wooden slats beneath her, soaking into her long blond hair and dying it a sickly red.

To Melinda's right, bathed in shadows, sat another figure; a brunette with dark waves. *Is that Kallie?* She was leaning over Melinda, watching her slip away.

The vision faded and Sarah squeezed her eyelids, waiting for the next scene to invade her senses. There had to be more.

"You can open your eyes now." Eve had broken contact, her cold fingers no longer wrapped around Sarah's wrists. "We've glimpsed everything."

What? No. Sarah swallowed; her throat raw. She needed water. Like a gallon of it. "Kallie's here looking for that amulet," she croaked. "She said the man who killed Josh's aunt is trying to find it."

Eve's features twisted. "The witch we just saw was Josh's aunt?"

Shit, Eve didn't know that. "Her name is… was Melinda," Sarah said. Would Josh be mad at her for telling Eve his aunt was gifted too? At least she hadn't spilled about his mom.

"I don't understand?" Eve said. "How can Josh be okay with Kallie if she was involved in his aunt's death?"

"Because she told him someone else killed her."

"You saw that vision. Did you see anyone else there?"

"It was dark." Sarah tried to picture it again. All she could see was Kallie watching Melinda die. "It didn't show her hurting Melinda," she pointed out. They saw so little. It couldn't have been all there was to the situation.

Eve scoffed. "You're so naïve, Sarah. Kallie was letting her die after inflicting that wound."

"And you know that for sure, do you? Why are you so certain? Is that what you would do?"

"Yes, it was in the murderer handbook. Lesson number one."

Sarah cast her eyes down. She knew this hadn't been a good idea. Her gaze swept the jar of spiders. They'd stopped moving again.

Eve got up from the circle, snatching her pillow and throwing it onto her bed. Her satchel sat on the end of the mattress and she pulled it open.

"What are you doing?" Sarah asked.

"You think we should talk to Kallie first, right? Find out her side of the story?"

She was thinking that. Was Eve going to be logical? "I agree that's best."

"Fine, let's go. You said she was staying at the Blackbirch Motel."

Sarah nodded, climbing to her feet and leaving the jar of dead spiders where it was. Eve had taken the knife from the circle and added it to her bag. "Do you really think that's necessary?"

"We don't have power, remember? The last time we went up against a witch, that blade was the only thing that saved us."

"Still, maybe we should talk to Josh first? Who's to say Kallie will listen if we go to her demanding the truth. Josh, on the other hand... she'd be more likely to confess to him."

Eve stopped packing her satchel. Had Sarah made her mad? She glanced at the doorway, trying to remember if it was locked.

"Fine." Eve nodded.

Another reasonable answer. What was going on?

"We'll speak to Josh first. How about you ask him to meet with you alone at home in an hour? I'll come by then."

"You want to split up? Why? What will *you* be doing?"

"Just in case this Kallie person is dangerous, like we saw during the glimpse, I will gather supplies for a protection spell. It might not work against her level of magick, but it's better than nothing."

"Do you really think she's that much of a threat?" Despite seeing what Eve had, Sarah couldn't help but feel they were missing something.

Eve threw her satchel onto her shoulder and strode toward the door. "Do you really want to find out?"

NINE

Landport. Four months ago.

Kallie placed her hands on her shaking thighs, her back hunched as her breath escaped her mouth in ragged heaves.

"Jerry... you have to... slow down."

He turned but kept running, skipping himself backward as a grin lit his face. "Come on, I thought you liked to run?"

She pushed her sneakers off the mushy forest floor. Five feet from catching him, she tripped on an exposed tree root. Her knees struck the ground first, ricocheting pain through her limbs. Her outstretched hands hit it next, forcing her to brace for the sharp snap she knew was coming. Instead, the image of Jerry floating face down in a body of water flashed through her mind.

"Jerry!"

He came thundering back toward her. "You okay?" His skinny arms reached down.

"Don't go in the water."

Jerry laughed, his concern slipping from his features. "We're going underneath it, remember? The cavern is under the water."

Kallie pressed herself further into the dirt, cradling her head. It was like the vision was attaching itself to her brain, clawing its way in so she wouldn't forget how blue he looked in the water. The images she saw had never done that before.

"Come on, we don't want to lose the light."

Jerry gently helped her sit up, and she studied the dirt path ahead that continued into a thicket of trees before dropping into the stream.

"What if I can't go on?" she asked.

"Did you hurt yourself?" His gaze swept her legs. There was no bruising or blood, just grains of earth clinging to her bare olive skin.

"No. I don't feel good."

"Wait here then. I can come back for you. I'll only be a few minutes."

"No!" Kallie latched onto his wrists, as Jerry's eyes widened. "I don't want you to go."

"Nothing will happen." He chuckled. "I've been in the cavern hundreds of times."

"Then why do you need to go back?"

"We talked about this." Jerry's voice softened as he slid from her grip. "We'll go in for a few minutes, just enough time for me to record something good."

Kallie glanced toward the stream again. The soft babbling of water rose through the trees, the edge of the tunnel planted in the forest floor as if it was a doorway. To go through it was a steady drop into a dark pit. Like Alice falling down the rabbit hole.

"It's not scary inside," Jerry promised. "Don't look so freaked out." He laughed at her again. "The cavern is large enough to stand in." He nudged a sneaker toe toward her. "Especially for two shorties like us."

She smiled and then tried to take it back, scolding herself for letting him break her resolve with an inside joke. Jerry was always coming up with nicknames for them. At least he'd finally moved on from calling himself Water-Boy and her Fire-Girl.

"It'll be dark underground," she said. "We should have brought a flashlight."

"Nah, there's plenty of light," Jerry promised. "Besides, if we need more, you can get some flames going, Fire-Gir—"

"Don't say it." Her hand flew up.

Jerry slapped it like she'd been looking for a high five and not a way to silence him.

"The water," Kallie said. "How much is there?"

"There are only trickles, I swear. Most of it's trapped behind the rocks and it all runs out of the cavern and into the stream outside."

Jerry's dark cheeks had a touch of color from their run. His black hair looked healthy out in the sunshine, the wayward strands ruffling in a light breeze. Staring at him now, the vision of him drowning seemed impossible. How could someone so full of life be in any danger?

"Come on, it rained last night which means there will be plenty of water flow." Jerry pulled a sound recorder from his pocket.

Surely it wouldn't take long for a recording? It didn't when she and Jerry visited the stream a few weeks ago. It was going into the cavern for the first time that was throwing her off. She didn't like dark places.

"Are we going?" He squeezed her hand.

She stared at his fingers wrapped around her. She'd never seen a vision as clearly as his death. The already fading image seemed forced, not as certain as that haunting car accident. That tragedy had happened, she knew it. Jerry face down in the water? It wasn't true. It couldn't be. He loved water. He was Water-Boy. Her imagination—her paranoia— was on overdrive. *Just like mom always says.*

"Okay." She squeezed his hand.

He pulled her from the ground, overacting the movement, gasping and clutching at his lower back.

"Stop it." She nudged him, prompting Jerry's laughter to fill the air. "Race you?" She pointed toward the sound of the water, scowling when he took off before she'd gotten into the starter position. "Hey!"

"Come on, Fire-Girl!"

Kallie watched him fly along the path, dust kicking up as his sneakers bit into the earth. She smiled and followed Jerry underground, where she had to wrap her arm around herself to keep warm.

The air circulating the bottom of the cavern bordered on freezing, fed by the cool water dribbling through the crevices of the hard walls.

She lifted her left sneaker and shook her foot, trying to rid her sole of the wetness seeping in from the floor puddles.

She had to squint to see the further they moved from the entrance, which was their only light source. Jerry might not need a flashlight to explore the cavern, but she did.

"Careful." He grabbed her elbow and guided her around a puddle.

"Not much water, hey?" She shot him an unimpressed look.

"Just follow me." He weaved over rocks, expertly scaling their uneven surfaces.

"You said it wouldn't be dark." Kallie stuck close to his back.

"It's not *that* dark."

"You also said there were only trickles of water. I'm hearing more than a trickle." She rubbed her right ear, trying to work out if the steady thrum was the water dripping around them or the forest stream on the other side of the wall.

"It's just a few drips along the walls, maybe some puddles." He slowed down and helped her avoid a big rock jutting through the surface of the floor.

When they cleared it, the ground became flatter and easier to see. Seems Jerry forgot to mention those trickles formed puddles someone could drown in. Kallie knew they were large enough—she'd seen him floating face down in one.

"We need to leave now!"

Jerry turned to her; eyes wide. "We just got here." He dismissed her, getting up on his sneaker toes and creeping over the slicker rocks toward the far wall.

Kallie held her breath as he felt his way along it and then stopped at a thick stream pouring down a jagged collection of rocks.

"A few drops of water, my ass," she muttered. This whole place was a tragic slip and slide waiting to happen.

Jerry activated his recorder, a stillness coming over his features as it taped the cavern sounds. He wouldn't hear her if she begged him to come back to her side. He was too focused, too mesmerized by the flow of the stream and the song it seemed to hum only to him. *What am I going to do with you, Water-Boy?*

She crept toward the same rocky wall, creating a distance between them and one of the largest puddles. If she could keep Jerry away from it, everything would be fine.

"Do you hear it?" He smiled when she got near. "Jump over." He circled his arm wildly, stepping back to make room for her.

She eyed the shiny sheets of rock beneath her feet and the water glistening over every inch, just waiting to trip her up.

"I can hear it." She stayed where she was. "It sounds great. Have you recorded enough now?"

Jerry examined his recorder, his fingers hovering over the buttons. "I'll need a few minutes to get enough water sound without you talking."

"Then stop talking to *me*!" She folded her arms across her chest, regretting her decision to not bring a jacket. Her short sleeve t-shirt did little to keep her skin warm. They needed to get out of there. She scanned the far end of the cavern, barely making out the walls in the scarce sunbeams. If the entrance collapsed, they'd be screwed.

Being trapped in the dark wasn't what she saw in her vision, though. *It's the water that's the problem.* She eyed the largest puddle again and tried to work out if it was the one that she saw in her head. "Are you almost done?"

Jerry was staring at his recorder still, watching the red light blink. It'd been two minutes. What was he waiting for? It's not like the sound was changing.

"I think I have enough." He finally jammed his finger into the stop button.

"Join me over here." It was closer to the entrance. Closer to safety. Away from the puddles.

Jerry backed off the wall and the invisible rope constricting her chest unraveled. He was coming over. They could leave and she could forget all about that horrible image. *Unless it's a future event?*

What if it happened the next time he came here alone? She glanced back at the big puddle. It wasn't rippling like it had in her vision, with tiny wrinkles of water that lapped around Jerry's cold, blue arms.

"Let me know when you're coming here again. I don't want to miss out," she said as her friend shuffled his way toward her.

"See, I told you the cavern was cool."

He stepped over a large rock. Five more steps and he'd be back with her.

"Wait! You haven't even seen the best part." Jerry suddenly stopped and turned around.

"Where are you going?"

"The witch's things. I mentioned them ages ago, remember? They're over here." He crept over to the far wall, the one with the thick stream running down it. Kallie's gaze followed the water to the ground. It fed right into the large puddle.

"You can show me next time." She took her eyes off Jerry to watch her feet as she chased after him. Maybe if she grabbed his arm and dragged him toward the entrance, he would leave? "I mean what if the witch comes here and finds us?"

Jerry snorted. "I guess we'd be cursed then, right? Turned into frogs or something."

"Yes, and we don't want that."

"I dunno." Jerry shrugged. "Splashing around in water all day sounds great."

Kallie's stomach flip-flopped at his words. He wouldn't be splashing. He'd be drowning. "We should go, just in case."

Jerry laughed again, stopping at the thick curtain of water. It cast a mesmerizing spell. He'd already fallen victim to it, his hand drifting toward the life-giving liquid and absorbing into its crystal-clear center.

He turned to her, his trademark grin stretched wide as he pulled his wet hand from the depths of the wall, a tiny jar nestled in his palm.

"The witch probably thought she was being clever, but I know where her treasures are hidden. There's lots in here. Jars full of dirt, rocks, dead spiders, and strange colored sand."

"That's awesome." Kallie glanced from the jar to his face, pushing a smile to her lips when he scowled at her.

"You don't want to see?"

"Please, Jerry, can't we just go? You got your recording."

He sighed and stared at the jar in his hand like he had his recorder, before lifting it to the stream's hidden hidey-hole. "You can look at it next time. There's supposed to be a huge storm next week, this whole place will probably fill. Wanna come back then?"

"Sure, we can do that." *Or not.* She kept the smile plastered to her face.

Jerry flicked his wet hand, spraying droplets at the ground.

"Careful." Kallie swallowed, pushing the fear out of her voice. "You don't want to slip."

"It's just water." He flicked his wrist at her, frowning when her skin and clothes remained drop-free. "That's not fair." He tugged on the wet edges of his shirt. "We can't be frogs together if you're not soaked too."

"You know water isn't good for fire." Kallie forced a laugh.

"True," Jerry said. "It's still not fair." He twisted sideways, stretching back toward the mini waterfall and skimming his hands through it.

"Don't," Kallie warned, keeping her eyes on the water in his cupped palms.

He smiled before thrusting his arms out.

Kallie's hands went to her face, shielding it from the inevitable icy splash. The water splattered onto the ground just in front of Jerry, exploding against the rocks. Her bare shins caught splashes, but Jerry's legs got saturated.

She burst out laughing. "You have the *worst* aim."

Jerry laughed too, shaking his wet hands. "You don't need to aim when you're a frog."

"Come on *Frog-Boy*, hop to it."

Jerry laughed again and raised one leg, hopping over the rocks. When his foot landed, it splashed into the new puddle he'd made and slipped out from underneath him. Before Kallie registered that he'd hit the ground, Jerry was sliding down the rocks.

"No!" she screamed. Jerry's whole body skidded across the slick cavern floor, racing toward the big puddle and falling into it before she had pushed her sneaker soles off the ground. By the time she reached the puddle edge, Jerry was underneath the water, somehow sinking right into it. "Jerry!"

His floundering arms and head broke the surface, the water he wanted to flick at her finally landing on her t-shirt.

"Ka-Kallie," he spluttered.

She kneeled, catching her stricken expression in the water's inky blackness. What she'd assumed was the rocky floor of the cavern beneath the surface was only the start of the puddle's depth.

It's not a puddle.

The waterhole ran deep, probably feeding out to the stream. "Swim," she begged, stretching out her hands.

Jerry focused on her shaking fingers; his eyes as wide as his mouth. Water lapped into his throat. "I-I can't." He coughed. His flailing arms flattened, drifting aimlessly as he lost control of them. His head lolled to the side as he finally closed his chattering lips. They were as blue as his skin.

"Jerry you have to fight." Kallie slipped off her sneakers, ice water soaking into her socks and sending a chill through her limbs.

"To-too c-cold."

If she jumped in, she'd freeze like Jerry, and she couldn't help him if she was an ice-cube.

Turning, she scanned the cavern. The rocks wouldn't help, the water was already doing all the damage. *The witch's things?* She scrambled over to the curtain of water and thrust her hand in. The hidey-hole was deep. It took precious seconds before she touched on anything other than a slimy rock.

The jars weren't any good; she slid her fingers off the smooth glass of one and bumped against something new. She grasped it. It has some length to it, a hard, thick surface. She pulled on the irregular-shaped end. *A stick?*

The dark wood cleared the hidey-hole and was almost her height when she stood it up. She ran back over to Jerry, thrusting it at him. He'd drifted to the middle of the waterhole, his skinny arms fighting a losing battle against the frosty water.

"Here." Kallie pressed the stick out further. The end of it glinted as if something was embedded in the point. The section under her skin felt extra rough, and she shifted her hands up, finding a carving etched into the dark wood. A witches' pentacle. *On a stick?*

The far end dipped as Jerry's weak hands grasped at the tip and Kallie almost lost it. She tightly wrapped her fingers back around the carving grooves and shoved the stick at Jerry. "Grab it!"

"I-I can't." His fingers slipped off and his head dunked below the surface before his dark hair bobbed up seconds later, rising out of the water a matted mess.

"Try again." She leveled the stick at him, holding it as steady as she could.

In between coughs, Jerry's hands finally wrapped around the end, but his frozen fingers could barely bend, let alone grasp. His eyes went wide again. "Kal-Kallie."

His attention shot behind her, just as it seemed like the surrounding light dimmed. The break in the gloom came from the sunlight filtering in from the entrance. They weren't near it now, yet Jerry's head fixed in its direction. Was that the thud of heavy feet jarring against the rocky floor? *Stop being paranoid!*

"Jerry, loop your arms around the end." She poked the stick at him. The end glinted again, or somehow caught some sunlight. It shone against Jerry's face, making it even bluer. *Could sunbeams be blue?*

"Ka-Kallie." Jerry's teeth chattered. "Ru-run."

"What?"

"Run!" Jerry's arms swung up above his head, knocking the stick away.

The end jutted into her shoulder, breaking her grip on the wood. The stick slipped into the waterhole, bobbing past Jerry, who was splashing toward her. She reached out to him, leaning as close to the edge as she could without falling in.

Did the light dim again? She caught something moving out of the corner of her eye, but Jerry's terrified expression stopped her from jerking her head to the side. Her eyes trained on his mouth as it dropped open, his small voice reaching her ears as the shadow morphed into the familiar shape of human legs.

"Ka-kal-Kallie. The witch!"

TEN

Kallie fell sideways, her shoulder taking the brunt as the stony surface pressed into her flesh. The rocks also did a number on her temple, the whiplash splintering across her forehead.

She rolled onto her back, wincing as the ice water filled her clothes. Her head twisted to the side; her view tainted by brunette waves moist with a warm redness that stuck to her skin. She raised chilled fingers to push the strands away.

Jerry had made it to the waterhole edge, his top half clinging on, while his lower half floated beneath the murky water. She watched his drenched gray shirt heave against the rocks, vapors of cold air escaping his chattering lips.

His head lifted, but not toward her, as the legs that knocked Kallie into the cavern floor strode to Jerry. They belonged to a lanky man, not the witch.

"Sir, please," she called out, daring to move her aching bones. "Help my friend."

The man turned in her direction, but didn't look at her, his beady eyes scanning the depths of the waterhole. Perhaps he was working out how to save Jerry? He wasn't a large man, his long limbs skinny underneath a collared shirt and belted slacks. Pulling Jerry out on his own might end with them both in the water. She should get up. They would need her help too.

Kallie forced herself to sit, the cavern walls tilting and whirling. She closed her mouth, swallowing back the vomit threatening to spill from her throat. The man was still skirting around the waterhole, dipping the pointy toes of his shiny shoes into its depths. He couldn't have been hiking, not in those clothes. She wondered how he found them underground.

Risking pain to shift her head, Kallie checked the entrance. It was a dull yellow dot in the distance. You'd have to know the woods to discover the opening, which plunged into the earth.

"Kallie."

Jerry's weak voice cut through the air. The man was on his knees, a long arm dipped into the freezing water. Fat droplets flicked out as he pulled the stick free.

What was he doing? They didn't need that useless thing now. She climbed to her feet, swaying as she took her first steps. With her shoes still discarded on the rocks, she dragged her wet socks through water as the man stalked toward Jerry, using the stick like a cane. *Or a staff.*

She hadn't noticed its narrowed end before seeing it click along the cavern floor. Or its thicker middle and pointed tip. Was something shiny buried in it or was it a trick of light? That rock really did a number on her brain.

She rubbed her eyes, trying to erase the sparkling glint running the staff's length. It was covered in lights, each one burning brighter the closer it got to Jerry.

Her Water-Boy was still blue, at least it looked that way under the glow of whatever was jammed into the top of that staff.

"Ge-get away fr-from me!" Jerry stuttered, glaring.

He was so weak his head wouldn't lift. Kallie could see all his strength channeled into his arms as he clung to the rocky edge. *Hang on, Jerry.*

The man raised the staff, spinning it until the end faced her friend. He held it toward him like Kallie had, a tether to escape the icy liquid, but Jerry didn't reach for it. The man didn't use his stick to save a life. Instead, he pressed it into Jerry's shoulder, the strange blue light cutting into him.

Kallie lifted her arm so she could pull Jerry from the water. She blinked at her blurry fingers, snatching at him. He was right there. Why wouldn't he take her hand? Her eyesight sharpened. They weren't within reach. She'd barely shuffled from where she'd fallen. *Where did my shoes go?*

"Kal-Kallie run!"

She flinched at her friend's voice, pressing her temple to steady the echo. Her palms were so sticky. She tried to focus on her waving fingertips. They were a warm red, not icy blue like Jerry.

"Water-Boy," she whispered.

He called her name again. At least she thought he did. Someone's screaming drowned it out. They sounded just like Jerry.

She wiped her hand on her shirt. Perhaps the water could clean away the red stains? She stumbled toward it, right where that man was standing. *Is he fishing?* There weren't any fish in the waterhole. Just that weird dark shape, floating with its arms and legs straight out.

Jerry would find that funny. He would tell her it looked like a body. *Where is Jerry?* She heard his voice a second ago. He was telling her something about a blue light?

"Hello," she called to the fishing man. "Have you seen my friend?"

His beady eyes flicked to her, a strange smile twisting across his thin lips. His fishing rod rose out of the water, making the dark shape bob. That blue light was back. Kallie cringed, shielding herself from the glare, wondering why her palm was so red.

It's blood. Your blood.

She hit her head. Jerry hit the water. The man hit Jerry.

Her eyes searched that stupidly deep puddle. The bobbing shape *was* Jerry, floating along the surface, just as she'd seen.

Kal-Kallie run!

His last words splintered through her mind. She turned, slipping across the rocks. The blue light struck the walls of the cavern, chasing her. She didn't dare look if the man was chasing her too. She just stumbled across the stony ground, toward the yellow-lit entrance.

Bursting into the forest, she blinked back the sunlight and plowed through the trees. *Don't let him get you or no one will find Jerry.*

She zig-zagged, fumbling through a pile of fallen branches. The tree limbs behind her cracked. He'd caught up to her already. That meant she was next.

Every step she made, he outpaced by two.

If she had shoes, she'd be faster. If the air in her lungs didn't feel like fire, she could breathe. If she hadn't gone into the cavern, Jerry wouldn't be... her knees locked up and she dropped to the ground, a guttural sob shaking her body.

Before she closed her mouth, a cold hand clamped over it, an arm around her waist, yanking her backward into a thick shrubbery of bushes.

This is it. This was where she'd die. Not drowning underground, but buried in dirt and mushy leaves that would rot along with her skin. They'd have to use her bones to identify her, if animals didn't steal them first. Her mom would have to take off work to go to the morgue. *She'd be so pissed.*

Red scratches erupted across Kallie's bare arms as the needle-like shrubs attacked her. Another cry formed in her throat, but before she could release it, the man sprinted past the bushes, his slim body a blur.

"Don't move," a woman whispered in Kallie's ear. "And don't scream."

The hand dropped from her mouth, followed by the arm around her waist.

"My friend," Kallie's voice cracked. "He's hurt."

"Your friend is dead."

Kallie shook her head, as if it would somehow erase the truth.

The woman's hand returned to her, fingers combing through Kallie's blood-tangled locks. Who was the person trying to comfort her? The lined face and long blond hair weren't familiar.

The woman tilted Kallie's face toward herself. They didn't know each other, yet the lady's blue eyes trained on her like she was staring at an old friend.

"Surely you knew about the boy. You foresaw it."

"How... how do you know about that?"

"I was watching the two of you when you entered the forest."

"Why didn't you help us?"

The woman glanced over her shoulder; in the direction the man had run. "I can't interfere."

What kind of bullshit was that? "Who is that man?"

"It would be better for you if you didn't know."

"It would have been better for me if you helped!" Kallie scrambled to her knees. The woman grabbed her wrists, holding her in place.

"Don't ignore the things you see, or you will lose everything."

Heat rushed to Kallie's cheeks. "Are you threatening me?"

"You threatened yourself. And that boy's life."

Kallie twisted her hand free, slapping it across the stranger's face. "I did not kill Jerry!" She flexed her wrist, her stomach sinking as finger shaped welts surfaced on the woman's cheek.

The lady touched her reddened skin. "When we don't ask for our gifts, they're hard to accept."

"I didn't ask for anything."

The woman nodded, the deep lines around her mouth sagging. "But you still have it."

Her hand reached back to Kallie's blood-stained hair and Kallie flinched, worried the woman was going to slap her back. Instead, her touch tapped across Kallie's forehead. How did this woman know about the pictures she saw in her head?

Kallie yanked herself away, spying a tattooed wrist. Black ink in the shape of a witch's pentacle stained the blond woman's skin.

"You're the witch! You did this!" Kallie clenched her hands. "I didn't see anything real until you started watching me."

"I started watching you *because* you began to see what was real."

"No! You made this happen. You knew Jerry would die, that's why you're here."

"You knew it too."

"My vision of Jerry wasn't real. It didn't feel like the others." Her usual visions came to her like snapshots, surfacing in her mind without any effort on her part. The image of Jerry in the water had been different, forced, jammed inside her head like an intruder. Like it was placed there... "By someone else," she whispered the end of her horrified thought out loud. "What did *you* do to me?"

"I helped," the witch said, her voice confident despite the guilt that seeped into her features. "It was necessary to show you. You have the ability, but you need to develop it. I had to help you so you could save your friend."

"But I didn't." She couldn't save Jerry when it felt so fake. That vision shouldn't have happened. *But it did.* She covered her mouth, swallowing the rancid vomit and feeling it burn its way back down her throat.

"*You* ignored my warning."

"No! This is your fault!" Kallie burst from their hiding place.

"Don't ignore what you see," the witch called. "For all of our sakes."

Kallie pushed the words from her mind, each one falling away as she ran. The witch and the man would pay for Jerry's death.

Kallie would make sure of it.

ELEVEN

Josh and Kallie sat cross-legged amongst the black birch trees, facing each other while they took turns focusing on the magick buried in the dark green leaves and brown trunks.

After Arden and the clearing, Josh felt there was something more to them, something more to everything. The air, the sun, the birds, even the grass beneath them had a presence that aligned with the power in his veins. At first it was like a whisper, but Kallie taught him to tune into it, and now everything hummed.

"The black birches have the strongest draw," he said, pulling his energy back. Kallie had advised him to keep his veil up and showed him how to summon his magick without it showing as a red glow on his skin. That meant his connection wasn't as strong as it could be, but even at half strength, he could tell the magick in the trees was the most dominant.

"I feel that too."

When Kallie connected, she allowed her blue light to show. Josh eyed the paleness and questioned if she was holding back. Her magick had been a vivid hue in their shared dreams; the nightmares where monsters and shadows chased them, but maybe he shouldn't expect the real-life color to be as exact.

"Did you know you can harvest the energy?" Kallie wiggled her petite fingers. She placed one glowing hand on the ground between them and flattened it into the blades of grass, lighting them up. The deep green vegetation softened and faded, while Kallie's pale blue glow deepened to a stronger shade. Now it looked the right color, and he scolded himself for questioning her.

"If your power ever needs a boost, the energy of anything living can give it to you," she explained.

Josh had seen a change in hue like that before. "Do you think that's what Arden tried to do to me? Harvest my magick?"

Kallie's expression darkened. "Harvesting only borrows a small amount. It sounds like he tried to take yours. That's different and requires a lot of energy."

"He couldn't have pulled it off?"

"Not alone. His body wouldn't handle the influx."

"The man was no longer alive. If the consequence for him was death, it wouldn't have mattered."

"It would have mattered," Kallie disagreed.

"Maybe he was only trying to steal some of it then?"

"He could have taken half." Kallie's voice dropped to a whisper. "It's possible to steal half."

"Is that what Cade tried to do to you?"

She met his question with silence, the kind that hung in the air, before shifting her attention back to the pale patch of grass.

Good going, Josh. Bring up Cade. I'm sure that's exactly what she wants to talk about. Heat flushed through his cheeks. "You don't have to say anything," he offered, "I'm sorry I—"

"Melinda stopped him." Kallie ripped at the ground, plucking fistfuls of grass blades from the dirt. "She wouldn't let Cade take everything he needed."

"And that was a good thing, right?" He eyeballed her hands. Did he miss something? She seemed angry.

Kallie unfurled her fingers, the crushed grass drifting back down to the earth. "I wouldn't be here if it wasn't for Melinda."

Josh was sure she meant her comment to be positive, but it was hard to say that when the tone of her voice sounded so bitter. He tried to read her expression, focusing on her eyes.

She met his gaze and her face brightened. "Melinda taught me a lot. Things that have saved my life. She was a talented witch."

So she was happy that his aunt beat Cade. His shoulders relaxed. "I wish I could have known her. It sounds like her grasp of spells was amazing. In only a few hours you've shown me more than any of the books I've read from the store. Even more than the knowledge my mom's memories put in my head."

"That was Melinda's ability. She didn't just know about spells, she wrote them. Her gift could imprint magick in any word and create castings that wouldn't be possible otherwise. It's a shame it's gone now."

"Gone?"

"We all get one ability. It died with her."

"I had no idea it was so... final." Did that mean his mother's gift was gone too? "Makes me wonder what my mom's ability was."

"You don't know?"

"No." If only it was a memory rattling around in his brain. Maybe then he wouldn't feel like he didn't know her.

"Well, there's also someone else's ability you don't know about yet." Kallie wiggled her fingers again.

"I thought your gift was the glimpsing?"

"I told you that was a spell."

"The visions?"

"All natural," she declared, puffing her chest, before descending into a hearty laugh.

"What secret have you been keeping from me?"

Kallie's eyes glinted in the sunlight. She activated her power and one of the trees behind her swayed, tilting toward them.

That's a weird ability. The angle of the black birch was so far forward it looked like it was going to...

Crack!

Kallie startled, her mouth dropping open as her head turned to the thunderous sound.

"Move!" Josh ignited his energy, throwing himself at her and using his strength to roll them both to the side. The tree slammed into the ground where they'd been sitting, flinging dirt into the air.

"Why did you do that?" He coughed.

"I didn't."

Crack!

The second tree was swifter. Hurtling faster than they could move. He increased his power, allowing it to coat his entire body. The trunk stopped against his protected back, but he didn't know how long he could hold it.

"I need more..." He prepared to drop his veil.

"Don't!" Kallie latched onto his arm and fed her glowing energy into him.

Heat rushed through his veins and the heaviness of the wood dissipated against his flexed back. His muscles pulled taunt while he stood and threw off the trunk. As soon as they were free, more black birches tilted, rushing at them like an oncoming freight train.

"Hide!" Kallie shoved him at a tree cluster.

"How do you know these won't come down?" He squeezed into the tiny space, scratching his exposed skin on rough bark.

"Because we're still out there." Kallie's glowing finger pointed over his shoulder.

Two figures crouched at the fallen trunks. He squinted at the boy and girl, gasping when they came into focus. "What's happening, Kallie? Are you seeing this?"

"Can you see us?"

"Yes!" It was them. Him and Kallie, hiding behind the trunk. "How is this possible?"

"Are we visible? Enough to be seen by anyone watching?"

"If someone is keeping track, they'll see us... them."

"Good." Kallie's blue energy faded. "And now you know what my ability is."

Josh grasped the bark he leaned on, as he watched himself cower behind the cracked tree. His other looked every bit as real as the broken roughage beneath his grip. "Illusions."

Another black birch bent at their copies, the roots ripping through the earth as the top half, flushed with leaves, rushed toward it.

It struck the illusions with a mighty thud, erasing them under a cloud of displaced dirt and shattered tree limbs.

"Do you think we tricked them?" He turned from the fake-carnage, hoping they'd fooled whoever was trying to kill them. Kallie's power was fading, only the pale blue looked like it was taking all her natural coloring with it. "Do you need more?" he offered. His energy buzzed beneath the surface of his skin, waiting to be unleashed.

Kallie's cheeks flushed, "I-uh. No." She tucked her hands away. "We'd better leave before whoever thinks they killed us works out they didn't."

Josh pointed behind her. "If we head back over there, we'll come out of the forest near Grace's house."

Kallie elbowed her way out of the branches ahead of him. The color had returned to her skin, but something was off in the way she moved.

"Kallie?" He touched her shoulder to slow her down. "Are you hurt?"

She curled her hand up to her chest and cradled it. "I'm fine for now."

He slid past her, pushing up branches so she could clear them without having to move her arms. She flashed a grateful smile, and he returned it before looking back at the fallen trees.

There was a lot of damage. Whoever, or whatever, pulled them down did it with force. He let his magick coat his hands, keeping the color hidden like Kallie had shown him. He didn't want her to know he was searching for another power source when she had other things to worry about.

His senses were immediately drawn to the felled trees, and he channeled more energy at them, his stomach knotting when the broken shards lit up in an eerie green glow.

TWELVE

Sarah dropped into the couch cushions, switching her gaze between the front door and her phone. *Where is everyone?* She'd left messages with both Josh and Eve and neither of them had gotten back to her.

As another five minutes ticked by, she sent a seventh text to Eve asking where she was.

It'd been three hours since they'd glimpsed Kallie's past, and Sarah had gone home and waited for Josh like Eve asked. He was still out, and Eve hadn't arrived with her promised protection spell. Sarah pounded her index finger into her cell screen, growling along to the ringing.

"Hello?"

"Eve!" Sarah stood, pacing away from the couch. "Where are you?"

"Who is this?"

"What? It's Sarah."

"Sarah?" Eve's groggy voice questioned. "What do *you* want?"

What do I want? "I'm waiting at home like you told me to—*for you!* You said you'd meet me here hours ago."

"Something came up," Eve replied, yawning.

"Are you coming over now?"

"What for?"

Sarah pulled the phone away from her mouth. "Don't throw it. It's not worth it," she muttered before putting the cell back against her ear. "You're supposed to be here when I talk to Josh about Kallie."

"Kallie?" Eve laughed. "She's no threat."

Sarah stopped pacing. "But this morning you acted like she was dangerous."

"I changed my mind."

"You changed your mind?"

"Yep." Eve yawned again.

"But I don't understand?"

"And you never really will, Sarah."

Her phone beeped twice and then went to static. Stunned, she considered calling Eve back just so she could yell at her. Her index finger hovered above the call button, shifting off it when the front door flew open.

"What's going on?" She stared wide-eyed at Josh and Kallie.

"Can you grab the first aid kit?" Josh guided Kallie to the couch.

Sarah ran to the upstairs bathroom, vowing to kill Josh if he went back out to the clearing. When she returned to the living room, Josh was sitting on the edge of the coffee table directly in front of Kallie and holding her hand.

"What happened?" Sarah put the kit next to Josh, scanning him for blood. He looked fine. *Thank god.* He was examining Kallie's swollen and oddly bent ring and pinky fingers.

"There was an incident out in the woods," Josh explained.

"The clearing?"

"No."

Good. Sarah smiled, tapering it back when Kallie shifted her hand from Josh's and gasped. "Those fingers look broken." She fished through the first aid box for a roll of adhesive medical tape.

"They are." Kallie's face screwed up as she lifted her fingers so Sarah could apply the tape.

The shape of them wasn't good and Sarah wondered where to start. "This tape won't do anything with the bones this bent. You're better off going to the hospital."

Kallie sucked in a breath and then cracked her broken fingers straight.

"Holy shit! Didn't that hurt?"

"Sarah, the tape." Josh hurried her.

"How are you not in a ball on the floor right now?" Sarah carefully secured Kallie's ring finger to her pinky. "Or at the very least, screaming to go to the hospital."

"They won't do anything more than what you are," Kallie said.

"Yeah, but they have drugs there. They could give you some pain relief."

"I can take you," Josh offered.

"I don't want to go to the emergency room."

"A doctor can set the bones properly, so they heal right." Maybe she'd never broken anything and didn't understand the comfort she could get?

"I won't go!" Kallie snapped.

First Eve and now her. Was it *Speak Rude to Sarah Day?* "I'm just trying to help you!"

"I didn't ask you to."

Kallie's hand pulled back, knocking the scissors in Sarah's grip. "Hey, watch it!" Sarah growled.

Beside her, Josh rose from the coffee table and Sarah felt his hand on the back of her shirt. "Let's get some water."

"What was that?" she complained as soon as she and Josh were alone in the kitchen. Why didn't he call Kallie out for being so rude?

"She's in pain," Josh said as he reached for glasses in the overheard cupboard.

"Pain," Sarah grumbled, flinging open the refrigerator door and scanning the shelves for the water jug. "She's a pain in the ass is what she is."

Josh was staring at her when she turned around, his jaw tense. If she wanted sympathy, she wasn't getting it from him. *No surprise there.*

"What happened in the woods?" She handed over the cold water.

"Someone tried to kill us."

Her jaw dropped, the angry heat across the back of her neck instantly cooling. "You *really* need to stop going into the woods."

"Yeah, I'm thinking that too."

As she was filled in on Josh's afternoon, including that he'd accidentally broken Kallie's fingers rolling her away from killer trees, Sarah suggested again that he take Kallie to the hospital.

"She doesn't want to go, and I don't blame her."

Sarah knew he didn't like hospitals, but why was Kallie so against the idea? "Don't you think it's odd? Her bones won't heal right, she needs an x-ray."

"She's on the run from a psycho. She probably doesn't want to leave a paper trail Cade could find."

"Maybe not just Cade." Detective Brewer was looking for Kallie too, although Sarah still hadn't told Josh that. Would now be a good time? He was leaning against the kitchen bench, the filled glasses ready, yet he made no move to rush back to his precious Kallie.

"What do you mean not just Cade?" Josh asked.

Crap. She had no way to reveal the news tactfully now. "I found some articles online about Kallie and there's a detective chasing her."

"A detective?" Josh straightened against the bench. His eyes darting to the doorway. "Why?"

"He suspects Kallie of being involved with Melinda's death."

"Involved how?"

"Well, she was there. Eve and I saw it—"

"Wait a minute. You and Eve saw *it*? Saw what?"

"Well, there were these dead spiders, candle smoke, and a glimpsing spell—"

"*You* and Eve cast a glimpsing spell?"

What did he mean *you*? Sarah was just as capable as anyone of casting a spell. "If you let me explain it without interrupting me..."

Josh leaned back into the bench, crossing his arms as he stared silently. Was he mad or jealous she and Eve had pulled off a spell?

"Are you *going* to explain?" he asked curtly.

Not jealous. Definitely mad. "We glimpsed Melinda saving Kallie's life. Then we saw Melinda dying and Kallie watching and doing nothing."

"You saw Kallie kill her?"

"Not exactly. It was dark, but—"

"But you think you saw it and that's good enough?"

"There were the articles too."

"The ones you showed to Eve instead of me?"

"I wasn't sure if you could—"

"Be trusted? After everything we've already been through?"

"I was going to say be impartial when it came to Kallie."

Josh unfolded his arms, reaching for a glass of water and taking a sip.

She doubted he was suddenly thirsty, more like he was trying to avoid saying something he'd regret. If only she had the same filter. "You need to speak to her about it."

"Speak to me about what?"

Sarah flinched at the sound of Kallie's voice, and the annoyance in her tone.

"I assume you're talking about me." Kallie eyed Sarah as she walked into the kitchen.

Josh picked up the other glass and handed it to Kallie.

Sarah couldn't see any anger in his expression when he looked at the brunette, but his eyes dimmed. Sarah knew he wanted to believe Kallie was there to help him. Now she hoped she was wrong.

Sarah cleared her throat. "We wanted to talk to you about some articles I found."

Kallie's eyebrows raised, and she carefully lowered the glass to the bench, misjudging the edge and causing the glass to clink against the marble top. "What articles?"

"First, how are your fingers?" Josh asked.

"They're okay."

"Do you feel well enough for a casting?"

"Um, what?" Sarah interrupted their conversation. Why was Josh asking Kallie about a casting now? They should be grilling her about the articles.

"Depends on what it is," Kallie said to Josh, ignoring Sarah. "And if I don't need to move my hand too much."

"Whoever tried to hurt us out in the woods had magick, right?"

Kallie nodded.

"Do you think you could find it? Like how you found me by zeroing in on my power."

"Yes, but that took months."

"What if you knew who to look for? A specific person."

"I could do that," Kallie said. "Who are we checking for power?"

"Yeah." Sarah folded her arms across her chest. "Who?"

Josh caught her eye, a steeliness in his gaze. He gave the same look to Kallie. "Eve Thomas."

Josh let Kallie settle herself on the couch before he drew the blinds in the front window shut.

Sarah had taken a seat in the armchair, arms crossed over her chest as she kept her stare fixed on their guest. He could see it in her resentful expression that she wanted him to confront Kallie about the articles and the detective chasing her, and he would. But first, he needed to know if Eve attacked them. He could only deal with one betrayal at a time, and if Kallie wasn't being honest with him, he needed to adjust to it first. *Sorry, Sarah.*

With the blinds closed, the dimness he'd created shadowed Kallie. It was a stark contrast to how she'd looked earlier that afternoon when her features were lit by the glow of the sun.

Josh had memorized everything about her then. The way the dark color of her brown eyes matched her thick eyelashes. The pink flush on her cheeks as they hiked into the woods. The light smattering of freckles along her nose, and the dimple on her right cheek that only showed when she smiled a certain way. He adored seeing her smile. It was something he'd always wanted to experience outside of his dreams; a secret wish he'd made before he knew she was real. Now he just wished that Sarah's quest to prove Kallie was hiding things was wrong.

"If you have something of Eve's, it would make it easier for me to concentrate my energy on her," Kallie said.

"I brought her work shirt home to wash," Sarah offered.

"That'll do."

Josh stayed by the window while the shirt was fetched, watching as Kallie laid the polo on the coffee table. Her spell started with a flare of her power, which reflected its soft color off the beige walls as her fingertips hovered along the shirt hem.

Josh's skin tingled with a light flush as Kallie's energy unleashed, and he used a trickle of his own to secretly chase hers. If Kallie found something and told him she hadn't, he would know she was lying. *Please, don't be lying.*

And then there was Eve. He'd scanned her for magick after that night in the clearing. He didn't believe she had power then, and he still didn't now. She can't have if she needed Sarah to cast the glimpsing spell. Eve would never work with others if she didn't have to.

When Kallie's energy faded back into her skin minutes later, she looked right at him and confirmed his hunch.

"This girl doesn't have the kind of power we're looking for."

He agreed. "There's a trace there, but it's weak." Eve wasn't out to get him, and Kallie wasn't lying to him.

"Are you sure?" Sarah asked. "I was with her today, she cast a high-level spell."

"I picked up her trace on the other side of town." Kallie named exactly where Eve lived. "There's nothing, at least not our level of power."

"Could she be hiding it?" Sarah asked.

"Eve's level of energy is so low it's practically undetectable. Unless she's got some secret stash of power she only channels when she needs it, which I doubt, she's not who we're looking for," Kallie said. "What was the high-level spell you saw her cast?"

Sarah's mouth dropped open, but no words came out. Josh wondered why she was waiting. She was the one who dug into Kallie's history and wanted to know more. Now was her chance.

"Sarah and Eve glimpsed your past today," he said, as the seconds passed and Sarah remained silent.

If the revelation shocked Kallie she kept it hidden. Her expression didn't change, she just moved her attention from Sarah to Josh.

"Is that what you wanted to ask me about earlier?"

He nodded.

"Then ask." Kallie looked back at Sarah. "I have nothing to hide."

"Did you kill Melinda?" he uttered the one question that mattered.

Kallie's gaze dropped to the floor. "No. I didn't kill her," her voice wavered. "I was there when it happened, but it was Cade who killed her."

"The glimpse didn't show anyone but you and Melinda," Sarah said.

Kallie's tilted head snapped up. "Do you know how much energy it requires to cast a decent glimpsing spell? You and your friend pooling together the minuscule amount of natural magick in your bodies would have given you hardly any. I can't imagine what you saw was anything but dark, fleeting, and completely wrong!"

Sarah shifted in her seat, her mouth opening and closing again before she threw him another look.

"Is that the vision you glimpsed, Sarah?" He'd seen visions brought on by magick and knew how chaotic and confusing they could be. *No wonder Kallie is angry.*

"I-uh. I also found some articles on you," Sarah said, listing the details.

The mention of Jerry Miller broke something in Kallie. Her scowl melted, a dimness washing across her features. "Cade was responsible for those deaths," she whispered. "No matter how much Detective Brewer wanted it to be me."

"Cade was a professor who murdered his students." Josh recalled the story. "He pushed one student off a cliff and buried the other alive."

Kallie nodded. "Earth and air."

"So he was using the elements." He'd thought the same after hearing the tale, saying it to Sarah before he even knew such a thing was possible. Her wide eyes glanced at him; her shock just as palpable.

"He was harvesting them. Earth and air for those students, water for Jerry and..."

"Fire for you." Josh concluded after Kallie's voice trailed off.

K.M. Allan

She nodded. "All he needed to complete his spell was the energy of a gifted human."

"Melinda."

"She wouldn't give it to him. She passed it to me, and it was protected so he couldn't take it."

"What about Josh's magick?" Sarah asked. "Can Cade take his?"

"If he finds him. That's why it's important to keep his power hidden in the veil."

No wonder she was so eager to stop him from dropping it that afternoon.

"I guess I owe you an apology," Sarah said.

Kallie folded up Eve's polo shirt and handed it back. "I know you're just looking out for Josh"—she glanced at him—"so am I."

"Still, I am sorry."

Kallie tried to give Sarah a smile, but the gesture turned into a wince as she shifted her hand.

Had she forgotten already that her fingers were broken? "I can take you to the hospital," he offered again. "If you want."

Kallie steadied her taped fingers, shaking her head. "I think I'll just go to my motel room and rest."

"Let me walk you back."

"It's fine. You're already at home." She scanned the living room.

"Let me walk you to the door then." Did he sound as disappointed as he felt? He must have, given the sympathetic look Sarah shot him before she took Eve's shirt upstairs.

"I'm sorry I hurt you," he said to Kallie as he opened the front door for her.

"It was an accident, Josh."

"Yeah, but hand injuries are bad. I cut mine a few weeks back, and it was really painful."

"But it healed, right?" Kallie said. "My fingers will be fine again in no time."

"It did heal." He turned his palm face up, staring at the smooth skin. "It healed by itself."

"Well, most injuries do eventually heal by themselves."

92

"No." He ran his fingertips over his palm. His wound had been deep. There should have been a scar. There should have been an injury that was still healing. "When I discovered my power, the cut went away. Maybe the energy healed it?" Why hadn't that occurred to him before?

Kallie paused in the doorway, her eyes searching for his hand. "It disappeared when you sparked your energy?"

"Yes. Have you heard of that happening?"

"Only if it's an ability, but we know strength is your gift."

"Maybe it was my mom's?" The idea made him smile. "My dad always used to joke she should have been a healer." He laughed at the memory of his father, stopping when Kallie frowned.

"If your mother's ability was to heal, it was hers alone."

"But her magick transferred to me." Was it really not possible for her gift to transfer as well?

"Yes, and with it you got your own ability. I told you there's only ever one. If healing was your mom's gift, then it died with her. Just like putting magick into words died with Melinda."

"I see." He tucked his hand away. Kallie knew more about the power than him. He should trust her word.

"I wasn't trying to lie to you," Kallie said, when silence settled between them.

Josh studied her expression, looking for a clue as to what she was talking about.

"Earlier," she clarified. "Those articles Sarah found. I wasn't trying to keep things from you... I just didn't want to have to..."

"Relive it all."

"Yeah."

"I understand. You've seen something I don't want to relive." Maybe that was why Sarah was so quick to jump to conclusions. She hadn't suffered a trauma like they had.

Kallie started to apologize again for glimpsing the car accident. He held up his hand. "Let's call it even. And from now on, when it comes to magick, we tell each other everything, okay?"

"Okay." Kallie nodded. "You should probably know one more thing."

"What?"

"It's not just power Cade needs to complete his spell. It's a certain type."

"Such as?"

"He needs the power to be tainted, to be dark. That's why he kills when harvesting the elements. The energy he draws from his victims has to be stained with death."

"So, if he finds me, not only will he try to steal my magick, but he'll kill me?"

Kallie nodded again.

"Are you sure it wasn't him who tried to murder us today then?"

"I know it wasn't. Cade's not in Blackbirch."

"We also know it most likely wasn't Eve, so who else could it be?"

"I don't know yet," Kallie replied. "But I promise you I'll find out."

THIRTEEN

The car broke down on the side of the road, close enough to the town that the driver could walk the rest of the way. He did so with nothing but the clothes on his back and the items he could carry.

He didn't need much, only ever staying in a place long enough to get what he needed, and leaving before being recognized.

The highway was quiet that night and he hadn't seen another car for hours. It was probably better that way. He'd had his share of Good Samaritans stopping to help, always having to repay their kindness with an action that ensured no one would know they'd helped their fellow man. He couldn't have anyone finding out where he was. Not now he was so close.

A seasoned traveler, he'd come across the outskirts of many towns. Some were dirt roads, others lush fields. Most were rows of houses, and a lot of them were trees. Towns with forests were common in this area, popping up like vermin.

The forest before him now was special, though. He knew it as soon as he approached. This township was proud and looked after their entrance. The trees were trimmed; the asphalt maintained and pothole free. No garbage, tacky statues or plaques like the other tourist towns this side of the highway, just a simple town sign constructed from dark wood.

The only blight was a broken bulb in the streetlight next to it. He strode to the sign to examine it in the shadows, pushing his most precious possession against it.

He thought he could make out the letters, but just to be sure, he twisted the crystal on top of his wooden staff and used the light to confirm he was where he wanted to be. Where he needed to be.

Cade had finally arrived in Blackbirch.

FOURTEEN

"That's him." Kallie tapped her finger against the foggy glass of the van windshield. "That's the guy I saw."

She kept her eyes on Kered Wheeler as he left the Curvers Rock Security office and there was no doubt in her mind. This was the man her vision showed had energy capable of pulling off an attack like the one in the woods.

"He looks like a normal guy." Sarah leaned forward, running her hands around the top of the steering wheel.

Beside Kallie, Josh stayed pressed against the back of the van's bench seat, only his eyes shifting. Like her, he followed Kered's walk from the office door to a beat-up lemon-yellow car parked in the small, empty lot.

"They always look normal." Kallie reached to the floor of the van, pulling her backpack onto her lap. The stiff tape wrapped around her broken fingers threatened to snag on the zip, but she lifted them out of the way, used to the week-old injury now.

"Maybe he is a monster." Josh shivered. "He's got to be cold-blooded to not feel the chill tonight."

"I'll say." Sarah snuggled into the sleeves of her white woolen cardigan.

Kallie glanced up. Kered was dressed in a thin light blue shirt and the dark blue slacks of his uniform. "It's not that cold." She shrugged her bare arms.

"Monster," Sarah whispered, snickering.

"What's the plan?" Josh asked.

At least someone was taking her seriously. Kallie retrieved a small quartz crystal from her backpack and held it up, watching Josh's forehead crinkle under the chocolate brown lengths of his hair. He looked so clueless. Cute, but clueless. If only she could go back to being in the dark about crystals. "This will help us." She gestured to the security guard.

Kered was almost at his car, his fingers flicking around the keys pulled from his pocket. The glinting chain caught the light of the one lamp post with a working bulb. He was smart enough to park under it, yet something wasn't right.

Physically, he was definitely the man she'd seen in her vision; tall and solid, with a mop of wavy, ash-blond hair slicked back with a thick layer of gel, but the dark presence she'd sensed when she glimpsed him wasn't there. Neither was a hint that he had power. She caught Josh's eye, knowing he would have checked for energy too.

"Maybe you're wrong?"

Kallie refused to believe that. "He's just hiding his magick. Don't worry, if he has power, this quartz will find it."

"Let's go then," Josh said, leading them out of the van.

Kallie's fingertips knocked against Kered's foggy windshield, the vibration hitting every nerve in her broken bones. She should have used her other hand, which was currently wrapped around the crystal, but it was better to keep it out of sight. She brushed off her mistake and ignored the pain, waiting for Kered to react.

Despite the parking lot being empty, it appeared he didn't notice the three of them move toward him. He jumped at the sound of her tapping, his hands immediately spreading across the passenger seat.

Kallie should have checked that he was alone before drawing his attention and scolded herself for that mistake. When the car window rolled down seconds later, she discovered that she shouldn't have bothered. The 'passenger' he was protecting was a lunch box full of sandwiches.

"You guys lost?" Kered asked, his mouth covered in crumbs.

Where was the person she saw in her vision? The mean guy. This one, who looked barely older than them, fixed her in place with a stare full of genuine concern.

She decided to switch tactics. "We're having some engine trouble. Could you help us out? Maybe come and look?" Perhaps he'd be different out of the safety of his car.

"Sure, no problem." Kered flipped his lunch box shut, finally wiping at the crumbs caught on his lips. "It's a long trip home," he explained, smoothing his fingers along his pants as he got out of the driver's seat. "If I don't eat now, I'll have to wait until breakfast."

"You don't live around here?" Josh asked.

"Nope," Kered said, gesturing for them to lead him to their car. "It's an hour and a half drive, even this late at night with barely any traffic."

Kallie didn't welcome the news that he didn't live in Blackbirch. That made it unlikely Kered was in the woods that day, or that he knew them well enough to track her and Josh amongst the trees. "But you must like Blackbirch, right? To drive more than an hour just to work here."

Kered chuckled. "I work here because the money's great. For some reason they can't get any locals for the night shift, especially the patrols for the companies bordering the trees."

So he *does* know the woods. She inched the quartz to the edges of her fingers for a better grip. She might need it after all.

Josh was walking ahead of her and she wished she could see his face. She wanted to know how he was feeling about the situation. If he was anything like her, he wouldn't want to be blindsided. That's how people got hurt.

When Kered reached the van, Kallie signaled for Sarah to open the driver door.

"Oh, right! We're having car trouble…" Sarah unlocked the van and popped the hood.

As Kered settled himself in front of the engine, Kallie activated the crystal. All she needed to do was get it near him. If Kered had power, the crystal would light up. She inched around behind him and waited. Nothing happened.

She scowled. "No reaction." *That can't be right.*

"Huh?" Kered turned at the sound of her voice, his arm swinging out and knocking the crystal from her hand.

"Shit!" Kallie cursed as the crystal hit the ground and shattered. It was probably in a million pieces, none of which would help her now.

"I'm so sorry." Kered bent down when she did, his forehead knocking right into her.

"Ouch!" Kallie straightened up, rubbing her head.

"Everyone okay?" Josh stepped over to them.

"Not really, I lost my crystal." She glared at Kered's big fat head.

"Crystal?" Kered's eyes went wide, the color draining from his skin.

"You know about crystals?" Kallie asked, her attention drawn downward when Kered's hands suddenly developed a twitch. She shot a look to Josh, hoping he would know it meant to get his power ready. If this guy knew about crystals, he might know about magick, and in her experience, that never ended well.

"I know I don't like them." Kered backed up a step.

"Why not?" Josh asked, his voice sounding more curious than accusatory.

Kallie couldn't sense Josh's energy or see its red hue on his hands. Why wasn't he prepared for a defense? "Spark your power," she hissed at him.

"The only energy I can feel is yours," he whispered back.

She'd taught him how to sense magick once and suddenly he was an expert? If it was being hidden by someone who knew what they were doing, they wouldn't feel it. That crystal had been their only chance to cut through any lies.

"Tell us why you don't like crystals," Kallie demanded.

"Fine. But then I'm out of here, because there's clearly nothing wrong with your van." Kered shut the hood with a thud that echoed in the quiet night. "I found a crystal, it was this funny black color, and it made me feel weird."

"Weird how?"

"Just… weird. Oh, and it disappeared."

"Disappeared or disintegrated?"

"I don't know. It was just gone when I woke up."

"You lost consciousness? For how long?"

Kered shrugged. "A few hours. I found the crystal at the start of my shift and I woke up six hours later in the dirt with no crystal."

"Where did this happen?"

"The Olsen factory."

Kallie glanced at Josh and then Sarah. Did they know the place?

"The Olsen factory was the last tree exporter in town," Sarah explained from beside the driver's door. "They shut it down after the workers sparked a fire in the woods that killed six firefighters."

"Arden Flynn included," Josh whispered.

"So this factory is near the woods?" She didn't like the sound of that.

"It's Blackbirch," Josh answered. "Everything is near the woods."

"If this factory is closed then why were you out there?" Kallie asked Kered.

"It still has all the expensive logging equipment inside. The owners don't want it stolen. I can take you out there if you want, show you exactly where I found it."

"You would do that?"

"Sure! If you promise to never ask me about this again."

"That would be really helpful, thanks," Josh said.

Kallie felt his hand pat her shoulder as if they'd won some type of victory. Josh might trust Kered, but she didn't. For all they knew, he was leading them into a trap. "Fine. Let's go together in the van." She didn't want Kered getting back in his own car, afraid he'd just drive off.

"I can't leave my ride here, besides, I can head home straight from the factory."

"Fine. I'll ride with you."

"Uh…"

"How about *I* ride with you," Sarah offered.

Kered smiled. "Sure, no problem."

"We'll follow." Josh held his hand out for the van keys.

Sarah leaned into them as she handed them over. "Here's an idea, why don't you guys come up with a new plan on the way over. One that's as helpful as the non-evil guy who's being so nice to us."

Kallie watched Sarah's blond hair bounce as she walked away with Kered. "You're happy for her to go with him?" she asked Josh.

"He seems pretty harmless."

"Or he's playing us."

"How about we see what you can glimpse at the factory?" He patted her shoulder again, guiding her toward the van.

Seated inside, Kallie cradled her broken fingers, absently playing with the tape as Josh started the engine.

"Your hand okay?"

A certain look always washed across his face when he saw her injury; guilt, regret. She knew he wanted to undo the damage he caused.

"I'm fine." She forced a grin.

Josh smiled back. His was more genuine.

"How long will it take to get to the factory?"

"A few minutes." Josh put the van into gear, following Kered's car as it pulled out of the lot ahead of them.

"Don't you just love living in small towns."

"It comes in handy."

"You don't miss the hustle and bustle of the city?" she asked.

"You've never been into a city before, have you?"

"Did the 'hustle and bustle' line give me away?" Her cheeks flushed.

"It's louder there. Like everything is always on. It's harder to switch off," Josh said.

"Not like out here." She stared into the deep blackness stretched before them. At least in a loud city your thoughts could get drowned out. In small towns all they did was echo.

"I like it out here," Josh said. "The company's better."

There was that genuine smile again. She pressed her hands to her cheeks to cool them. "Let's just hope our new friend is also good company."

"What do you think that crystal did to him?"

"According to my vision it wasn't anything good."

"You still think what you saw was right after meeting him?"

"You don't?"

She didn't know why she asked. Josh looking away from her and back at the road all but confirmed his answer. He didn't know about crystals like she did though. He must not know about liars either, and how the good ones can hide who they really are.

As they drove into the night, through the empty streets of Blackbirch's industrial area, she kept her eyes on the brake lights of the lemon-yellow car. They barely lit up, Kered speeding ahead when they got onto a straight stretch of road before his car disappeared on the next bend.

"Where'd he go?"

"Relax, he's driving the right way." Josh turned into a darkly lit road lined with concrete warehouses. He pointed to the largest building up ahead. "That's the Olsen factory."

Kallie sparked her energy, the heat slowing her racing heart. She wanted to be prepared for what they found. Already she could sense the presence of another source of magick.

"Do you feel that?" Josh asked.

"Yes."

"What is it?"

She knew but didn't want to say. Not until she could confirm. She waited for Josh to pull into the grounds of the factory so she could see the magick tainted area with her own eyes.

It drew her instantly; a dark spot where the trees started on the outer edge. She summoned her energy so that it sat below the surface of her skin, ready to be used.

"Keep your guard up," she advised Josh as he drove across the concrete lot. "And your veil."

FIFTEEN

Sarah leaned against Kered's hood, pulling the sleeve of her cardigan tighter around her waist. She'd been happy to get out of the car, considering his lead foot, but now the cool air was getting to her.

How far behind is Josh? He was a cautious driver thanks to his parents' fatal accident. Kered didn't have such reservations. He drove fast and with his music loud. As soon as his engine started, the familiar beats of *The Dudes*, a local band from The Playhouse, blasted through the speakers. Sarah knew them too and was able to get on Kered's good side by talking about the songs. He was quite a chatterbox when not being questioned by a stranger with a crystal.

During the short drive, she'd learned Kered was twenty-one and studying to be a mechanic, paying for his tuition with his security job. He'd only been working as a guard in Blackbirch for a few months. It was just him and another guy rotating between shifts for the businesses on the Curvers Rock roster. He'd told her some shift work had dropped off as the factories closed, but the money was still more than he could make closer to home. He said his boss would joke it was witch-hazard pay, a notion Kered had dismissed until the crystal incident. Even then, he claimed he tried to convince himself it had been a weird dream. That was until tonight when they showed up.

"Your brunette friend seems kinda... intense."

"Yeah, she takes this stuff pretty seriously." Sarah leaned further onto the hood, trying to soak up the residual heat from the engine.

"It wasn't serious. That crystal didn't hurt me."

She snorted. "You can't know that. It knocked you out for six hours."

"Yeah, but I was only over there, lying in the dirt." Kered pointed to a dark section of trees planted where the factory's concrete parking lot ended.

Sarah scowled at the spot and leaned forward to get a better look, trying to convince her brain the silhouetted trunks weren't familiar. That those dark branches didn't lead to the exact place Josh had driven the night they first went into the clearing. Maybe she should be taking this more seriously. She glanced at the road. *Hurry up, Josh.*

As if answering her plea, headlights appeared.

"It's go time." Kered pushed off the closed car door, stepping out to meet the bookstore van, but overbalancing. He almost fell right into the path of it, throwing himself backwards at the last second and landing on his ass.

"Are you alright?" Josh jumped out of the driver's door and immediately bent down to help.

"I'm fine." Kered brushed off Josh's hand, dusting the dirt from his pants.

"That was an impressive save." Sarah rushed over. Kered had taken that fall like a seasoned pro, practically bouncing off the concrete and back onto his feet.

"Wish I could say that hasn't happened to me before." Kered shrugged, his face turning red.

Kallie appeared with a scowl on her face. "Have you only been falling over since finding the crystal?"

Sarah tried not to roll her eyes at the question. Josh must not have eased Kallie's paranoia on the ride over.

"I wish that was true." The color on Kered's cheeks deepened. "Then I could say the crystal made me do it instead of my clumsy feet." He laughed, the sound petering off when Kallie threw a look that made it obvious to everyone that she didn't have a sense of humor.

"How about you show us the spot," Sarah suggested.

Kered led them straight ahead, right to the place he'd already talked about. If he really was the evil person Kallie saw in her vision, why would he be helping them so much? "He isn't exactly the villain you said he'd be, is he?" Sarah dropped back a step, whispering at Kallie.

"Or he's the perfect villain and hiding his true self."

Kered reached the trees ahead of them, smacking the top of his head on a low-lying branch.

"Yeah, that klutz is really hiding stuff."

"I found the crystal here." Kered pointed to a circular pattern in the dirt that was clear even in the dark. "Can you see it?" He grabbed at a flashlight clipped to his work belt, pulling it out to switch it on. A baton next to it flung out, hitting the ground at the right angle to extend out.

"Ow!" Sarah jumped back, the baton slamming into her ankle. "Son-of-a-bitch!"

"I am so, so sorry." Kered abandoned his flashlight.

Sarah bent down and examined the lump already visible on her left ankle, blinking back the tears threatening to spill.

"I have an ice pack in my car," Kered offered.

"How about you go and get it?" Kallie suggested.

Now she's sending him away? She couldn't have done it five seconds ago? Sarah gently rubbed her swollen skin.

Josh stepped up behind Kered. "How about I help you?"

Help *him*? Sarah's mouth dropped open. Josh was just as bad as Kallie. She squinted at her ankle. For all anyone knew, she was injured so bad she was bleeding to death.

There was definitely a dark mark that could be blood. She pressed her fingers against it to check, but the mark suddenly changed shape, disappearing as it got lighter. It wasn't blood, just angry red skin. Sarah glanced up. Kallie's power was on her hands, the blue glow illuminating their immediate area. That's why Josh was so quick to usher Kered away.

Kallie's power surged, tinging the air as it pooled into the circular dip in the earth. Kered better have been speaking the truth. If Kallie was trying to see what happened and it was different to his story, there's no telling what she would do. She may have forgiven Sarah for her accusations and explained the glimpse surrounding Melinda's death, but that didn't erase from Sarah's mind the look she'd seen on Kallie's face—the utter lack of empathy in her eyes for the woman dying before her.

Sarah watched the blue energy spread into the moist earth like water pooling, before splashing into Kallie's waiting hands. Her eyes closed as it flowed along her arms and sank into her temples. The whole process lasted seconds, the energy siphoning quickly through the dirt. *Is that it?* The dark night flooded back as Kallie's power dissipated, but Sarah still saw her eyes snap open.

"What did you see?"

"Don't let him leave!"

Kered was in his car, Josh outside the driver's door, holding onto an ice pack and a lunch box. Kallie's scream was so loud, both boys physically startled and Sarah saw Josh's face twist into an expression of utter panic.

"Kered, don't run." Josh lunged at the car.

Run? The security guard wasn't on foot, he was behind the driver's wheel. "Oh, shit."

The engine rumbled to life like a sudden thunderclap, trailed by the thumping slam of the driver's door. Josh hit the ground trying to avoid colliding with the fishtailing bumper, the icepack and lunch box flying from his hands.

Sarah's nostrils filled with the scent of burned rubber as she raced toward Josh, pulling him up from the concrete so fast it felt like she'd ripped his arms out of his sockets.

"You're bleeding." She grabbed his wrist, twisting it around to get a look at the graze on his palm.

"It's okay… I'm fine."

"He got away." Kallie jogged over.

Sarah spun toward her disappointed voice. "You yelling like a psycho didn't help! What was that about?"

"What did you see?" Josh asked, more calmly than Sarah thought Kallie deserved.

"I saw Kered."

"Doing what, torturing puppies?" Whatever it was, it must have been bad to warrant Kallie's reaction.

"It wasn't anything he was doing specifically. It was his presence."

What was it with her and Kered's presence? "Was it apologetically clumsy?"

"No! It was the same as what I saw earlier. He was evil."

"Evil? That guy?" Sarah nodded in the direction Kered had taken off. "Really?"

"You didn't see what *I* saw."

"It's fine," Josh said. "We know where he works, we can find him again."

"If he even comes back to Blackbirch," Sarah argued. "I know I wouldn't."

"Let's just get out of here." Josh fished the van keys from his pocket, his wrist covered in dripping blood.

"Home to the first aid kit again," Sarah sighed, wincing as her adrenalin wore off and the pain swelled in her ankle. She limped beside Josh, the two of them following Kallie to the van.

"Maybe we need to convince Grace to open a pharmacy?"

"Or maybe Kallie can conjure up some healing balm?" Sarah muttered. "That's if she's not too busy sensing everyone's evil presence."

"I think if she could make a healing balm she would have already," Josh whispered back.

Kallie had stopped at the van door, but was staring back at the spot Kered showed them while she fiddled with the medical tape strapped to her broken fingers.

"Maybe I should drive?" Sarah signaled for him to toss her the keys.

"You might as well, you're the only one without injured hands."

She clicked the button to unlock the doors, shaking her head. "And yet you two have all the magickal power."

SIXTEEN

Silence greeted Josh when he opened the front door. For a second, he thought Grace was still at the bookstore until he glanced at his watch and realized it'd be too late for that. She'd be in bed sleeping, so he turned to the girls behind him with a finger raised to his lips.

"I'll sneak upstairs for the antiseptic," Sarah whispered, making a limping beeline for the stairs.

"She knows where all the creaky steps are," Josh told Kallie, as he crept across the living room, groping for the armchair he could just see the outline of.

"The lamp's over here, yeah?" Kallie's voice came from somewhere to his right.

"Near the couch." Josh blinked when the corner of the room burst into light, his eyes adjusting to find Kallie's face contorting into a pained grimace. "You okay?"

She nodded, pulling her broken fingers from the lamp switch and cupping them gently.

"I don't know how you keep forgetting you're injured." He met her at the couch, patting the cushions. As much as Kallie tried to hide it, he knew she was in pain.

"It's not about forgetting." She sat next to him. "I can't afford to be hurt right now."

Josh chuckled. "You can't just pretend your fingers aren't broken."

"Who says?"

A smile appeared with her answer, but it twitched at the corners of her mouth, threatening to come undone. Her mask was slipping. The one he knew all too well.

"You don't have to fake being fine," he said. "Not around me."

"I am fine." Kallie's smile wavered.

He picked up her injured hand and felt the rough tape against his skin. "I wish I could fix this for you."

"It's not your job to fix me."

"Why not? You seem to think it's yours to protect me."

"It is."

"Who says?" Josh asked. That's right, he could be just as stubborn.

"I'm bad at my job. I put you in danger."

"And here I am, blaming myself for the same thing."

Kallie's gaze drifted to the broken fingers he held. Seconds later, she lifted her other hand to his as a replacement. *Well done, Josh, you were hurting her.*

With her good hand, Kallie traced her index finger across his upturned palm. He closed his eyes to concentrate on her touch, feeling it sink into the grooves of his skin. This was the hand he'd cut open. The one that had miraculously healed when his energy first sparked. *No, that's not right.* It'd healed when he first touched the cloth-bound notebook that belonged to his mom, the one full of her energy.

He opened his eyes. "Do you trust me?"

"Of course."

He gently pulled his hand from Kallie's and called on as much power as he could without lowering his veil. Kallie straightened, tilting her head to the side as she eyed his lit fingertips.

"May I?" He pushed his glowing hands toward her.

Her eyebrows raised, but she gave him a quick nod. He gently re-cupped her fingers, hoping he didn't look as unsure as she did.

That wasn't how he felt. He was acting on instinct, closing his eyes to concentrate as his power moved along with his thoughts. A flash of light erupted in the darkness behind his closed eyelids, before fading to leave a dark void. In a place that seemed distant, he became conscious of his hands and the heat that warmed throughout. It was fed from his veins and the power that lined them. It waited for him to activate his gift. The strength was always there, even during the times he didn't feel powerful. It wanted to help him, but such a gift would not heal Kallie's bones. It had been responsible for breaking them.

What he needed was the other gift present in his body. The one that had been hidden even deeper than his own ability. The more he thought about it being there, the stronger it called to him, confirming his hunch and begging to be set free.

He stroked Kallie's taped fingers and connected to the cracks that snaked through them, wishing more than anything that he could fill them in. His energy rose to his demand, but not in a way he'd ever experienced before. Instead of hardness, there was softness, instead of destruction, restoration. His gift weaved itself around Kallie's damaged bones and knitted them back together.

When it was done, his skin cooled, the light flash making another appearance before he opened his eyes and blinked. The yellow glow of the lamp hit him before he focused on Kallie. She was staring at her hand, still nestled in his. Josh unwrapped the tape and watched Kallie's fingers bend like they'd never been broken.

"How did you get your magick to do that?" She wiggled her healed fingers.

He parted his lips, but no words came out, just a smile so wide he could feel it in his cheekbones.

Kallie gave her ring and pinky fingers another stretch and flex. "Was it a spell?"

Her eyes darted from her hand to his face, slowly morphing from wonder to what looked like worry. Why was she so concerned about something so awesome?

"It wasn't a spell," he said. "It was my power."

"Like an ability?"

"Yes. It was the same as calling on my strength."

"You shouldn't have been able to do that." Kallie's voice dropped to a whisper, as if she believed speaking about it any louder would cause something terrible to happen.

"I know you said the magick only gives one ability, but there's so much we don't know about the origins of the power and what it can do. Isn't it possible that rule is wrong?"

"It's not wrong," Kallie insisted. "Healing is also a very rare gift. Even though you and I have power and we can manipulate the energy around us, healing is on another level. To heal using your own magick *is* a big deal."

Had what he'd done been that monumental? Despite the headache brewing in the deep spaces of his brain, healing Kallie's bones had been almost effortless. It was as natural to him as breathing. It also reminded him of the car accident. He knew his mother had cast the Beginning to save his life, but before that... *she tried to heal my wounds.*

"My mother was a healer. Her ability *must* have come over with her power when she saved my life."

Kallie's lower lip dropped, the same disbelief settling into her features as the last time they'd talked about his mom's power. He'd healed Kallie though; she couldn't deny it.

He sparked his power again and filtered his energy through his wrist's fresh graze, wiping away the dried blood.

"Okay." Kallie eyed his smooth skin. "There *may* be some truth to your theory. Before your mother, no one had ever successfully cast the Beginning. That means she had great power."

Great power she'd hidden. He understood why, but that didn't mean it wasn't frustrating. If he knew about the magick, if his mother had prepared him, he wouldn't be playing catch-up now. He might have known something was off with Kered before he ran. He might even be good enough that Kallie could trust him to lift his veil. She was so worried Cade would find them. The fear that clouded her features when she talked about him was the same as an expression that struck her tonight at the Olsen Factory.

"When you glimpsed Kered and his crystal, was it darkness you saw?"

Any joy present in Kallie slipped from her then.

"I saw total darkness in Kered. The kind I've only seen in one other person."

"Cade."

"Yes."

"Do you think the crystal was his? That he infected Kered with it?"

"I didn't see that when I glimpsed. I hope not. Even if Cade isn't involved, when Kered ignites that darkness, I'm worried it'll call him here."

No wonder she was so concerned about finding Kered, and about him not running away. Josh didn't want Cade in town either, or anywhere near Kallie.

"We'll stop Kered before that happens," he promised.

Kallie leaned back, her head resting on the top of the couch.

The night's events had only added to her omnipresent fatigue, and he wished that was something he could have healed too. He wanted more than anything to erase the last few months of her life, and to obliterate the non-physical scars left by Cade, by loss, by death, but would she want him to? Would he do the same for himself? They wouldn't be the same people then, and they wouldn't have crossed paths now.

Kallie's touch brought him out of his thoughts, her healed fingers stroking his skin.

"I should go."

He lifted his hand to her cheek and brushed away a stray hair strand, letting his fingertips linger. Kallie's eyes focused on his and his breath caught in his throat. He wanted them to stay there. He wanted to lean closer to her, to her lips, but her attention drifted behind him.

Josh turned. Sarah was sitting on the stairs, her head resting against the banister and her ear cocked toward them. *How long has she been there?* In her hands was a bag of cotton balls and a bottle of antiseptic.

"I should go," Kallie repeated, standing. "We'll catch up again tomorrow to work on finding Kered."

"Why do we need to?" Sarah asked, not moving. "He isn't the one in your vision."

"Not yet."

"So you keep saying."

113

Josh shot Sarah a now-is-not-the-time-look. "I'll drive you back to your motel," he said to Kallie.

"It's fine. Stay here and rest."

"Are you sure?"

"We have early morning shifts at the bookstore," Sarah reminded him. "It's the weekend and we'll be busy."

"You'd better get some sleep then." Kallie patted his arm. "Besides, I could use the fresh air."

"How about you meet us at the bookstore in the morning?" Josh suggested. "You can look in the stacks while we work. I'm sure if there's any worthwhile books, you'll find them."

Kallie gave him a smile. He ignored the eye roll from Sarah.

"Tomorrow morning, around nine-ish." He walked Kallie to the front door.

"See you then." She waved at Sarah, who surprised Josh by waving back. She'd voiced her annoyance, though, and that was usually enough for her.

As soon as the door was shut, Sarah rose from the steps. "So, you get two abilities and I get none? That's not fair."

Josh eyed the way she stepped lightly on her swollen ankle and brought his energy to his fingers again, reaching down and wrapping his hands and power around Sarah's bare skin.

Now that he knew the gift was there, it surfaced naturally, melting the lump caused by Kered's baton with barely any effort on his part.

"Right now, I'd trade both gifts for the ability to get some decent sleep." He glanced at his watch. They had to be up again in four hours.

Sarah flexed her healed ankle and smiled, pulling her cell from her back pocket. The act wiped away her good mood.

"What's with the frown?"

"Nothing." She slipped the phone away.

She wasn't fast enough to hide the fact there were no notifications. Usually Max texted her goodnight. "Everything all right?"

"Yeah. Do you think Kallie will be okay getting home?"

Was Sarah really concerned or being sarcastic? He couldn't tell. Not this late. "She might as well have stayed." He yawned. "And driven in with us in the morning."

"Oh, yeah?" Sarah tilted her head. "And where would Kallie have slept?"

It was also too late to be made fun of, but at least he'd made her happy again for a second. "Good night, Sarah."

He felt her fingers poke his back as he ducked past her, her giggles following him all the way up to his bedroom.

SEVENTEEN

Sarah sighed as Josh rushed up the bookstore stairs for the fifth time since his shift started, ending the forced-out breath with a growl.

He was supposed to be restocking the candles but kept going to the stacks to talk to Kallie. Even her mom, who was due to leave on a delivery run, had spent all morning upstairs chatting with her.

"We should be paying Kallie, with all the organizing she's doing up there," Grace said, pawing through Sarah's immaculately stocked counter drawers. "I didn't know there was a market for half of the stock sitting in those old boxes. Have you seen my address book?"

"It should be in *your* desk drawer." She nudged her mom's fingers away. *Go and destroy your own workspace.*

"Kallie knows a guy who will buy our unsold inventory."

"Great," Sarah replied, hoping her remark didn't sound too sarcastic. Kallie should be finding information to work out what happened to Kered when he found his crystal, not sorting the stacks.

"It is great." Grace smiled. "If only she was staying in town. She could have Eve's old position."

"Speaking of... have you heard from Eve?" Even with all this new Kered business, Blackbirch's resident witch and her strange behavior hadn't been far from Sarah's thoughts. Neither were the unanswered texts she'd sent to Eve over the last week. Sarah was sure Eve was up to something, even if Kallie and Josh had deemed her harmless. They didn't know Eve like she did.

"No. I asked her to come in and pick up her final paycheck, but she hasn't. Could you follow it up?"

Sarah pulled out her phone. There weren't any messages from Max yesterday either, which was even stranger than Eve's disappearing act. She texted him asking where he was, smiling when she got an instant reply. *So, he is still alive.* Good, now she could kill him.

'I'm right behind you.'

She laughed at the message on her screen, tapping her fingers across her cell. She almost dropped it seconds later when a heavy hand hit her shoulder. She spun. Max was literally behind her.

"Long time no text." She waved her phone at him.

"You can't do without me for one day?" He placed a small taped-sealed box next to her on the counter.

"What's that? And why are you coming through the back entrance? You don't work here. Unless you want to? I still haven't found a replacement for Eve."

"What's with the million questions?" Max wiped his hands through his cropped hair.

He only did that when he was nervous. "Is everything okay?"

"Of course. I've got some things of yours." He tapped the box. "You left them in my room."

"You cleaned?" Sarah slapped a hand on her cheek and let her jaw drop. "Now I know something is wrong. Did the world end and I just don't know it yet?"

"Maybe not your world."

A forced smile followed Max's reply. Was he trying to pass that comment off as funny?

"What happened?" she demanded.

Max wouldn't look at her, his blue eyes darting around the busy bookstore. "Can we go somewhere quieter? Upstairs?"

"Josh and my mom are up there. How about outside?" She reached over to lock the register, her fingers hovering over the key as a customer piled the counter with books.

"You can't," Max said. "Don't worry. I'll talk to you later."

"No, wait." Sarah grabbed him, but he pulled out of her grasp, disappearing down the hallway to the store's back door.

Josh propped the front door open, stepping aside as Kallie shimmied past him juggling a bag of books.

"Are you coming in too?" He turned back to Sarah.

"Huh?" She halted on the porch; her eyes glued to her cell.

"Max still hasn't called?"

"I spoke to him." Sarah barely glanced up. "He came into the store, but something was up, and he left without telling me what it was. Now he won't reply to my texts."

Josh leaned out of the door frame and squinted through the black birches lining the side of the yard. He couldn't see all of Max's house through their full, green branches, but he saw enough to know the garage was open. "Someone's home. Why don't you go and check if it's him?"

Sarah raised her head and narrowed her eyes at the trees. "Don't eat my sandwich."

He jiggled the tote in his hand, packed with food from The Cheese and Grill café on Main Street. "I don't know, they smell good." He inhaled the toasty scent of melted cheese and butter wafting from the bag.

"Don't eat my sandwich." Sarah spun on her heels, striding across the porch.

"Don't take forever," he called out. Any longer than twenty minutes and her grilled cheese was fair game. He licked his lips as he walked into the kitchen, his stomach giving a rumble in protest of its emptiness.

"Where's Sarah?" Kallie asked.

"She'll be back soon." He threw the wrapped sandwiches onto the dining table. It was well past lunch, closer to dinnertime, the day having slipped away between store cleans and customers.

"So you only found a few useful things in the bookstore?" he asked Kallie as they settled down to eat.

She nodded. "Grace has a fantastic collection. It's not as helpful as Melinda's, but then again, she wrote a lot of her own spells."

"But you found some possibilities for what the magick in Kered's crystal could be, right?"

"Yep. I'm positive it's magick that will change him."

That didn't sound good. "If Kered isn't yet this dark, violent person you saw in your vision, then who attacked us?"

"I've been wondering the same thing." Kallie put down her half-eaten sandwich. "Didn't you say that someone has gone after you before?"

He remembered the text conversation they had last week, when she said she could always tell when the maid had been in her motel room because the air was different. Josh had felt something similar a few weeks ago, when he woke to find his bedroom ransacked. "It was during that dream we shared when you showed me the tarot cards." Hadn't he mentioned that detail? Maybe he hadn't because she didn't give him a reply at the time. During the dream, Kallie said she would stop whoever was in his room. "You don't remember seeing anyone?"

"No, but those dreams were all over the place and so confusing. It was hard to know what was real."

Is that what she thought of them? "They were real to me."

"Well… what's unreal is this sandwich. Who knew melted cheese could be so good, right?"

"Ah, yeah." Josh picked at the gooey yellow cheese clinging to the paper. "It's the best."

"Josh?"

Kallie's hand reached across the table, her fingertips barely touching his before pulling away. He'd been wrong about how much the dreams meant to her. He must have been wrong about their connection too. She didn't even want to touch him.

He glanced up. Kallie's eyes were glazed, her palms pressed into her temple, like that day in the clearing. *Not again.* "What's happening? Are you okay?" He jumped up, his chair toppling and clanging into the floorboards.

Kallie was out of her chair too, swaying unsteadily on her feet, stumbling and then heading toward the ground with no hands out to break her fall.

Josh lunged, his arms wrapping around her waist and pulling her up, inches from the hard floor. She convulsed once, her whole body shaking as the heat of her skin burned against his.

Kallie's fingers loosened, their fierce grip falling from her forehead as she rapidly blinked.

"What is it?" Josh asked.

"It's Kered." She pushed out a heavy breath. "He's changed now. We can't help him anymore."

"That was a vision?"

Kallie nodded, resting her hands on the table. They didn't sit flat, her fingers shaking against the wood.

"Are your visions always so physical?" He placed a hand on top of hers to stop it moving, to offer some comfort, but she slid it away.

"We should find Kered before he uses his darkness."

"Do you know how to contain it?" Josh followed Kallie's movements to the kitchen door.

"I know how to stop him."

"You found a spell?"

"I told you there is no way to remove the darkness once it becomes a part of him."

"Then what are we going to do?"

"What we have to."

What we have to? Did that mean what he thought it meant? Surely he'd misheard her. "You're not talking about killing him, are you?"

"I'm talking about stopping him before he hurts us or someone else."

"There's got to be a way we can save—"

"The Kered you met is gone now."

"But—"

"But nothing! Either you help or you don't. I can do this alone if I have to."

They were supposed to be in this together. "I want to help you," Josh assured her, "but there has to be another option. Please."

Kallie's hard gaze softened. Was she considering his suggestion? She had to see that they could think of something else, a plan that didn't involve killing anyone.

His cheek twitched, his skin shifting against the faint fluttering of a loose hair strand. He pushed his dark locks behind his ears, ignoring the sudden rush of heat making the hairs on his neck prickle.

Kallie's hands raised, energy lashing every inch of exposed skin, melding together into a ball of blue fire at the center of her palms.

"What do you need all that power for?" Had she sensed something? He glanced beyond her to the back door. Grace and Sarah never locked it. Someone could have snuck in.

"You don't look well, Josh. You should stay here and rest."

"We should both stay." He swallowed, the thick air lining his throat like hot cocoa.

"I can't." Kallie pulled her hands apart, the blue fireball doubling. "Not while Kered's out there."

Josh stumbled forward. Maybe he should have stumbled back. The direction didn't matter in the end. Neither option gave him the chance to duck.

EIGHTEEN

Sarah found Max in the garage rifling through a cardboard box. His father was there too, loading boxes into the back of his car. The trunk was so full she wondered if they were clearing out the whole house. *Max's mom must be on one of her cleaning sprees again.*

She eyed the boxes at Mr. Ryan's feet and wondered which decluttering trend had inspired this round. He was getting rid of clothes, shoes, and office files. That seemed odd to her. Wouldn't he need those?

She scanned Max's box. There wasn't anything scribbled on the side in his illegible handwriting, but she could see the corner of one of his monitors poking from the cardboard edge. Max wouldn't get rid of that. Even if his mom told him to.

Mr. Ryan was packing up everything he owned. Max was packing up everything he loved. They were moving out. Max's world really had ended.

"Max." She moved up behind him, blinking back the tears that threatened to spill.

He looked up from his box, rising from his crouched position beside it. "Hey."

Just a 'hey.' No, 'Hey, Sar?' Not even a smile? His face looked weird without his lopsided grin. Maybe because she couldn't remember the last time she'd seen him without it, especially for her. Max always had a smile for her.

"You left in a hurry today." She glanced toward Mr. Ryan, who was so focused on his task he didn't even look up at her arrival.

"I came home to pack. My dad's moving."

"It's good you're helping him out." Although she didn't understand why Max was giving his dad one of his computer monitors. Didn't Mr. Ryan have one in his home office he could take?

"I'm not helping him." Max's gaze shot to his dad's car, but he didn't focus on anything before leaning down to hoist his own box up. "These are my things. I'm moving in with my uncle."

Sarah's heart jumped into her throat. "You won't be living next door to me anymore?"

Max snorted, half laughing. "Sorry to disappoint *you*, Sarah."

How could she say something so unimportant right now? "Sorry, I—"

"It's fine." He cut her off.

The look was back. The heavy one he'd worn to the bookstore. It pooled into his hunched shoulders, dragging them down. They were practically the same height, something they hadn't been since they were eleven. "I'm sorry I haven't been around."

"It doesn't matter." Max shrugged.

Yes, it does. If he didn't care, he'd have his reserved-for-her lopsided smile.

"My life has been so messed up lately, I wouldn't want to hang out with me either." He jammed another box into the trunk.

"That's not why I haven't seen you." She wanted to tell him about everything from the last few weeks, all the unimaginable things she'd learned. Sarah didn't think there'd ever be a time when she and Max kept things from each other. Now they had, it created a strange distance. One that stopped him from coming to her with his problems. "Can we talk?" She glanced at his dad. Mr. Ryan's back was to them, but he was within earshot.

"They don't want me."

Sarah shifted, her whole body turning to Max. She had to look to confirm it was him who spoke. The hushed words were so bitter, so tainted, it was as if another person uttered them. Someone she didn't know.

"What?"

"*They* don't want me."

"Who?"

"Mom and Dad. I'm going to live with my uncle because they don't want me."

"That can't be true." Max always joked about his parents not caring about him, and she'd seen the way they ignored him sometimes, but they were still his parents. They were still a family.

"They're selling the house and they both got new jobs out of town. Neither offered for me to go with them." Max slammed his trunk shut. "Like I would have, anyway."

Mr. Ryan finished packing too, his trunk echoing Max's thud. As he turned from the car, he looked at Sarah. There was no polite nod this time, just the lowered head of a coward, slinking to the door and disappearing into the house.

"They gave me every excuse in the book," Max said. "I'll be eighteen in a few months and finishing school this year and probably moving out on my own soon enough anyway, but the real truth is they don't want me."

"Why didn't you tell me this sooner?"

"When Sarah? You're always hanging out with Josh now, and when you're not with him, you're talking about him or his new girlfriend, or whoever she is. You don't have time to hear my problems."

Her palm went to her cheek. Her stomach in knots. Yeah, she might have been busy with Josh and Kallie, but Max knew where she lived, where she worked. He drove her to school every weekday morning. They'd been in the car earlier that week, when she was researching security uniforms after Kallie told them about her vision. Max could have said something then. She would have looked up from her phone. She would have listened. *Maybe if you'd looked up, you would have noticed before today how flat his eyes are.* She raised her hand toward him, to comfort him and playfully mess with his hair like she always did, but he stepped away before her fingers got near. He'd never done that before. He must be really mad. "I'm so sorry."

"Yeah. You said that already."

"Why don't you text me when you've settled in? I'll come over and we can overdose on pepperoni pizza and watch a movie."

"Sure. If you can squeeze me in."

She didn't know what was bigger; the knot in her stomach or the lump in her throat. She turned to leave, drifting. *Please stop me.*

Max didn't call after her. He didn't ask her to stay. He let her go. Not even saying goodbye as she walked away.

She reached the edge of the open garage door, her hand going to her eyes to shield them from the setting sun. The brightness surprised her, she couldn't feel the sunbeams heat and had forgotten it was there. Maybe that's all Max needed right now? To remember the warmth.

She turned back to call to him, to ask him to join her, but all she found was two packed cars.

Sarah looked up when the edge of her ballet flat hit the tiled step of her front porch.

She was so focused on holding in her tears; she hadn't noticed she'd crossed back into her yard. That was the problem though, wasn't it? Her failure to notice she'd been a bad friend, unable to see that Max's family had finally fallen apart, and she wasn't there to help him deal with it.

She sniffed, wiping at her nose as she dragged her feet to the front door and slipped inside.

"Josh?" He sat sprawled on the same stair she'd been on last night, leaning against the banister just like she had. But he wasn't eavesdropping and hanging on the words of others—it looked as if he was hanging on for dear life. "What happened?" She rushed over.

His face tilted toward her voice, the effort ricocheting through his whole body and forcing his banister-clamped hands to shake. The stairs squeaked like he was running up them. The poor guy could barely move.

"Ka-Ka Kallie." Josh closed his eyes, all his features tightening.

Sarah couldn't see her, but the books Kallie brought home from the bookstore were strewn across the floor. Sarah darted along the disheveled trail and into the kitchen, worried the person from the woods had found them.

Was Kallie's body sprawled across the dining room floor? She almost didn't want to look, keeping her head up until she had no choice but to scan the floorboards.

"N-o-o," Josh's shaking voice called to her. "Sh-she shocked m-me with her pow-power, then left."

Sarah turned and sprinted back to him. "What? Why?"

"Sh-she's going after Ke-Kered. She did-didn't want me to go wi-with her."

And this is how she stopped him? "Take in some deep breaths." Sarah returned to the kitchen and got him a drink of water. He seemed better once he'd finished the glass.

"Why did she want to go alone?" Sarah helped Josh stand and move to the couch.

"S-she said Kered has... turned. That we can't help him anymore."

So that gentle klutz had become the violent person Kallie feared? And she didn't stick around to say, I told you so? "Kallie's not going after Kered to help him, is she?"

Josh's face cracked, like it was shattering along with his heart.

Sarah fished her phone out of her cardigan pocket and called Curvers Rock Security, speaking to the owner. "Kered's working the Olsen factory tonight," she said after hanging up. "His shift starts at nine."

Josh's head moved, but she couldn't tell if he was nodding or shaking. She watched his still trembling hand put the glass on the coffee table edge, her mom's voice already in her head telling her to move it. Sarah was too late. The glass slipped to the hard floor before she could reach out, shattering.

Her hands flew to her ears as the smashing echoed with a sharp ping. Beside her, Josh's hand had flown up too, only his went to his temple, latching onto his skull so tightly she worried he would burrow through to the bone.

"Josh? Josh!" She shook his shoulder roughly, watching his head roll to the side and his brown eyes surface from under an unfocused glaze.

"Kallie's in trouble." Josh straightened.

"Forget about Kallie. We just have to worry about Kered."

"No. Kered is the problem. Kallie won't be able to stop him, he's too powerful for her."

"How do you know that?"

"Because I saw it."

Wait. He *saw* it? "You had a vision?"

Josh stood, using the couch arm to steady himself. "Kallie's vision wasn't real. It's all a trap."

NINETEEN

Josh swiped his hand along the frosted glass, wiping away the condensation, only to have his breath fog it up a second later.

Next to him, Sarah shifted in the passenger seat, her hands closing around her mouth to stifle a yawn. They'd been sitting in the van for an hour, watching the night sky deepen from streaks of orange to the darkest shade of black. Where were the stars? He swiped the window again and squinted, but the clouds must have been too thick or the lights from the Olsen factory too strong. He couldn't get a glimpse of the tiny sparks shining in the dark and wondered if it was a bad omen.

"Do you think Kallie will remember how to get here?" Sarah asked.

"If she doesn't, she'll feel the pull of the energy." He could. Even parked away from the grounds. But he couldn't feel her. Kallie's presence had been absent since she shocked him, and he missed it.

He couldn't say that to Sarah, though. She wouldn't understand. Not after the look she gave him when he lowered his veil for a few seconds looking for Kallie and didn't find her. Sarah had said it was a good thing, her lips almost forming a smile before she caught herself and straightened them out. She was ready to crucify Kallie for what she'd done. He just wanted to find her and make sure she was okay.

"Do you see that?" Sarah's neck stretched, her right arm raising to point through the windshield.

The Olsen factory might have had lights, but they barely lit the concrete parking lot. After the first half hour, Josh began to think he had it wrong. Maybe his vision had been a trick like Kallie's, and whoever sent them was laughing about the time he was wasting, waiting for something to happen in a place void of a living presence. Now, a lone figure emerged from the back end of the lot, just outside the far building.

"It's Kered." He studied the security guard's face as he passed under a bulb fixed to the factory wall. "He's in his uniform."

"We knew he was working." Sarah's hand reached for the door.

"Wait." Josh scowled, watching Kered pull back and forth on the handle of the factory door, the sleeves of his shirt crumpling with every move. "He wasn't in a uniform in my vision."

"Maybe he gets changed after his shift?" Sarah suggested. "It's not like you have an exact time, just that it's happening tonight."

"Maybe," Josh murmured, but tightness still gnawed in his chest.

Kered continued to stride his way down the empty lot, pulling his retractable baton from his waistband and twirling it as he went. The closer he came to their end, the clearer his features. Josh's only experience with darkness came from facing the twisted, dead monster of Arden. When he saw his true face, it was steeped in death, his eyes empty, his burned lips spitting cruelness and lies. Kered's lips were pursed. Josh cracked open the van window. In the silent night, the merriness of Kered's whistled tune easily reached them.

"This isn't the Kered from my vision. He was cold, dark, like Kallie predicted he would be."

Kered reached the end of the building and sauntered across the yard, reaching the black birches fenced off by a thin wire. As he walked beside them, running his baton along the makeshift fence, he stumbled on the uneven ground, and almost landed on his face.

The tightness in Josh's chest traveled up and formed a noose around his neck. Either Kered was a fantastic actor, playing the bumbling fool to a T, or something sinister was happening. "The Kered from my vision never would have fallen like that." He'd been confident, cocky, almost like a different person. Was it possible Kered hadn't been changed yet? That they could still stop this without anyone getting hurt.

"Let's find out what's going on," Sarah said.

Kered was still following the line of black birches as they stalked after him through the lot. The tree's silhouetted branches bordered the area, letting them know their boundaries against the starless sky. Josh didn't need the visual. He could feel their hum. It grew stronger as he filtered his magick to his skin and it mixed with the tainted energy coating their surroundings. In the symphony of power, another note was added.

"Kallie." Josh paused, scanning the concrete.

"Where? Do you see her?" Sarah whispered at his back.

He shook his head. She was hiding from them, but her energy was unmistakable, and she was summoning something big.

"We need to find Kered, now!"

Josh sprinted ahead of Sarah, aiming for the far building where Kered and his whistle echoed.

"Kered!" He flailed his arms above his head.

He should have called out to Kallie. Maybe it would have stopped her.

Kered's face lit up. Was he happy to see Josh running at him like a madman? No, that wasn't it. It was the glow of Kallie's blue energy coloring Kered's skin, giving it light as it exploded across him in a fiery flash.

"What is she doing?" Sarah let out a shocked cry.

Kered crumpled to the ground, drowning in a sea of electric blue waves.

Still sprinting, the horror of what was happening jumbling before him, Josh finally saw her. She darted out from the trees, closing the gap between herself and Kered before he had covered half of the same distance. She really was a runner.

"Sense me," he begged. "I'm here to help." He couldn't warn her that what she'd seen was wrong because Kallie was too fast, too focused, too determined to deal with Kered's darkness. Was she even going to check he had changed before doing the unthinkable?

"Kallie!"

His shout was ignored as she pressed Kered into the ground with lashings of her energy. Blue power flooded the concrete, spilling from her hands forcefully, wildly, like she couldn't control it.

Kered squirmed, his baton still gripped in his hand. His eyes went wide at the sight of it, as if he'd only just realized he held something that could help him.

Josh's sneakers slapped the pavement as he forced his legs to increase their pace.

Kered's baton struck up, slicing through the energy like a sword, and slamming into Kallie's ribcage. She doubled over, almost falling into her puddle of power. Her hands splayed open as she used them to break her fall, the flood of magick, disrupted. "God dammit!" her voice hissed.

Now was Josh's chance.

He summoned his own energy, the red lighting Sarah's face as she drew alongside him. In the darkness, it was like the sun. Kallie and Kered turned; his face breaking into a look of utter relief; hers, a scowl.

Hate me later, Kallie. Josh copied her earlier move and molded his power into a ball. It soared into the sky, briefly flying above them, before it raced back to earth and found its target.

The air in the space between Kered and Kallie exploded. Josh wanted to separate them, and it worked. His red energy broke Kallie's hold. Kered ditched his baton and scrambled to his feet, rushing toward Sarah.

She pulled ahead of Josh, her arms stretching out for Kered. Josh made a beeline for Kallie, his lungs burning as he skidded at her. He slowed his pace, the tips of his sneakers digging down into the concrete as he forced himself to stop. *I know this.*

The scene before him was familiar.

Kallie's hands twisted at her waist, her fingers frantically shaping her energy into a rounded sphere. He'd seen her do that hours earlier when the image was jammed so violently into his head. Slower in real life, the pieces of his vision slotted into place.

Kallie would raise her arm and throw the ball past him. He planted his feet, determined to not accidentally step into the energy's explosive path. "Play it out. Throw the ball," he whispered.

The energy flung from her hands, sailing over his head like he knew it would. His ears picked up the high pitch whistle, his hair blowing back at the force of magick rushing by. He whipped sideways, following its path. Something he'd failed to see, what the vision hadn't shown him, was the ball's real target—Sarah and Kered.

"Duck!" he screamed.

They couldn't.

They didn't.

Scattered across the ground in opposite directions, Sarah and Kered landed roughly on the concrete. How could Kallie do that? Did Kered deserve punishment without evidence of a crime? Was Sarah just collateral damage? *Am I?*

Josh summoned another energy ball, throwing it at Kallie before she could do the same. He aimed off to her left. He didn't want to hurt her.

The ball exploded next to Kallie, sending her toppling onto the ground.

He took off, darting at Sarah and Kered, reaching Sarah first.

"Are you hurt?"

Her scattered blond locks clung to her face, strands near her right temple held in place by sticky blood.

"Help Kered!" She used grazed palms to push him toward their fallen new friend.

Kallie, on her feet, was racing to the security guard. Josh couldn't outrun her. He couldn't even stop her.

She looked possessed. Her eyes focused squarely on her prey, her mane of dark waves loose and wild as she bore down on Kered.

Passing under the yellow glow of the factory lights, Josh spied the blood dripping from her nose, the shake in her fists as her skin frothed with energy. It was taking everything she had to summon it. How far was she willing to go?

"You have to stop her!" Sarah screamed, her bloody hands waving frantically.

Heat rushed through him, warming his skin as fast as the movements of his contorting palms. This time he aimed his energy ball directly at Kallie, pushing the essence of his strength gift into its edges. If she was unconscious, she couldn't hurt Kered—or herself.

His arm wound back, the magick dancing on his fingertips. It'd been years since he'd thrown a ball, but the skills his dad taught had helped so far. Ready, his body shifted, sending him to his knees when a sudden sharpness splintered his forehead.

Snap!

Thud!

The searing pain tore through his temple, bubbling into his brain as the hardness of the ground gave way beneath him. He didn't feel the concrete as his knees smashed against it, or his bones sinking into it like they'd hit sand.

What he could feel was the invasion. The flood of images cramming into his synapses and lighting them on fire.

Not now! Not another vision.

TWENTY

Josh squeezed his eyes shut, but all that did was give his vision a canvas to play on.

"I know this," he growled, watching fractured, stilted images of Kallie shaping her energy and throwing it at him. After this, she would attack Kered, running at him like she was now. Then things would change. She would be somewhere else. In the dark? A warehouse? It must be the Olsen Factory. There would be a brick pillar. She'd be tied to it with rope, trapped, tricked. Kered would be there. Dressed in red? No, black.

Josh tried to picture his previous vision and work it out, but it was no longer clear. The faces were missing. Was it Kered he was seeing? Kallie?

Show me. He surrendered.

The energy ball in his hands cooled, and he pushed every ounce of magick in his veins to breaking point, forcing it all to his fingertips.

He searched his mind, through the tangle of images, for the edges of his veil and lifted it. Heat coursed through his limbs. His knees held him up against the cold concrete, his hands carried the energy ball.

He could see it in his mind's eye, in the new vision, bright, vibrant, and blood red. It sailed from his fingers, streaking across the night sky to the far end of the factory where it landed next to…

Oh, God!

"Josh!"

Kallie? His eyes flew open, her scream forcing the images to flee. It was fine. He'd seen enough.

Kallie had Kered in her energy-infused hands while Sarah ran at them with Kered's discarded baton raised over her head.

Josh had to stop Kallie. She needed to know the truth.

"Kallie, wait!" His shout echoed across the concrete lot, bouncing back at him, at all of them. Sarah slowed, her torso twisting, her bloodied hair whipping around her face. Kered's head swiveled in Josh's direction, his ashen face terrified.

Please listen. If I mean anything to you, stop and listen.

Kallie's head turned, her whole body freezing as her wide eyes settled on him.

Raising his energy ball, Josh flung it, watching it color the night sky as it had in his vision. It careened toward Kallie and Kered, her eyes narrowing as the ball drew closer. Her grasp on Kered loosened. Her blue power flared out like a flame, twisting its damaging energy at him, at the sky. *Just wait. Please.*

The ball sailed over Kallie's head and her flaming wall of energy to Josh's target; the shadows at the far end building.

"Two!" Josh pointed to the fifth person. "The crystal split Kered in two!"

Clang!

Kered's baton slipped from Sarah's hand. She'd stopped running when Josh's energy ball flew over her. Now she turned to face him. "Oh, f—"

"Run, Sarah!" He blasted past her, toward Kallie who had dropped the uniformed Kered, and was studying the Kered clad in dark jeans and a black shirt. That was the Kered from his vision. That was who they needed to stop. "Get up!" Josh reached security Kered and pulled him from the ground, summoning his healing ability and filtering it across the limp in Kered's left leg.

"What's happening, man? I-I. Wait! How did you fix that?"

"We don't have time."

Sarah appeared and took Kered's hand. "It's go time," she said.

"Find shelter inside the factory if you can." Josh ushered them away, checking on the other Kered. He strode toward them—then broke into a run.

Josh searched for this Kered's energy and wondered what his ability would be. Was he building his power, keeping it from them until he was close enough to strike?

"How do we play this, Kallie? What about his gift?"

"He doesn't have one."

"What?"

"Can you feel his energy?"

"No."

"He doesn't have power, which means he doesn't have a gift."

"So, he's just a man?"

"I... don't know?"

She doesn't know? What was coming toward them?

Kallie's energy flared across her skin, exploding like a flame, with the heat to match. Josh once again copied her, lining every inch of his exposed skin with red power. Around them, the parking lot lit up, swallowing the shadows the other Kered had been hiding in. Every speck of space was so visible there wasn't a place for escape. *Come and get us.*

But he didn't. This thing running toward them changed direction, darting off to Josh's right. "Did we scare him off?"

"He's not here for us," Kallie said, her energy light following the other Kered as her body shifted to keep track.

Josh looked at the trajectory. "He wants him." Other Kered was going straight for actual Kered—and Sarah.

Kered and Sarah probably thought they were hidden, their backs straightened against the side of the Olsen Factory wall, but their haven was exposed. Kallie took off toward them, Josh no match for her speed. He twisted his power into another ball and pitched it.

His aim finally faltered, the energy falling short of the other Kered and coloring the ground of the parking lot instead. "Shit!"

Kallie skidded through his power, scooping it up and expertly using it to boost her own. A laser beam of energy shot from her fingers, striking the other Kered in the back and knocking him to the ground. Kallie's power then splintered, multiplying the factory wall and Kered and Sarah until there were so many of them it was impossible to tell what was real and what was an illusion.

The other Kered remained on the ground, now on his knees. Josh darted sideways, making a beeline for him. The back of his red t-shirt cooled, the material clinging to him like it'd suddenly shrunk three sizes. Cold air flushed across Josh's exposed skin and his feet no longer felt the ground. The light concrete beneath his sneakers flashed red, blue, brown, and yellow. "What is that?"

Josh's knees buckled, the wind at his back so strong and suffocating it briefly lifted him then slammed him into the ground. His elbows took the brunt, the top layer of skin ripped off as the oxygen in his lungs flung out of his body.

Rolling onto his back, he gasped, trying to take a decent breath. Finally, he could see the stars. Tiny blobs of light pulsated against the night sky. They were so close. He blinked, his right hand shaking as it reached to grab one. It was blue. The one next to it yellow. His fingers broke through the blue one and it tingled. *Magick?* His eyes focused. The stars were scattered shards of power. Someone hit him with power.

Josh opened his mouth, air rushing past his tongue and filling his throat. The oxygen cleared his head, giving him the strength to sit. Colored magick floated around him. He scooped his fingers through a larger blue blob. It shattered, leaving wet droplets on his skin.

He raked through a yellow clump, which instantly dried the droplets from his fingers, and snatched at an orange bubble, flicking the hot magick from his skin as he winced. *Fire. Air. Water.* It wasn't just magick—it was the elements.

He pushed himself into a sitting position. The power had come from behind, knocking him down as he ran. Josh searched for the person responsible and his instincts pulled him to the black birches.

There was something in the shadows, someone? He tried sensing them, but before he could get a grasp, Sarah's scream pierced the night air.

Springing forward on his feet, Josh barreled toward the multiplying factory walls. Kallie was still building on her illusion, working on keeping his friends safe. She had her back to him, to the other Kered, who remained on the ground, crawling. Josh ran over and flipped him.

Staring at each other face-to-face, the other Kered's lips twisted, the muscles in his cheeks twitching like he had something to say. Josh tilted his ear, waiting for the words. The other Kered stayed mute, his mouth forming a grotesque smile. It couldn't have meant he was happy. That emotion didn't show in his other features; his eyes as empty as the star-less sky above.

Goosebumps rolled across Josh's skin, but it wasn't brought on by another gust of wind. It was something in this Kered's eyes, or to be exact, it was the *nothing* in his eyes.

This perfect copy of Kered only matched him in looks. Everything else—the essence of who Kered was—was absent.

"What are you?"

The grotesque smile stretched further, making Josh question if this was even another human.

An eerie spark ignited in the man's eyes as his fingers clawed for Josh's face. Pushing strength-tinged power into his hands, Josh held him down, causing the spark in other Kered's eyes to grow. It raged like a fire, fed with the desire to cause pain. He was human. The worst kind. One whose only intent was to hurt others.

"You won't get to them," Josh threatened. Even if Kered and Sarah were hidden. Even if Kallie could handle herself. He wouldn't let this man near any of them.

His threat caused a catastrophic change. Other Kered's lips hardened into a thin line. His new expression matched his true nature.

It hadn't been an equal split. Only the physical aspect of the crystal's spell had worked. The body was there, but there was no soul. That half was missing, filled instead with pure darkness.

Kallie had been wrong when she said Kered turned. What she'd glimpsed was this copy of him—this dark half.

Josh pushed his power outward. It was in vain.

Dark Kered's anger gave him strength, and he shoved Josh back. Unbalanced, he fell, landing hard against the ground. He scrambled to get onto his knees, to bring his arms in front of himself with enough power for a defense.

He was too late.

Dark Kered sprung to his feet, towering above Josh with eyes that weren't blueish green like the man he'd been split from, but a blue so deep the irises were practically black.

Take him down! Josh willed himself, sparks of red flashing off his fingertips.

The air swelled, bringing that familiar chill. It fluttered through his hair and he braced himself. The wind ripped past him, sailing over him in plumes of red, blue, and yellow. Each stream of energy slammed into Dark Kered, drenching his skin.

The magick blotted out his features. His soulless eyes disappearing without their stare leaving Josh's face. He couldn't look away either, the horror of that twisted smile searing itself in his brain as Dark Kered's lips survived long after his cheeks melted away.

"Josh?"

Kallie's voice roused him, her hand on his shoulder, her touch enough for him to turn from the horror. Dark Kered was nothing more than a stain now; a puddle in a parking lot.

"Pull back your energy," Kallie said.

Josh didn't know it was still summoned. He couldn't feel it on his skin, or the warmth of Kallie's hand on his shoulder. He shook his head, trying to dislodge the images, but they were stuck to him like tar, black and thick. Just like the puddle.

He forced his eyes to find something new to focus on. Kallie filled his vision. Her brunette waves a halo around her head. "Are you okay?" he asked. There were still traces of blood on her skin.

"Are *you* okay?"

Why did she ask like that? Her voice, hesitant and strange. He shifted his shoulder, flinching when her hand clamped down on him. "What are you doing?"

"What am I doing?" Kallie pointed her free hand to the puddle formally known as Dark Kered. "What did *you* do?"

TWENTY-ONE

"Is he gone?" Sarah's small voice broke through the night.

Josh shifted his attention from Kallie to her. Along with Kered, she was gingerly moving closer to them. Kallie's illusion had disintegrated, the true factory wall the only thing up ahead. Without her energy, his own no longer burning on his hands, and the elemental magick absorbed into Dark Kered, the air was stale, still. Real.

"He just disappeared," Josh said.

"I don't know what you did." Kallie bent to inspect the puddle. "But whatever it was, it worked!"

She was happy with him? "I thought you were mad."

"Why would I be mad?"

"It was awesome, Josh." Sarah reached down to help him up.

"Yeah!" Even Kered joined in, giving Josh's back a playful slap.

They were all pleased about what happened. And he should be too, they'd won, but it wasn't because of anything he'd done. "Well, I—"

"So that thing was me, right?" Kered interrupted. "I mean like me, *me*. We looked exactly the same."

"I don't know about that, he seemed to have a better dress sense," Sarah teased.

"This uniform is not flattering, okay."

"That *thing* was the consequence of picking up what doesn't belong to you," Kallie said, but her stern warning only made Kered laugh.

"Well, I guess I'd better not make that mistake again!"

"I'm sure there's lots of mistakes *we* won't make again, right?" Sarah narrowed her eyes at Kallie, nodding toward Josh.

Subtle, Sarah.

Kallie nodded at him and mouthed the word 'Sorry.' So she did feel bad for shocking him. Sarah caught his eye and smiled. He would have liked to have seen it without the smugness.

"Maybe you should be thanking Kallie for hiding you," Josh said to Sarah. Kallie might have started the night out badly, but she ended it well.

"Oh, yeah! That was so crazy!" Kered pointed back at the factory wall. "It was like being in one of those mirror fun houses where there's like a million versions of yourself."

Josh found it strange, watching Kered be so animated after he'd stared down his dark half. He couldn't shake the emptiness in Dark Kered's eyes. Josh's focus drifted from the stain on the ground to the trees. Who had helped them?

"Is that why you attacked me?" Kered asked Kallie, rubbing his arms where there was sure to be bruises. "Because you thought I was that thing?"

Her series of nods continued, and Josh wondered if that would be her only acknowledgment that she'd been wrong. Her expression was hard to read.

"You're not going to attack me again, right? Now that thing is a puddle?" Kered chewed the bottom of his lip, his gaze pleading.

"I promise." Kallie crossed her heart.

"Well, that's a relief. Am I right?" Kered spun to Josh, his nervousness gone and his hand up like he was looking for a high five.

As Kered shifted, he overbalanced and almost fell into the puddle. Josh shot his arm out, stopping Kered before he did any damage.

"Wow! That would have been messy!" Kered laughed.

"Just stand still for one minute." Josh summoned his healing gift and ran the red power over Kered, erasing a dark bruise that had surfaced on his temple.

"Wow, thanks! I feel like I just woke up from an eight-hour nap."

"You're welcome."

"Fix me. Fix me." Sarah pushed her left arm out and he healed the bloody graze running along the back of her forearm.

"Did you fall?"

"Me versus the building." She nodded back at the Olsen factory.

With Sarah healed, he ran his gift over his own elbows, patching the raw places where the skin had been ripped off by spills onto the concrete.

When he was done, he stood in front of Kallie. The dried blood let him know where she was injured, but he took care of the bruises on her forearms first, then the cracks around her nails. All that summoned energy made her fingertips bleed. Her hands trembled as he fixed them, the shake staying even after he'd finished.

"I didn't want anyone to get hurt," she whispered, wiping at the final stain of blood still on her face. "Especially you."

She had a funny way of going about protecting people, but he understood where she was coming from. "It all worked out."

"No thanks to me."

Kallie squeezed his hand before rounding toward Kered and Sarah and apologizing to them.

"Everyone warned me about taking a job in Blackbirch," Kered said. "The rest of this shift will feel pretty boring now."

"Don't knock a quiet night," Sarah scolded. "They're underrated."

Kered's throaty laugh echoed around them, before his eyes shifted to the ground and his smile slipped. Would the dark stain be something Kered needed to explain to his boss, or would he take it further and tell friends? That kind of rumor spread like wildfire in Blackbirch. It wouldn't be believed, but it wouldn't be easily dismissed either.

Josh shifted his feet as Kered nodded at his wringing hands.

"Hey, there's no need for that," Kered said.

"You're not going to mention this, are you? Or tell people about my magick?"

"Tell people, are you kidding? Trust me, no one would believe me."

Josh's relief must have shown on his face because Kered's hand raised toward his back again. Josh braced, waiting for the jolt, but Kered's palm landed on Josh's shoulder instead, giving it a squeeze.

"Thanks for saving my life. From that thing,"—Kered pointed to the stain—"and her." His arm shifted up.

"Kallie? She wouldn't have seriously hurt you."

"Are you sure about that?"

"Yes."

Kered let go of Josh's shoulder. "If you say so, man. You know her better than I do."

He did. Kallie didn't want anyone to get hurt, including Kered. "Maybe on your next patrol you should stay away from the woods," Josh suggested, grinning when Kered responded to the remark with a gleeful look of his own.

"And other people when you've got this thing." Sarah came up beside them, handing Kered his baton.

"Don't worry, guys." Kered slotted it into his belt, amazingly without dropping it. "I'm never setting foot amongst those black birch trees again."

The conversation ended with another burst of Kered's laugh, but as Josh scanned the tree line one last time, he couldn't help but think Kered was onto something.

"Do you want to make sure she's okay?"

Sarah's question mulled in Josh's ear before his brain processed it. He was too focused on looking out of the van windshield, watching Kallie fumble at the door of her room.

"It was weird how quiet she was, yeah? She barely spoke once we left the factory."

"Totally. She should have been gloating about being right that there was an evil Kered. Go and see if she's okay."

He had his fingers on the door handle; the van switched off and in park when Sarah's hand tapped his shoulder. "If she talks, listen to what she has to say. You never know what people are going through."

He patted Sarah's hand. "You're a good friend." He meant it as a compliment, yet she seemed upset, a sadness flashing through her eyes before she cast them down, now distracted by her phone. "Are *you* okay?"

"I'm fine. Go." She didn't look up from her cell.

He slipped out of the van and shifted around parked cars to the row of identical motel doors, finding Kallie pushing hers open after finally mastering the lock. She didn't turn on the light, staring ahead into the dark room as he closed in. Her head shifted first, her eyes searching for him over her shoulder.

"You saw what was going to happen," she said.

Kallie stated it like a fact rather than a question, but he replied as if he was answering. "Yes."

Did that make her happy? He could have sworn the corners of her mouth tugged upward, but before he could decide for sure, she turned and led him inside.

Her motel looked the same as the first time he visited it. Clean. Neat. Kallie's bag packed in the corner, ready to grab and go at a moment's notice. Was it possible for a motel room to feel like no one lived it in, even when hundreds of different people did every year? That's how this place felt. That's how *she* made it feel: a ghost occupying a space until it was time to move on. She didn't live here. She didn't live anywhere. Not anymore.

"You're better at interpreting the visions than I am." Kallie moved to the foot of the bed, lowering herself to its neatly tucked quilt and sinking into the beige fabric. "You took note of what you saw. If you didn't stop me, I would have killed both of them."

His lips parted, but no words came out. He didn't have any. Would she really have taken it that far?

"Can I show you something?" She patted the bed.

Josh closed the door behind him and eased next to her on the mattress.

"May I?" Blue energy surfaced along her hands, rolling like waves toward her fingertips.

He nodded, closing his eyes. The darkness of his shut eyelids brightened as Kallie's fingers danced lightly across his forehead. Her magick was cool, rolling down his cheeks like tears. The iciness seeped into his skin, and with it, a vision of water so suffocating he gasped for breath.

It wasn't Josh struggling to breathe, but another boy. In a dark, lonely cavern, underground.

"I was helpless the day Jerry died. So frozen by my fear. I didn't have power. I couldn't help him. I couldn't stop Cade. I never wanted to feel that way again. Then he came to my house, and he killed my mom."

Josh opened his eyes, muddy river water clogging his throat. Thanks to the restored memories of his parents' car accident, he already knew what it was like to choke to death on your own blood. He didn't know which was worse. "You couldn't have known, Kallie," he croaked, swallowing thickly to clear his airway.

"I knew. I saw Jerry drown before we went in the cavern. I saw a fire at my house for *weeks* leading up to the one that killed my mother. I could have saved them, and I didn't. I vowed I wouldn't make that mistake again."

She folded her hands in her lap, staring at them even after she'd pulled back her power. She had her weapon now; her means to keep people safe. And he remembered what it was like to have it used on him.

"With hindsight, it's easy to say you could have kept them safe, to think that." As he spoke, he wondered if that was how his mother thought. Is that why she'd hidden everything from him, his dad, everyone?

"Hindsight. Foresight. Current sight. It doesn't matter. I *always* get it wrong. I was looking right at Kered and didn't see he wasn't the man from my vision. I didn't want to see that I was... wrong again."

"To be fair, I don't think any foresight would have flagged a dark half."

145

"A what?"

"A dark half. It's what I dubbed that Kered-thing. I mean the physical half of him was there, but the inside half wasn't him. It was just… darkness."

"Like an evil twin?"

"Yeah, but not as amusing."

"I was wrong about you."

"You were?" Wrong about what? Was it something that made her not like him anymore? Had she ever liked him in? At least in the way he hoped she did.

"I thought I was here to keep you safe. That's why I knocked you out, to stop you from being there tonight. But you don't need saving. You don't need me for that."

"I don't know if that's true. You know more about magick than I do."

"You defeated the dark half."

The empty factory tree line flashed through his mind. Josh didn't defeat anything, but how could he say who did when he didn't see who it was?

He glanced at Kallie's hands. Her fingers were twisting together like she was forming an energy ball, practicing the moves. She probably didn't even know she was doing it. She was a fighter used to fighting. A runner always ready to run.

"He's gone. Neither of us have to worry about it. Not tonight." He slipped his hand over hers, stopping her busy fingers. She wrapped her fingers around his. *That's how you stop being a ghost, Kallie. You reach out to the living.*

"We might not need to save each other, but there are other things we can do," he said, suddenly worrying his palm was sweating and she could feel it. The room seemed to have heated up, and he scanned it, looking for a window. His gaze fell onto the rest of the bed before he realized Kallie was following his line of sight.

"What did you have in mind?" Her left eyebrow raised.

"Not that." What he meant was 'yes that, one day.' *Wait.* Did he just say 'Not that' out loud?

Now both of Kallie's eyebrows were raised and her mouth was open. Great. He'd insulted her.

"What I'm trying to say, very badly, is that we can support each other. You know, work our way through all the bad, together."

"That sounds nice." She gave his hand a squeeze, resting her head on his shoulder.

Josh could feel the weight of her responsibility as she pressed against him. That tonight's events hadn't just been a horror, but a culmination of everything that had happened to her during the last few months. He could relate to some of it, but he could never have dealt with all of it. Or carried it. Not like she had.

"It wasn't your fault."

He could have been talking about tonight, her mother, Jerry, Melinda, it didn't matter. He knew Kallie just needed to hear the words.

Her fingers untangled from his and her arms went around his waist, pulling him into a hug.

Kallie fit into him, with her head nestled against his heart and her soft waves cushioning his chin. Breathing in, Josh could smell her shampoo, a sweet flowery scent that reminded him of the cherry tree blossoms that used to bloom in his old backyard. Kallie smelled like home. She *felt* like home.

He returned the embrace, chuckling when she pulled away and blue and red energy sparked around them as it had when they first met in The Playhouse alleyway.

It seemed like months ago now, and strange he'd only known her a few weeks. How was that possible when he felt the way he did?

Kallie leaned away from him; her cheeks flushed. He missed her warmth already. She was right there next to him, within reach, yet he missed her.

"What would you say if I suggested we both have a night where we're out having some fun, as opposed to battling for our lives?" he asked.

"I would say where and when."

"We could see a movie. Or get some dinner at The Playhouse. Or both."

"It's been a while since I've done anything that normal."

When was the last time he'd done the same? Not since before his parents died. "Tomorrow night? I'll pick you up here around seven."

Kallie smiled. "It's a date."

The happiness stayed on her face as she followed him to the door, almost making it impossible for him to leave. He couldn't wait to be back there tomorrow night, picking her up. He'd already decided he'd kiss her then, no matter how much he wanted to turn and kiss her now. Tomorrow night it'd have to be, when he wouldn't have Sarah watching from the passenger seat of the van.

"Tomorrow," he confirmed from the doorway.

"See you then, Josh."

He loved the way she said his name, and he had to will his legs to carry him across the parking lot and climb back into the van.

"Is she okay?" Sarah asked.

"Yeah, she's good."

"Is she grinning like an idiot too?"

"Yeah."

"Do I want to know what you two were doing in there?"

"We were just talking."

"Must have been a hell of a conversation."

"Are you ready to go home now?"

"Yes, I am more than ready to get out of this van."

"Think Grace will let me borrow it tomorrow night?"

"Have you got some book deliveries to make?" Sarah teased.

Josh stretched his lips back into his idiot grin. "Put on your seat belt." He shifted the van into drive, inching it out of the motel parking lot. It was late, the sky's darkness waiting to be erased by the morning light.

Maybe he'd remember the night's events differently tomorrow and the bad stuff would be easier to deal with. That's when he'd tell Kallie about the magick that wasn't his. She deserved one night of rest, one span of time where she didn't have to worry that there was another gifted person out there.

He glanced at her door, picturing himself knocking on it tomorrow night and resisting the urge to go back now. They would have plenty of time to deal with everything later. Together.

TWENTY-TWO

Kallie slipped her boots off, allowing each one to drop to the floor with a light thud. There was dirt on them, caked through the lined pattern on the base of the sole. When had she collected that? Hiding in the tree line at the Olsen factory? Waiting for Kered to show for his shift? It could have been worse. It could be blood instead of earth staining the soles of her favorite shoes.

Josh stopped you.

Her fingers skimmed the hem of her t-shirt and swiped at the flaking dried droplets of her own blood. *He stopped you.*

Kallie lifted her arms to peel the shirt away, stopping abruptly when a knock echoed off her door. Her attention flicked to the end of the bed, checking to see if Josh had left something. Maybe he wouldn't have an excuse and wanting to see her again was good enough.

"Can't wait until tomorrow?" she asked as the door swung open.

The panel of light spilling from her room caught the features of her guest. Sharp gray irises trained on her, the thick brows above them matching the color of his unkempt black hair. A pointed nose, large in profile, sat above thin lips that twisted into a smile that could have been enchanting if it wasn't formed with such malice.

"No. This couldn't wait." Cade pushed his way in, slamming the door shut behind him.

Kallie backed into the middle of the room, almost tripping on her discarded boots. Her hands went to her chest, but they couldn't do anything to calm her thumping heart. Slipping them down to her stained t-shirt hem, she smoothed it into place, her shaking fingers flaking off more dried blood.

"It seems you had an interesting night." Cade scanned the empty walls of the motel room before he spotted the armchair in the corner and made himself comfortable.

He lifted his staff as he turned back to her, arranging it so she could see it. *As if I've forgotten what it looks like.* She studied the dark wood before finally finding her voice. "You were at the factory?"

"I was out amongst the trees. I only popped out to take care of the security guard's double."

"It was your magick that took care of it?" That made more sense. Josh had seemed so stunned by what happened. She almost broke into a grin picturing his confused face staring at that dark puddle, but she kept her mouth straight, determined not to show weakness in front of Cade. "So you should have. It was your mistake, right?"

Cade smiled; stretched lips and malice. "You weren't exactly taking care of the double either. I've never seen you flounder so badly. Do all the boys have that effect on you, or just this new one?"

Kallie gritted her teeth. "It was *your* error throwing me off. That thing was more than just a double." *What did Josh call it again? A dark half?* "Something was wrong with it."

"The split was a little off. It's likely all the darkness from the crystal went into it."

"You think?"

"It still knew its objective and tried to merge back with the security guard."

"And it tried to take me out with it."

"I stopped it before it did you any real damage." His gaze swept across the blood on her shirt.

"What about your precious darkness now?"

"I'll find it somewhere else." Cade twisted his staff around, showing her a new, empty crystal embedded halfway down.

"When you do, don't drop it this time. This town is full of bigger fools than Kered Wheeler."

"Does that include Josh Taylor?" Cade smirked.

Kallie didn't have time for this. All she wanted was to put on clean clothes, crawl into bed, and fall asleep. She looked at the beige quilt longingly. "Is that why you came here, to gloat about saving me from danger *you* caused? Did you send me those visions too? Tricking me into tracking down Kered even though he wasn't who I was looking for and sending me to the factory tonight without a warning that there was two of him. I don't appreciate being played with."

"I didn't send you any visions. I suspect it was the same person who sent Josh his."

Kallie closed her eyes and let out a growl. "I told him to keep his veil up. She can't be allowed to reach him."

"She knows how to work her power, even better than you. If there's the tiniest crack in his veil, she'll find it."

"I thought you had her under control."

Cade waved his bony hand with a flick of his slim wrist. "She can't get to him. What's more important is we have Josh under control. Does he trust you?"

"Yes." *Too much.* She glanced at the end of the bed. It was probably still warm where they'd been sitting.

"Good. I'll let you know where to bring him."

"I'll take him wherever you want, just as long as you bring the box and hold up your end of the bargain."

"You'll have your chance to take care of her."

"You better hope she doesn't warn Josh again. Not now you're finally this close."

"Nothing will stop me this time." Cade twisted his staff around, bringing focus to the new empty crystal.

"Maybe you need to take care of the security guard then. I don't trust that he won't tell anyone."

"Fine," Cade agreed, a small chuckle escaping his thin lips. "Anyone else to add to the list?"

Did he think this was funny? "Josh's friend Sarah, the blond girl. She looked into my past and could be trouble."

"Then I'll take care of her too."

Kallie nodded. "Don't come here again either. It's a small town and you prancing about with your staff won't go unnoticed."

"Fine." Cade stood; the crystals embedded along his staff glinting under the overhead light as he headed to the door. "Anything else I need to know about before we finish this?"

She shook her head. With Kered's dark half gone, there weren't any immediate threats. They could be done with this town, and she could finally be done with Cade. Once she had the box, she could even be done with him permanently. "Your magick." She tilted her head at his staff, eyeing the multicolored crystals. "Is it strong enough to bend trees?"

"Yes, but what would be the point in that?"

What would be the point? It'd been quiet since the forest incident. Whoever had come after her and Josh hadn't tried it again. They'd also given up easily once her illusions came into play. It made her wonder if it was a test, something to force them into action. Why? Just to see what magick they could do? It couldn't have been the dark half like she originally thought. It wasn't Cade either. He was aware of what she was capable of, and she'd already told him about Josh's strength. She eyed the staff and wondered if Cade had a crystal that could combat such an ability. Even if he could hurt Josh, Josh could always…

"Heal himself," she whispered.

"What?" Cade paused at the door.

"There is one more thing." She spoke louder, berating herself for forgetting about Josh's second ability.

"What is it?"

"Josh's gift. It's not just strength he possesses. He can also heal."

"Two gifts?" Cade's eyes widened. "Are you sure?"

Did he think she was lying? To him? "I've seen Josh heal. He said it was his mother's gift. Could it be a side effect of her casting the Beginning?"

Cade's fingers ran over the pink scar marring the skin above his left eyebrow, and he chuckled.

"You think that's funny? You told me we only ever get *one* gift."

"That's true for most." Cade's face twisted into an expression she'd never seen him wear before. "It would appear Josh is not like most people."

"What do you mean?"

"Well, if what you're saying is true, your good friend Josh Taylor is a Collector."

TWENTY-THREE

Boom, boom. The music poured out of the club as the mid-tempo beat kicked in. Josh leaned against the wooden bar and squinted through the haze, finding himself surrounded by dancing silhouettes in the gray dim and wondering how he got there. He searched his jean pockets for the van keys, coming up empty.

The bass grew louder, swirling around him as the soft vocals drifted through the club and out the entrance. The crowd outside was drawn to the switch in melody and moved back in. A girl was amongst them, pushing ahead, her brunette waves catching his eye.

"Kallie."

He sailed toward her and a cool breeze pulled them together. Her hand reached for his and led him to the dance floor where she slowly swayed in time with the tempo. *Kallie dances?* Like the others around them, he couldn't keep his eyes off her. They stared at her beauty as he often did. Wanting her like *he* wanted her.

Josh pulled her close, wrapping his arms around her waist, but only seconds passed before Kallie leaned away and looked at the stained-glass window decorating the back wall. Something moved behind the colorful panes; shadows threatening to spoil their fun.

The rest of the club seemed unaware of the trouble stirring outside. He looked to Kallie for direction, her hardened stare now focused on a man standing to their left.

The man eyed Josh, his beady eyes sweeping him from head to toe while a staff balanced in his bony hands. This must be Cade. Josh sensed for power; his, Kallie's, Cade's crystals. There wasn't a crackle in the air or a hint of the static before the electricity. It was all missing.

Kallie's touch left his body, her hands reaching behind her back to retrieve a small pistol from the waistband of her jeans. With steady arms, she aimed it at her enemy.

Why does she need a gun when she has power? Josh flayed his fingers, willing his energy to flood his veins. They remained cold and void of magick.

Cade walked up to the pistol, positioning his chest in front of it. He smirked at Kallie. "You know that can't kill me."

She pulled the trigger.

Josh blinked, rushing to shield his eyes from the bright flash of orange. It took forever for his hands to reach his face. Then it felt as if it was all happening at once.

The music stopped. The crowd ran.

Cade was swept into the throng, that silly smirk still on his lips as he disappeared in the panicked mob.

"We have to get out of here!" Josh turned to Kallie. She lowered the pistol and strode toward the exit. *Move, feet!*

He raced after her but lost Kallie to the crowd too. Multiple hands pressed into Josh's ribs. Heavy shoes bashed into his ankles. Bodies slammed into him, pushing the air from his lungs. His sneakers caught on the floor and he went down.

Forced against cold tiles, he tried to get his bearings. Where was he and how did he get here? Why couldn't he remember?

Waves of people washed past him, and he let the horde thin before trying to stand, worried that Cade would still be outside.

Josh stumbled through the exit, stopping to catch his breath. Frantic faces gathered around him, but thankfully no one appeared hurt.

He squinted through the crowd looking for Kallie, finding only sinister shapes against an even darker night sky. A sliver of white caught his eye, the dress of a girl in a sea of people.

Most of the club-goers were wearing dark clothes, including Kallie before he lost her. She'd been in her jeans and a black shirt. Still, the brunette waves of the girl in the white dress lured him, and he followed as she weaved in and out of the crowd. Who was she looking for and why did he want it to be him?

Josh's hand reached for her shoulder and she stopped, turning to him.

"Kallie?"

It was her. His eyes took all of her in to make sure. He scanned her new clothes as she spun, feeling the heat rush from his body as the dark red blot spoiling Kallie's white dress appeared.

He shivered as her fingertips reached out and caressed his cheek. He wanted to close his eyes and enjoy her touch, but it was over too soon. Kallie collapsed on the ground; her hand ripped from him as she fell.

Following her to the cold concrete, he counted the shallowness of her breaths.

"I don't understand what's happening?" Where was all the blood coming from? He pressed his hands into her stomach and found the source. All this damage couldn't be because of one tiny hole, could it? *It's what made the hole! The bullet.* "Didn't *you* have the gun?"

He stared into her eyes, transported to the first time he'd seen them, when he'd dreamed about her in the hospital waiting room. It'd been a nightmare then, just like now, right? This *had* to be a bad dream!

Her eyes drifted to something beyond him and the little glow left in them faded.

"What is it?" Her body gave way beneath Josh's bloodied hands, vanishing into the pavement like the concrete was quicksand. There wasn't even a trace of blood to prove she'd been there. This *was* a nightmare.

Back on his feet, he spun. Kallie was behind him now, dressed in her dark jeans and shirt. In her hand was the gun, the barrel still smoking. *What kind of the dream is this?*

He inhaled sharply as Kallie raised the pistol.

"Please! No!"

She pulled the trigger.

TWENTY-FOUR

Sarah ripped at the cardboard box, pulling apart the sticky tape. "So, you think it was just a dream?" she asked Josh.

"Yes."

"Even after you stopped having those kinds of dreams weeks ago?" She ignored the exasperated look he shot her.

"Yes."

He might be sick of the conversation that had sound-tracked their drive to the bookstore and the first half of their shift, but she wasn't. "Maybe it was a vision?" She shrugged.

"It didn't feel like a vision."

"Well, did it feel like the dreams you used to have?"

"It felt like my subconscious was messing with me, after everything that happened with Kered and his dark half. My brain must be trying to make sense of it." He ripped the top off his own cardboard box.

"Or maybe your subconscious is letting you know Kallie can be two-faced and has a mean streak." Sarah smirked. "Didn't we know that already?"

"She was trying to keep everyone safe. To stop anyone else from dying."

"Right, I know, so you said." Sarah lost her smile, blinking to erase the memory of Jerry Miller's picture from that news article. It was hard to not link it to Josh's story about the vision Kallie showed him; of that poor boy drowning.

If Sarah had witnessed the same thing and been helpless to stop it, maybe she'd go to any length to make sure it didn't happen again too.

"Kallie saved your life as well, remember?" Josh reminded her.

"And in exchange, I have forgiven her for shocking you and trying to kill Kered," Sarah nodded.

"But you still don't trust her?"

"If you trust her, I trust her."

"I trust her."

"Then we both trust her." She conjured her best smile.

The store was quiet for the moment and they were using the lack of customers as a chance to restock the shelves. The job was usually Eve's, but since she'd quit—and apparently dropped off the face of the earth—it was up to them to pick up the slack.

Sarah's mom was practically living at the bookstore and was in the stacks after spending this morning making a help-wanted sign. It was taped to the front window now and a few people had stopped to read it, but no one had come in to ask.

"I've got to visit some suppliers in Freemont," Grace said as she rushed into the lobby. "This is not what I needed to be doing today, but someone has to, right? I'll need the van."

"No problem." Sarah turned to her mom, cringing at the dark circles under her eyes. "Slow down, okay? We can always help you out." She nudged Josh, who nodded along.

"I'm sure you kids have more exciting things to do then spend all your free time in the store." Grace moved up beside Josh. "Like go on dates."

His mouth dropped open; around the same time his cheeks took on a pink glow. Sarah stifled a laugh.

"Thanks a lot, big mouth." He glared at her.

"Mom, you weren't supposed to make a big deal out of it."

"I think it's great." Grace beamed at Josh.

The continued gushing only reddened his cheeks more. Was that a small smile on his lips? Sarah tried to get a better look, but Josh turned away, busying himself with stacking books on the shelf. It was totally a grin. Her mom was acting like his mom would have, and no matter how much he tried to pretend he didn't, Sarah knew Josh secretly loved it.

"Do you know what to do if someone comes in asking about the job?" Grace called as she headed to the front door.

"Give it to them."

"Thanks, sweetie." Her mother blew a kiss, scooping up her handbag and her order book as she disappeared from the store.

"Now it's been brought up, let's talk about your date! You'll need to eat before seeing a movie," Sarah advised. "It'll be easier to get a table if you go for the food first."

Josh returned to the boxes and ripped open another one, giving her half a smile. She knew it! He secretly loved it.

"Do you know if Max will be working tonight?"

"Maybe." She shrugged. "Probably."

"He's still not answering your texts?"

There was a tone behind Josh's question, matching the saddened accompanying look. He thought it was his fault she and Max weren't exactly on speaking terms, even after she'd explained about Max's parents and him moving in with his uncle. It made sense. Neither of them could deny her relationship with Max had changed now she was spending more time with Josh. Unlike Max, they both knew why. Sarah wanted to tell her best friend everything. If Josh showed him his power, Max would believe it. But Josh still didn't want anyone else knowing. Especially after what happened with Kered. *Curse that stupid dark half.*

Ding.

The brass bell above the door echoed from the lobby.

"Please be someone looking for a job," she muttered, putting down her armful of books and striding toward the tinny echo.

"Hey, guys." Max appeared at the archway into the library.

Sarah stopped short, her heartbeat jumping three speeds. *Speak of the devil.* She crossed her arms, staring at him.

"Hey, Max." Josh waved, slinking off and busying himself with the shelves.

Traitor. Sarah glared at the back of Josh's head. "Hey…" she muttered, turning to face Max.

He gave her one of his lopsided grins and it broke her resolve. "Can I talk to you upstairs?" he asked.

His hands fidgeted at his sides, like always, but there was something odd to the movement, as if he'd downed a large coffee or two. *Max hates coffee.*

"Sure, you can talk to Sarah upstairs," Josh answered for her.

Betrayer! She made her way to the stairs, knowing Max would follow.

Inside the stacks, Sarah gestured for him to take a seat at her mom's work desk, but he leaned against the wall. Sarah perched herself on the corner edge of the dark wooden desk and waited for Max to speak, wondering what he was going to say. He was the closest person in the world to her and she had no clue what he was thinking.

"I know you're angry at me," she said, after Max did little more than fiddle with the buttons of his light blue shirt.

He let go of his top and smoothed the material down his torso. "I'm not angry at you, Sar. And I'm sorry for yesterday. I was upset with my parents and I shouldn't have taken it out on you."

"Thanks." Sarah accepted his apology. "I really am sorry I haven't been around more." She was, and he must know that. He was always saying he knew her better than she knew herself.

"You and Josh have been hanging out so much lately, I didn't want to be a third wheel," Max replied.

"You're not a third wheel."

Max shrugged. "Maybe a fourth, then. I've seen you at your place with that girl you were stalking on my computer. No one asked me over to meet her."

That statement hurt, especially when there was a good reason behind Max having not met Kallie.

"That's Josh's friend Kallie. Again, I'm sorry if we made you think you weren't welcome. That's my fault, but we can work something out. Maybe one day after school, or next weekend?"

"What about tonight?" He raised his face.

"Josh and Kallie have a date. They're going to The Playhouse, actually."

"What if we went as well..." Max's voice trailed off. "Together?"

"Won't you be there already? I thought you worked Sundays."

Max pushed off the wall. "I must be saying it wrong or something," he muttered.

"Saying what wrong? Do you want me to come down to The Playhouse and wait until you finish your shift?" She usually got bored doing that, but if that's what she needed to do to make things right, she would.

"I don't want to *just* hang out with you, Sarah." Max circled a stack of books, his jittery hands tapping along the spines.

Okay, how much coffee had he had, and why was he suddenly drinking it? Stress over his parents? That must be it. Why else would he be saying he didn't want to hang out with her? "We'll always be friends. I don't want to change that."

Max stared at her from behind the book stack. His brows kept furrowing, and he kept sweeping his hair out of his eyes, but his mouth stayed shut.

"I... I can't *just* be friends with you anymore, Sar. My life has changed so much lately, and I want to be happy again."

"I want you to be happy too." Why would he think she wouldn't? His smile was back. She mirrored it.

"You make me happy, Sarah."

Good, they made each other happy. Why did Max even want to have this conversation? She replayed it in her head, picking up her mistake. Max had said he couldn't *just* be her friend. In fact, he'd said it twice. "Wait! Do you want to be *more* than friends?"

Max nodded, following the gesture with a confused frown. "Didn't we just establish that?"

"But why?"

"What do you mean why? It must be obvious how I feel about you."

Obvious? There was nothing obvious about it! They were best friends. Just because they hung out all the time, going to dinner, the movies, spending every spare second together... "I had *no* idea."

"You've never thought about us being a couple? Not even once?"

"No." She honestly hadn't. It was Max.

Awkward silence filled the room.

"Is it too much to ask?" He broke the quiet.

Max had hope in his voice. Something she hadn't heard from him in a long time. She was a bad friend who hadn't even noticed his life falling apart in front of her. How was she supposed to be his girlfriend? "I don't know if I can even think of you like that."

That was the truth, right? She also still had to keep things from him. Not being honest had already strained their friendship. What would it do to a romantic one? *A romantic one?* Was she considering it? *Why doesn't it feel as strange as I thought it would?* "We're best friends."

"And that's enough for you?"

She didn't know.

"Because it's not for me," Max said firmly. "Not anymore. It's this or nothing."

Nothing? Sarah's cheeks flushed. "How can you put such a demand on me?"

"Because for once I'm doing what *I* want."

"And I'm supposed to just go along with that?"

"I've gone along with you for the last few months. You weren't even there when I needed you."

"Don't you dare throw that back in my face! You didn't even tell me what was going on."

"When was I supposed to? When you were off having secret conversations with Josh? Doing background checks on Kallie? How about when you were hanging out with Eve Thomas? Someone you've *hated* for the last few years, but who you'd rather spend more time with than me!"

"There's more to it!" She gritted her teeth. Screw Josh, she should tell Max everything.

"Oh yeah, I forgot about the explanation you *never* gave me."

Okay. This conversation was going nowhere. "Max," she said his name calmly, swallowing her anger. If he would just look at her, everything would be okay. It usually worked, but when his blue eyes met hers, she could see there was nothing she could say. It wasn't often

Max was serious, but when he was, there was no changing his mind. She couldn't decide what she wanted here and now. "I'm sorry." She blinked back tears. "That it's ending like this."

For a second, Max's face fell, his jawline going slack as a sheen hit his eyes. Then his features morphed into a scowl. "Fine. Just remember that it was *your* choice."

He slammed the door, shutting it on Sarah.

Shutting her out of his life.

TWENTY-FIVE

The heat inside The Playhouse hit Josh as he pulled open the door, breaking the cool outside breeze in a swirl of warm, recycled air.

He gestured for Kallie to step ahead of him, and her red overcoat brushed against his arm as she slid past. He couldn't feel it through his own jacket, but his palms became clammy anyway, simply because they'd touched.

"I guess Sarah was right when she said it'd be better to eat first." Josh eyed the mob of people lined at the movie theater entrance. They practically filled the entire back half of the restaurant.

"You won't tell her that, right?" Kallie joked.

"I don't know." He shrugged. "She could probably do with some cheering up."

Josh had told Kallie about Max's ultimatum during their walk from her motel. He was van-less, with Grace still out on her stock run. That also meant Sarah was home alone, which was something he didn't want, given her day. But she insisted he leave for his date and even helped him pick out a shirt and jacket to go with his jeans.

The charcoal-colored long sleeve was dressier than his usual tee and had buttons and a collar that kept poking into his neck. It was the fanciest thing in his wardrobe, and he was worried he'd overdressed until Kallie opened her motel door. Her overcoat perfectly matched the red lipstick blended into her lips. She looked positively radiant. A far cry from the evening before.

"This building goes on forever," Kallie said, her attention moving beyond the booths surrounding them to the rows of pinball machines. "I didn't realize when I was first here. It's very deceiving."

"It's in the right town then." Josh eyed the game area and the way it sectioned off the restaurant from the twin movie theater. "The place where nothing is as it seems."

Kallie laughed at his quip, her hand slipping into his.

They joined the line for a table as he tried to read the movie times scrolling across the electronic board. They hadn't decided what to see yet, but he figured they could while they ate dinner.

They'd been waiting for the hostess less than a minute when a large door opened to his left, revealing a huge kitchen. They really did underestimate the size of this place. As he peered into the buzzing cookhouse, a familiar person waved.

Max, wearing the same uniform as the other staff, made a beeline for them.

"Hey, Josh."

"Hey." Josh nodded, searching for a harder tone in the friendly greeting. He was still convinced he was to blame for the rift in Max and Sarah's relationship, but Max only nodded politely back, his head tilting toward Josh's side. "This is Kallie."

"Nice to finally meet you." Max leaned over to shake Kallie's hand. "You guys want a table?"

"We're happy to wait," Josh replied.

"Don't be silly." Max waved his arms, insisting they follow him. He led them to a booth next to another wide door.

Josh waited for Kallie to take her seat and then slid in opposite her, knocking over a reserved sign with his elbow.

"I'll take that." Max picked up the plastic sign, his thumb swiping over the gold printed words.

They must be at Max and Sarah's regular table, where the two of them hung out every Friday night. At least they used to.

"So, what's good to eat here?" Kallie asked Max.

"Definitely the burgers," Max answered after a beat, tucking the plastic sign into his pants pocket. "Best in town." A forced smile stretched across his lips.

"Sounds great." Kallie glanced at Josh.

"Agreed! Make it two."

"I'll put a rush on the order, so you guys aren't waiting too long."

"Guess it pays to know the nephew of the owner," Josh said.

"Especially in a place this busy." Kallie nodded.

Was she uncomfortable around the crowds given her history? Maybe he should he have suggested somewhere quieter?

"It'll get even busier soon." Max pointed over his shoulder to a blueprint pinned on the far wall. "We're in the middle of gutting out the warehouse next door."

"What are you turning it into?" Kallie asked, reaching for the buttons of her coat.

"I'll show you." Max took off toward the wall. Josh got up to follow him, pausing for Kallie.

"Go. I'll catch up."

When Josh reached Max, he was excitedly dancing his long fingers along the blueprint. There was a planning permit pinned next to it. "I've been begging my uncle to do this for years!"

Josh scanned the plans. They looked like random lines. "Are you creating a secret lair?" he joked about Max's love of spy movies.

"I wish!"

"A bowling alley?" Kallie had joined them, her voice breaking in over Josh's shoulder.

"No, but that would have been awesome!" Max laughed. "It's going to be a club. You know, with a dance floor and a proper bar."

A club? Did Josh hear Max right? His whole jaw stiffened, the freeze running down his back and into his arms. His dream had been in a club. He could even picture the dance floor and bar.

"Sounds cool," Kallie said.

Would she go to such a place? He wouldn't. Not after that nightmare. Josh spun, his arms heavy and throwing him off balance.

Kallie reached to steady him. Without her coat, he could see the dress she was wearing.

It was white.

Oh, god. Heat rushed through his limbs, the stiffness melting under the energy lining his veins.

Kallie's painted lips dropped open at the sight of the power flaring across his forearms. Josh clenched his fingers into fists, the magick retreating. He pulled on the collar of his jacket, then his shirt. He missed his usual tee.

"How about we get some air?" Kallie's hands fell onto his shoulders.

"Everything okay?" Concern entered Max's voice.

"We're just going to step outside for a minute," Kallie explained. "Can you put our order in, please?"

"Sure. It'll be ready in fifteen."

"Thanks, Max." Kallie gently pressed into Josh's back, guiding him to the side door they'd both tumbled out of only weeks ago.

Like that night, the alleyway was empty, with each end illuminated. The closest was lit by the lights in the parking lot, the far end of the alley by the sign over the movie exit. He lurched halfway up, trying to reach the middle. It was darker and quieter there. That's what he needed, right? A place he could calm his racing heart and mind.

He turned when he reached it, Kallie behind him.

"You okay?" she asked.

He eyed her dress. Was it the same as his dream, or was his mind playing cruel tricks on him?

"I should have grabbed my coat." Kallie rubbed at her bare olive skin.

Her red coat? The one that was the color of blood? *Now you make that connection?* he scolded himself, wriggling out of his jacket and handing it to her.

"Thanks." She slipped it over her shoulders. "Are you going to tell me what's wrong?"

Maybe he should just let her read his mind? The images were all there. The gun. The blood-drenched dress. The dance floor and the club. The place he was sure she would die in. He glanced at the far side of the alleyway; the brickwork made up the building he was already vowing not to step foot in.

If they didn't go to the club, Kallie wouldn't get hurt. That was how destiny worked. That was the advantage of knowing it ahead of time. If his parents had never gone for that drive. If Kallie hadn't gone in that cavern with Jerry. If she'd been looking out for the fire. But she had known, hadn't she? She told him she'd known those things and ignored them. Would she ignore him if he mentioned his dream?

He took in a breath. It smelled like buttery popcorn. They should have gone straight to the movies.

"Josh?"

Her voice was as soft as the hand on his shoulder. He lifted his head, but didn't look at her, his attention going to the moon above. That's why it was so dim in this spot. The only respite from the dark was the pale milk of the moonbeams. *Why isn't there a light in this busy passageway?* He twisted his neck, his eyes falling on a dark box-like shape. There was. It just wasn't working.

"Josh?"

Kallie called his name again. He should answer her. He was being a bad date. "I think I'm just being paranoid." He couldn't turn from the broken light. Maybe if he stared at it hard enough it would turn on? The idea was ridiculous, but it kept him distracted. When that no longer worked, he leaned his back against the building and closed his eyes.

All he could see in the darkness was pictures from his dream; the panicked club-goers, Cade and Kallie, both Kallie's. The Kallie with the gun, and the one in the white dress who looked at Josh as she lay dying on the pavement. He flung his eyelids open and shook his head to dislodge the images, to stop them from staining his brain.

Kallie reached for him.

"I had a dream…" His voice cracked as he spoke.

She listened carefully, her warm fingers stroking the back of his hands as he described seeing her die.

"It may have seemed real, but it was just a dream," she said when he finished.

That's all she had to say? After everything he'd told her. "But the club… it's being built right here. It can't be a coincidence."

Kallie shrugged. "You're friends with Max, you probably overheard him talking about the plans and your subconscious made up the rest. Everything else that happened in your dream is silly." She laughed. "I can assure you I'd never go dancing at a club."

Now she was laughing at him? If anyone was going to believe him, it should have been her. "It felt real. Like those dreams we shared before you came to Blackbirch."

She scowled as she had the night they met and he mentioned the dreams. Sarah was there then, a stranger hearing about moments only they shared. That's why Kallie had scowled then. What he'd revealed was private. But now? They were alone. The only two people in the world who knew exactly how those dreams were and that they weren't something to scowl at. Or laugh at.

"You remember the dreams, don't you?"

"Of course." A smile spread over her blood colored lips. Her eyes avoided his, her focus at the opposite end of the alleyway.

Josh let go of her hands. "But I guess this nightmare wasn't the same kind. If it was, then you would have had it too."

"That's right." Kallie nodded.

She looked at him this time, confident, like she'd now gotten a hold on herself.

"And the dream would have ended in the usual place," Josh continued. "That strange orange room."

"Yes. The orange room." Kallie took his hand again, all the warmth in her skin gone.

She pulled him off the wall, dragging him back to the restaurant door. He didn't want to go with her—not now he'd caught her in a lie.

"There was never an orange room." He flared his power, his red energy swamping the hand in Kallie's grasp. He pushed his strength behind it and forced her to stop. "You've *never* shared a dream with me. Who the hell are you?"

He stared at the back of her head, at the cascade of dark waves washing down her shoulders. They were moving, all of her was, her muscles shuddering underneath the material of that damn white dress.

A noise split the air. Kallie was laughing at him, her chuckles shaking her whole body.

"What's so funny?" Josh flared his power. Kallie's hand tensed, pulling on his as she turned. The laughter stopped, but a smile still sat on her lipstick mouth. "Answer the question."

"I am Kallie Jacobs, just not the pathetic version you're so hung up on."

The air left his body, taking his will with it. "Does she even exist?"

"I wouldn't be here if she didn't. But there's only room for one of us in this world, and I call dibs."

He dragged her closer. Her features lit up in the glow of his red energy and her brown eyes glared at him, always darker than he expected. He'd been too blind, too naïve, to realize what that meant.

A dark half.

Heat rushed into his body, flaring through him from the pit of his stomach. Bile came with it, burning up the back of his throat and threatening to spill out of his mouth. His grip on her faltered. Hadn't he wanted this? To spend the night holding her hand and touching her skin. *Not this Kallie.*

Dark Kallie's wrist twisted, squirming out of his grasp before he'd registered it gone. His own fingers flexed open and closed, reaching for what was no longer there. Coolness traveled his forearm, snaking its way along his bicep, twisting around his chest and closing off his heart. *Good.* He didn't want to feel it anymore.

Josh's knees bent, slamming into the concrete as he lifted his head, the only part of his body that wasn't a weight pulling him down.

Dark Kallie towered over him, raised hands and dancing fingers. She was working her magick, coating him in suffocating energy that he couldn't see because she'd hidden the color.

"What do you want from me?"

"It's not what I want, it's what Cade wants."

171

Her dark eyes scanned the alleyway. They'd had it to themselves for too long. They both knew it wouldn't stay that way.

He needed to pull her trick and summon his power with no color so she wouldn't know he was planning an escape. He could be just as deceitful.

"Save your energy and your strength," she said. "You'll need it soon enough."

She forced him to his feet, using her magick in a way she'd never taught him.

Pushing him to a door on the empty warehouse side of the alley, she gestured to a thick padlock.

"Break it."

He curled his fingers into his palm.

"Fine." Dark Kallie clamped a hand over his, spilling her energy across his skin. His own power surfaced in defense and she turned it into a weapon, scooping up the red glow and slamming it into the lock.

No wonder she hadn't shown him that trick. He pulled back his energy, hiding it in his veil where she couldn't touch it.

"Now you're learning." Dark Kallie smirked. "It's a shame you're too late."

She opened the door and shoved him into the darkness. The soles of his shoes caught on the hard floor, his waist constricting as the pull of Dark Kallie's energy kept him from crashing into the ground. A faint blue hue seeped into the clear power, giving enough light for Josh to see the pillar he was being marched toward.

His sneakers slipped again, the rubber edges teetering on broken brick pieces. This is where he'd be found; half buried in construction rubble or fully buried in concrete. His disappearance could be a mystery until the day the dance floor of The Playhouse's club gets ripped up and his bones discovered. Would anyone look for him before that? His parents were dead, his family gone.

Sarah and Grace's faces flashed through his mind and his chest tightened. They were his family now—and Dark Kallie knew where they lived.

Lifting his veil, he filled his hands with colorless energy as he was secured to the pillar by a dusty rope, cringing when Dark Kallie fed her power into the rough nylon. *Did she give it invisible teeth?* He squirmed as his restraints bit into his skin, allowing his anger to color his cheeks. He wanted her to think he was too distracted to fight back, too scattered to form a plan, too inexperienced to know what they both knew: his magick was stronger than hers.

"Don't you worry." Dark Kallie tied the rope firmly in a knot, cutting the circulation off to his hands, before rounding the pillar to face him. "This will be the last you see of me."

"Too afraid to stick around?"

"Too bored. Besides, I've got my other half to get rid of."

"That's your next move?" He wanted to keep her talking, to find out where the real Kallie was. His fingertips tingled with pins and needles as his hidden energy pushed against the blue power on the rope.

Dark Kallie's head cocked to the side, and she eyed the invisible power as if she could see it. "It's a bit late for that now, isn't it?" Up on her toes, she drew level with his eyes, pressing her body against his as she wrapped her hands behind the pillar and tightened her knot. "Bet you didn't think this is how our date would end."

"I'm sorry I ever asked you out."

Her mouth opened at his comment, a hearty laugh escaping before she pressed her lips into his. Soft at first, then harder.

"Ow!" Pain pinched his lower lip and his head swung back against the brick pillar, the metallic taste of blood tainting his mouth. Not her. He didn't want to kiss *her.*

Dark Kallie stepped backward, her lipstick smeared, tinged a deeper red by his blood. Another smile crept onto her face as she reveled in his disgust. He flinched as her hands raised to his head, the glare of the blue energy stinging his eyes. He forced them to stay open. He wanted to see her expression when he unleashed his magick and broke free.

"I know your power is stronger than mine." She allowed a flicker of her energy to lash at him, singeing his cheek.

"Then why are you still here?" he growled.

Dark Kallie licked his blood from her lip. "Because, silly." She placed a hand on each side of his temple. "All your power and strength doesn't work when you're unconscious."

TWENTY-SIX

Josh scrapped his nail along the surface, searching for the roughness of the brick. The solid object pressed against him was strangely smooth.

Get out of the ropes.

He followed the thought with a flex of his arms, but a restraint no longer bound him. The pillar was gone, and the rope. He couldn't even feel Dark Kallie's magick crawling across his skin.

He rolled his head up, only realizing now his chin was buried in his chest and his eyes were closed. Opening them made no difference. He was simply blinking into the same suffocating darkness.

Stretching his fingertips, he groped behind himself, getting a feel for the wall he was propped against. It had gaps and grooves running horizontal, and a sharp, woody smell that tickled his nostrils when he breathed. *What place in Blackbirch has wooden panels?*

Hands off the wood, he flexed his fingers and waited for his red energy to set them alight, wondering if his veil was still up. He searched his subconscious for its edges, willing them to peel back. They weren't there. None of his power was. *What did Dark Kallie do to me?*

"Your magick won't work in this place."

The feminine voice was so faint he almost missed what was said.

"I... I can't see." He turned his head left, right, straight ahead. Every direction featured the same vast blackness.

"Are you sure you want to?"

What kind of question was that? "Yes, of course I do."

A shock of blue sparks erupted in the air, growing into a light big enough to show the emptiness of the tiny room. It was just four walls, him, and the sitting silhouetted shape of someone else.

He crawled toward them, settling on his knees.

"Are you sure you want to see?" the quiet voice asked again, and it was obvious now she was referring to the conjured light.

Objects moved within it: colors and shapes. He couldn't look away. He didn't want to. It felt important. "Will you be watching too?"

The light expanded, the ball flattening into a square. The colors and shapes were bigger now, but they made no sense. He rubbed his eyes, trying to blink away the blurriness.

The silhouette moved beside him, morphing into skinny fingers that trembled as they tried to keep the light steady. Slender arms attached to the small frame of a girl became clearer as the square of light expanded again. A petite figure, drowning under the weight of blue jeans and a white shirt sat next to him, her face partially covered by a mane of dark waves that smothered her sunken features.

"Kallie?" Josh whispered. It was hard to utter her name, to tie his memories of her with the gaunt body before him.

"Hello, Josh. I'm sorry, I don't have the strength to appear as I usually do in our dreams. Not if I'm going to show you what you need to see."

"This is a dream?"

"Yes." Her forehead wrinkled. "But it doesn't feel like you're asleep."

"I was knocked out."

"We'd better hurry then. You need to see it all before you regain consciousness."

"What are you going to show me?"

"What he did to your aunt."

"Cade?"

"Yes."

"Why?"

"So you'll know how to beat him when he comes for you."

"I'll make him pay for what he's put you through," Josh promised.

"It doesn't matter about me."

Kallie's hands pushed toward him, allowing the light to take on the hue of her blue glow. The color was barely visible, a watered-down tinge clinging to the edges. Her bony fingers shook, struggling as she ignited more. He focused on his own veins, on sparking anything that could boost her energy, but they were void of magick, empty and dry.

"He cast a spell when he found out we were communicating. He made it so the entire room blocks magick, but I've been able to get around his binds." The corner of her mouth twitched into a smile. "Cade thinks he knows all about the power and how it works, but he doesn't even know the half of it. And he's nothing without that staff."

Josh didn't know if that last remark was for him or for her. Kallie's grin continued for a few seconds, her attention fixating on the empty floor until she seemed to become aware of her surroundings again. Her gaze met his, and he finally recognized something familiar. Her soft brown eyes shone back at him, the ones he'd only ever seen in dreams. Dark Kallie's eyes were never this light—or this kind.

"I have enough power gathered," she said. "To allow you to see."

"Show me."

"First, you need to understand I didn't want any of it to happen," she paused, correcting herself. "I didn't *mean* for any of it to happen."

Her fingers were shaking again, but not because she was struggling with her energy. He recognized the guilt in her movements, the desire to keep busy and do something other than think about everything you did wrong.

Was it survivor's guilt like his? Another familiar feature of the real Kallie dawned on him: the red tinge to her fingers. It was always present in their shared dreams, and now he saw it for what it really was—blood on her hands. Did she blame herself for his aunt's death? For her mom and Jerry?

Everything he'd heard about Melinda's death came from Dark Kallie, so he didn't know how much of the story had been true. The only certainty he had was that the real Kallie wasn't at fault. She couldn't be. Not after the risks she'd taken to help him, the horrors she'd survived. They were not the deeds of a murderer.

K.M. Allan

"I'm sure you didn't mean for Melinda's death to happen," he said. It seemed Kallie disagreed.

"I wanted to hurt her, for sitting by and letting Jerry die. I wanted Cade to suffer the most, and I thought her magick would do that. That maybe they would punish each other if I brought them together." Kallie's voice cracked, her watery eyes finding her red fingers. They were nothing more than bones. "But Cade was more ruthless than I gave him credit for, and Melinda's death is on me."

Josh reached over, past her hands which she hid away, and softly touched his fingertips to her hollow cheek.

"I don't blame you and I'm sure Melinda wouldn't either."

Kallie's face crumpled, her guilt falling with it.

"Show me," he encouraged. "Let the truth play out."

More tears welled, rolling down her colorless skin. She closed her lids and dispersed her blue glow into her fingertips, placing a hand at his left and right temples.

"You'll see it as I lived it."

Josh allowed Kallie's power to sink into him. Her hands were ice cold, but the magick, was warm. In his own personal darkness, shapes and colors formed in his mind's eye. They became a story for him to follow—and a nightmare for Kallie to relive.

TWENTY-SEVEN

Kallie hid in the shadows, the darkness soothing her tired eyes. Usually the things she saw were pictures from a dream she could only just remember, or something so real she thought it was happening right in front of her. Those images didn't cause her pain, not like the last ones had—the visions that took her to the house of the witch.

Only days before Kallie had wanted to hurt her. The woman had invaded her mind and let Jerry die. She wanted the witch to feel as bad as she did, for her to suffer as she was. So she led him to her; the man with the staff.

Kallie went back to the cavern, after Detective Brewer had processed it and collected the evidence that proved only she'd been there. She left the murderer a message, and he followed it.

He found the witch's home, but also Kallie's. He started that fire, its deadly flames ignited by the orange crystal embedded in his wooden staff. He watched by the roadside as it consumed her house and chased her into the field where it suffocated her with thick smoke. She could still taste it now, the bitter, smoky ash. Maybe she'd taste it forever. Maybe she deserved to.

She was only alive now because the witch came with her magickal amulet, scrubbing the soot from Kallie's soul and giving her another chance. When the vision hit her, Kallie vowed to return the favor. The head-splitting force invaded her mind as she sat, still covered in ash, at the police station. The man with the staff wasn't done. He would use the witch the same way he had Kallie and Jerry—and she couldn't let that happen.

When two officers took her from Brewer and his verbal assaults, she used the chance to escape, running deep into the woods and reliving her favorite pastime before she learned that running couldn't help you escape your problems. No matter how fast you went.

The witch's house was dark when she came upon it. The smell of smoke still hung in the air. It was almost as thick as the silence. She couldn't even hear any crickets. Heavy shadows covered the small porch, and she used them to sneak to the door.

That's where she stood now, hunched over in a bid to slow her racing heart and calm the pounding in her head.

The images didn't want to leave, flashing constantly through her mind. The man with the staff would burst through the screen door. The witch would be in the largest room: a library of books. The murderer would trap her there.

A thump echoed from inside the house and Kallie worried that she was too late. She pressed her fingertips to the round doorknob and let the chill of the cool metal seep into her skin. It easily pushed open under the pressure of her touch. Another thump greeted her, rattling the handle as she used it to keep herself upright while she peeked inside.

The witch was on the floor, surrounded by scattered books and an upturned coffee table. *I'm too late.*

Blood dripped from the witch's face, shed from the gash above her eye and the skin split across her cheekbone. How has this already happened? Kallie's visions warned of the future. They always came *before* the event. Her hand gingerly wiped against her pounding temple. The headaches were never part of it, the images she saw never so clear. They were just like Jerry in the water. The witch had sent them to her. She'd played her tricks again, but why?

Another thump; the echo of books battering into the floor, tossed from the shelves by the tip of a wooden staff.

He was there. Still dressed in clothes too fancy for a murderer. His outfit wasn't perfect. The blood splatter would never wash out completely. Those fat droplets would always be there, even if they reduced to faded stains. They would cling to the material like shadows on his soul. But would they haunt him? Probably not in the way he deserved.

Kallie crawled into the doorway, her eyes trying to catch up with the visions crammed into her mind. The man had forced his way into the house, taking the witch by surprise. He wanted something from her. Something she refused to give.

Kallie mirrored the movements the witch made in the jumble of images. She touched her left cheek to soothe the imagined sting, her other hand going to her ribs to protect them from the swift blow. Beats echoed through her ears, books hitting the ground, furniture cracking under blows from his wooden staff. Those same sounds rang out in real life. She'd caught up to her vision. *Now what?*

The witch stared at her from the floor, her fingers covered in her own blood. They twitched at Kallie while her wide blue eyes darted back and forth, keeping track of the man. His rage kept him blind to Kallie, his focus on the shelves he continued to clear with the pointy end of his staff.

"I know it's here! I know you still have it."

What was he looking for? Kallie moved her own hands, wildly gesturing for the witch to crawl to her. If she could get to the front door, they could both escape. They knew the woods, even in the dark. They could hide in its trees until the man went away.

The witch's bloodied fingers violently thrashed the air again, pointing. Kallie turned. Was it the door? Why would the witch call her here only to signal that she should leave? *It can't be that.* She looked back into the house. The hall stand? It stood inside the doorway, but there was nothing remarkable about it. There wasn't even a drawer. Just four tall legs and a flat bench.

Kallie rose onto her knees to get a better look. There were three small trinket boxes on top. Each dark square was layered with dust, the grimy film filling the decorative swirls etched into the lids. They hadn't been opened in months. *Maybe it's something else?* She eyed them again, the third box differing enough from the others to catch her attention.

Her fingers went to it before she could think, drawn there automatically. The lid was slightly ajar, and the dust disturbed. She lifted the corner.

The amulet.

The silver disk with the cutout tree and crystals, the very object that had saved her life, was hidden in the third box. *This is what the man's looking for.* Kallie stashed it in her boot.

"Well, what do we have here?"

The man's voice cut through her. She hadn't heard him speak as he killed Jerry, in fact he never uttered a single word in the cavern. Each syllable that left his mouth now crawled over her skin. How was it possible for someone to make an innocent question sound so menacing?

She eyed the door. Even before her brain finished forming the thought to run, footfalls thundered behind her, the lids on the trinket boxes rattling around and freeing themselves of the dust.

Kallie's hands flew to the back of her head, as fistfuls of her hair were snatched and yanked, pulling her body backward. The man dragged her into the library and threw her at the witch. Their bodies tumbled together, pain shooting up Kallie's elbows as her limbs jarred against the floor.

"You've already served your purpose to me, girl."

Sharpness shot through Kallie's lower back. She arched it, trying to get away, but she couldn't escape the pinch of the staff. The man shifted it off her, allowing her to roll sideways, before stabbing at her again and slamming it into her ribs.

The crystal poking out of the staff's side snagged her shirt. It was orange. No, it was clear. The inside was orange, the flames captured in a prism and bottled up. They blazed, even through her clothes, singeing her skin and filling the air with the bitter scent of burned flesh.

"Get it off!" She squirmed, her ribs screaming in pain, her back protesting against the hardness of the floor beneath her. Lashing out, she tried to beat away the staff, but it wouldn't budge.

"Stop it, Cade!" The witch screamed.

"So, you do know who I am." He lifted the staff.

Kallie gingerly rubbed her shirt where the crystal had pressed into her, being careful not to disturb the tender skin underneath. She slid up, sinking her back into the bookshelf behind her. Maybe he'd forget about her now his attention was on the witch. She still sat beside Kallie, wiping at the blood dripping from the gash above her eye.

"I know you." The witch nodded at Cade.

"Then you know why I'm here."

"There's no point to you being here. I'll never give you my power."

Crack!

Cade's staff slammed end first into the ground between them. He twirled it, spinning it so the crystals glinted, drawing Kallie and the witch in. They were so colorful, sparkly blue, a deep chocolate brown, yellow like the sun. Then there was the orange one, the trapped flames that had already hurt her so much. The burned skin underneath her shirt throbbed, pulsing in time with the flickering glow.

"I've harvested the elements and I'll do the same with your power, Melinda." A smile spread along his thin lips. "That's right. I know who *you* are too."

Melinda's hands lashed the staff, gripping it with purple lit fingers. Kallie recognized it as what had overcome her in the field. It had run through her, filtering from the amulet that was currently stuffed in her boot. Her veins warmed at the memory. She still didn't fully understand what it was, what had happened to her tonight, or what was happening now, but she knew Cade should not be part of it. "Stop him," she begged Melinda.

The witch's purple power increased, the glow snaking its way up the staff. Kallie lifted a hand to shield her eyes from the glare. It was so bright. Too bright. A clear crystal near the apex lit up like it was decorating the top of a Christmas tree. It sent its silver light down the length of the wood, rebuffing Melinda's magick.

"You can't destroy it. Tailor-made protection spell, specifically against *you*." Cade yanked the staff from Melinda's grip, sending her crashing into the floor.

Without the threat of her power, the silver crystal dimmed. Cade slammed the end of the staff down again, punching a hole in the floorboard. "Even with all your magick my staff is too strong for you to break."

Melinda propped herself up, crawling backward on shaky arms. "It makes no difference. There's no crystal on that monstrosity that will ever make me give my power to you."

"I don't need you to give it to me when I can just take it." Cade twisted his staff, revealing another colorless crystal embedded in the back half of the wood.

Kallie didn't want to know what that one did. She kicked out her left leg, the heel of her boot digging into Cade's calf. His whole body momentarily dropped, but his strong grip on his staff kept him upright.

He glared at her, pulling the clear quartz free and slotting it into the apex.

Kallie's shallow breath caught in her throat, her stare fixed to the shine of the crystal, sharp and unforgiving, like the edge of a knife. Would it matter what he did to her now? Anyone who knew her, who cared about her, was dead.

"Try it," she shot back.

"I'll get to you." Cade lifted the staff, flipping it in his hands and bringing it down in one swift movement.

She waited for the now familiar crack of the boards, realizing too late that he was aiming for the witch.

"I need a gifted human to complete my spell," Cade said. "And to harvest that element, you need to die!"

Kallie's hands flew to her eyes, not to cover them, but to shield out the glare. As soon as the staff swung toward her, Melinda's purple glow spread into a barrier, blocking Cade. If Melinda could stop him from hurting her, why had she waited so long?

"Did you get it?" Melinda's whisper reached Kallie's ears.

She nodded.

All hell broke loose.

Melinda's hands twisted, her power-lit fingers working furiously, whipping back and forth in the air. The movement shaped her barrier into something else; a giant ball of sparkly magick.

Hurled at Cade's smug face, the ball ricocheted off his cheekbones and sent his whole body flying backward. Now he hit the floorboards. Him and his staff.

Kallie watched Melinda crawl to the hall stand as Cade sat up. His face was slack, his eyes unfocused, but those bony hands were working on autopilot, grasping at his staff and raising it up, aiming it at the witch.

She had her hands on one of the trinket boxes and spun it through the air toward Cade.

The clunk as it collided with his skull assaulted Kallie's ears. A maroon line sprouted above his eye as the box's unforgiving corner edge split his skin.

Crack!

Cade fell backward onto the floorboards again.

Kallie climbed to her feet and sprinted toward Melinda, the door, freedom.

The witch ran past her back into the main room.

"What are you doing?" Kallie growled at her.

"I have to stop him first."

"You did!"

"Not completely. Not enough."

Kallie glanced at the door. It was ajar, unguarded and within reach. With five steps she'd be at it. Within five seconds she'd slip through it, out into the woods and running through the trees like she used to. She could smell them already, their earthly scent tickling her nostrils as they would when her feet crunched through the dirt that fed them.

But she knew what happened when she ran. When she ran toward the cavern, Jerry died. When she ran from her house, her mom died. It was time to stop running.

"What are you doing?" She stood over Melinda in the main room. She'd crawled next to Cade, her hand alight with power, skimming down the length of the staff beside his unconscious body.

"I'm seeing what magick he holds in these crystals." Melinda's fingers hovered over a peach tinted one.

Cade's limbs twitched.

"He's waking up."

Melinda ignored her, and Cade's movements, spreading her palm over the peach crystal. "Bring me a box."

Knowing it was empty, Kallie grabbed the one she'd pulled the amulet from. Now in Melinda's hands with the lid lifted, Kallie noticed the inside wasn't made of wood like the outside, but a smooth substance reminiscent of a pebble.

"What kind of boxes are these?"

"They hold magick," Melinda said, pushing the empty box toward the staff and transferring her cupped hand along it. As her hand shifted, the peach magick inside the crystal pooled into the box. "Once Cade has collected all of his elements, he needs to bind them. That is the only way he can unlock the full potential of the power he found in that crystal there." She pointed to a ruby quartz. "I have now taken his ability to bind the elements together and hidden it in this box."

"Good, let's go. You've stopped him."

"Not yet." Melinda's shaking hands continued to explore the remaining crystals.

Kallie glanced back at the door. Why wouldn't she leave already? *Come on, Melinda!* Cade's eyes were still closed. At least unconscious the sneer had been wiped from his face. The corner of the box had dug sharply into his skin. The wound continued to bleed. His scar would be deep. He deserved a reminder of tonight, for what he put them through.

"Melinda, lets g—"

Kallie's words cut off, the witch thrown back into her as Cade's staff flung up and knocked them astray. The box in Melinda's grip slid along the boards, slamming against the edge of the wall-long bookcase.

Kallie hated that shelf. She hated the floor. She hated slamming against the floorboards. But most of all, she hated the man responsible for those things. He stood above them now, one hand wiping crimson blood from his open wound, the other flipping the staff over and thrusting it toward them.

Kallie waited for the return of his sneer, for hateful words to spew from those thin lips as he threatened them again. But this time there was no demeaning insult.

The crystal at the tip of the staff ignited, a black, void color blurring past Kallie's eyes as Cade speared it through the witch.

A cry broke the silence of the room, a pitiful yelp barely escaping a closed throat. Kallie's gaze shot to Melinda's sealed mouth before she wrapped her hand around her own neck. The sound had come from her.

Cade kneeled, those fancy dress pants soaking in Melinda's blood. The staff pierced through her stomach, her red liquid sinking into it. Cade's gray eyes studied the wood, the glow of his crystal. Whatever he was waiting for didn't appear to be coming. The furrow in his brow deepened.

"What have you done to it?" Words finally spewed from his mouth, spat with such hatred his voice didn't need to be loud to make Kallie shake.

Sound escaped from Melinda. A low, rumbling laugh that turned into a cough as she choked on her own blood.

"You think it's just death you need to harvest the magick." She glared. "You need the darkness."

"What darkness?"

"The darkness in the act of killing. The darkness it brings out in your victims, created from the hatred they have when you take their life. Kill me all you want. I have no darkness in me."

Cade scanned the room, the hall, the final wooden box on the stand. "You clever little witch." He ripped the staff from Melinda's body.

Kallie's hand went to her cheek, wiping at the warm liquid that splashed her. When she pulled her fingertips away, they were red.

Cade's back was to her, but he faced the door. Was there a rear entrance? She checked her surroundings. A small kitchen with a window barely large enough for a child to crawl through, and two separate doors, each leading to darkened rooms. *There's no escape.*

"Behind you," Melinda whispered.

Kallie glanced over her shoulder. The bookshelf didn't help, unless the tomes were hiding a secret tunnel. She studied the spines, the empty gaps where Cade had knocked things from the shelf. Then she saw it.

A fourth box.

Identical to the other three, Kallie reached for the square object and slid the lid off. The inside was as stony smooth as the others, but darker. Depths of hell darker.

"What do you have there?" Cade demanded, rushing at Kallie from the hallway.

She pressed the lid back over the sticky tar-like substance coating the box and smashed the whole thing into the ground.

The box's wooden sides crumbled, the insides dissipating into a sludgy mess that seemed to evaporate into the air.

"You'll regret that!" Cade's staff swung past her head, tearing books from the shelves. In his rampage he came across the box Melinda had siphoned the binding magick into.

Would he be furious when he lifted the lid? Would he spear her like Melinda? The witch remained tight-lipped on the ground; her hands pressed against her wound as if it was a papercut in need of a band-aid. It was more serious than that. It had to be, given all the blood on the floor.

"You think you're so clever." Cade stalked back over to them, shoving the box in Melinda's face. "You aren't the only one who knows their way around a spell."

The crystals in his staff lit, springing to life like fireflies at twilight. One crystal grew brighter than them all. Cade tilted the staff until the shining quartz pointed at Kallie, his lips muttering words she couldn't understand.

The power unleashed hit her like a freight train. Her insides twisted, a sharpness pinching through every nerve. Heat tingled along her forearms, building up until it felt like her fingertips would burst. She raised her hands, half expecting to see steam, not expecting to see what she did. The same black substance from Melinda's box pooled from Kallie's fingertips and into Cade's crystal.

She tried to pull it back, to stop it free-falling from her body, but didn't know how. She glared at Cade, the sludge only thickening.

"That's it. Keep hating me." His lips curled into a smile.

As the crystal filled and darkened, a new light took its place.

Spewing from Melinda's bloodied hands, the purple power formed a barrier, a wall of magick between Kallie and the stream from Cade's staff. Undeterred, he increased the flow from his crystal.

It was too much. The assaulting forces of both spells tore at Kallie. The magic buried itself in every cell. Her body flushed warm and then ice cold. Her skin soft, then as hard as the floorboards she writhed against. Her very essence broke, ricocheting pain through her nerves and muscles. She absorbed a full minute of agony before everything in her world went dark.

TWENTY-EIGHT

The silence was so thick when Kallie slipped back into consciousness that she wondered if her hearing had been damaged.

Her eyesight was off too, the room a blur of colors that melted into each other. What if it was permanent and Cade had taken her sight and hearing from her too?

She waited for her rage to boil up, for her darkness to fuel her limbs and force her to move. She couldn't feel it. She couldn't feel anything.

"Kallie?"

The witch whispered her name. Melinda was still alive? Something ice cold brushed Kallie's lower legs, and she shifted her feet and flexed her ankles, sending pins and needles up through her calves. She waited for the sensations to reach her face, for her eyes to focus. The swirling colors became solid shapes, and then the shapes became objects she recognized.

Cade stood over her, his knuckles white as he gripped his staff. Melinda was near her, not next to her like she expected. There was a fourth with them now, making Kallie wonder how long she'd been knocked out.

She shifted herself away from the new person, feeling as if she was detaching from them. They twisted toward her and their features came into focus. They were *her* features. Kallie was staring at a living, breathing, mirror image version of herself.

"H-how? she gasped.

"Well, well…" Cade relaxed his grip, barely settling his attention on one identical girl before it flitted to the next. "Isn't that a neat trick?" Trick? This wasn't a magic act?

She glared at his gleeful expression. The crystal on his staff had done this. It was no longer clear, filled with the sludge that had poured from her fingers. *My darkness.* He'd been stealing it from her while Melinda tried to stop him. It'd been their warring magick, their need to defeat each other, that had created this… mistake.

Kallie caught Melinda's eye. The witch would know what to do. Her attention was also darting back and forth between Kallie and her copy. Her expression was not wonder filled like Cade's, but rightfully stricken with horror.

Cade lit his crystals, spinning his staff until it became a blur of light. Kallie lifted a hand to shield herself from the painful glare. The girl next to her leaned forward, her eyes unshielded. The crystal glow highlighted each brown iris. They were darker than Kallie's—the only physical difference between them.

Cade smiled. "This one is pure darkness."

Melinda's lips cracked open. "She's an abomination."

"Or she's just a witch without her power." Cade was back on his feet, his hands wrapped around the staff and everything in it pointed at Melinda.

Still on the floor, with colorless lips and blood-stained hair, Melinda's hand reached for Kallie. Did she want the amulet? Could it even save her now? The witch should have been dead. The blood loss alone was enough to have killed her twice over, yet she was still with them. No wonder Cade wanted her magick, if this is what it was capable of.

Another clear crystal lit his staff and began its process, ripping at Melinda, siphoning what was hers and giving it to Kallie's double. He was turning the abomination into a witch, giving magick to the thing that contained darkness instead of a soul. He'd have his dark-tainted magick then. After that, he could murder the double for it and unlock his crystals.

"Do something," Kallie hissed at Melinda, grabbing at her own boot to get the amulet herself.

Melinda grasped Kallie's hands. She wasn't reaching for the amulet; she was reaching for her.

"I'm sorry." Melinda's pale lips formed the words.

"Sorry for what?" Sweat beaded across Kallie's forehead, the heat of the room suddenly doubling as the purple energy swirling around Melinda brightened. She'd been holding back, allowing her power to filter to Cade, to let him think he was winning. Seconds later, Kallie knew why.

The moment the energy being fed into Kallie's double turned blue, empowering it, Melinda forced the rest of her magick into Kallie.

The power Cade was stealing couldn't keep up. Melinda was freely giving her power to Kallie—the full strength of it—and transferring it at a rapid rate.

"Stop!" Cade demanded, stamping his foot. He shut off his crystal and struck Melinda with another blow. She didn't have the strength to fight him off while she continued giving her power to Kallie.

"Stop!" Kallie begged her. "Save yourself."

Melinda kept the magic flowing. Her pale lips parted; words pushed from them in hurried whispers. If Cade caught it, he may have heard the ramblings of a dying woman. For Kallie, it was a spell, magical words only she could understand. It was a transfer of knowledge to go with the power. Everything Melinda knew about magick so Kallie could survive.

She listened hard, absorbing it all, her soul changing as the knowledge and power sank into her bones and became part of her. Melinda wouldn't live much longer, but her legacy would.

Kallie understood it all now. How the magick worked. Why Cade wanted it. How she could use it to stop him.

She reached for the staff and flooded her hands with energy. A bright blue color erupted from her skin, fed through her veins and encouraged to spread to the silver crystal Cade had activated earlier. He'd used it to protect his precious staff from Melinda. Kallie had a new use for it.

"Let's see how you like this," she muttered, pulling the magick from the crystal and coating herself in it. She reached for the double next to her and smothered her too.

"Good girl." Melinda nodded; the gesture weak.

Kallie had protected herself and her double from Cade, as he had protected his staff from Melinda. He couldn't kill either girl, which meant he couldn't steal their magick or collect their darkness.

She reached for Melinda, to protect her too, but she pushed Kallie's hand away.

"It doesn't matter about me anymore."

Melinda's final spell was cast, her power now passed to Kallie completely, save for the amount that went into her double. Melinda was no longer an empowered woman, or in possession of the magick to stave off her mortal death.

Cade's staff struck at them again, slicing across Melinda's chest and cutting her so deep Kallie could see bone. The staff then leveled at her, inches from her face, trembling in Cade's hands.

"You think you're clever, don't you? Stopping me from killing you, from harvesting what should be mine!" He pulled the staff back, snatching Kallie by the collar of her stained shirt and dragging her to one of the darkened doorways.

Shoved inside the tiny room, she stumbled backward, regaining her balance as Cade touched the tip of the staff to the doorframe and coated it with a shimmer of gray magick.

"I may not be able to kill you, but I can make you suffer." Cade strode back to the double and stood over her as they both morbidly watched the life finally drain from Melinda. It felt strange for Kallie, watching herself smile over the loss of a life.

"Keep looking for the amulet," Cade barked, giving Melinda's body a final kick. "And start going through these books." He knocked more tomes from the shelf next to the double. "If you don't want to be trapped in that room too, you work for me, and your job now is to learn how to work your magick." He shot an icy stare at Kallie. "And to find me a witch whose power I can take."

Josh sat back, the light of the vision fading from his mind as the reality of darkness replaced it.

That's what happened to his aunt. That was how Kallie became empowered, how Dark Kallie was born. And that was Cade, the monster. Not just for what he'd done to Melinda, but for the way he'd kept the real Kallie prisoner all this time.

"Is that where you are now?" he asked her. "Trapped in Melinda's house."

"Yes."

"But why hasn't anyone found you? I know the police found Melinda's body."

"I'm hidden in an illusion my double cast. No one who came here after Melinda died could hear or see me."

"And Cade just left you here to rot?"

"Nothing done by him can kill me." Kallie wrapped her hands around her starved body.

"I'll find you when I'm done with Cade and get you out of here."

"It doesn't matter about me anymore," she repeated her earlier statement, echoing Melinda's last words.

"The dark half—your double—is coming for you."

"I know. She wants to complete the merge; she's been doing Cade's bidding in exchange for what she needs."

"I should have stopped her when I had the chance. I let her capture me."

"I led them to you. Cade forced us to find others with magick so he could finish his spell. I tried to hide you from him for as long as I could." Her eyes glistened with unshed tears. "I contacted you too many times. I should have stayed away from your dreams."

Is that really what she wanted? Didn't she know meeting her in his dreams had helped him, saved him. He reached for her. "I'm glad you didn't."

"I tried to help, to make up for what I've done wrong. I can't see everything that's going to happen, but I tried to share what I did. I sent visions, and dreams, and warnings..." her voice faded as her bony fingers gingerly rubbed her forehead.

"I know, and you did help me."

A tear rolled down Kallie's pale cheek. Her face softened, all her features did. The room too. Had his hands touched her yet? He could have sworn he moved them.

"You're waking up, Josh."

The surrounding darkness didn't just deepen, it disappeared. The wooden panels disintegrated, dissolving into watercolors that couldn't cling to the canvas. They washed away, taking the room and Kallie with them. *No! I'm not ready to leave her yet.* "I'll find you," he promised.

She nodded, her mouth moving as Josh strained his ear toward her. He didn't catch it at first, but as his body began to rouse, Kallie's voice echoed in his mind.

"He's nothing without that staff."

TWENTY-NINE

Josh's neck cracked as he rolled his head to the side, the popping sound loud in the surrounding silence. Pain seared across his forehead, dragging him back to full consciousness.

The gutted warehouse.

He was still inside, tied to the dusty brick pillar. He stifled his breath to listen and willed his eyes to make out shapes in the pitch-black. There was no sound to the outside world. No chatter in the alleyway from movie patrons, no thuds of car doors, or echo of music from The Playhouse restaurant.

That world was silent and well past closing time. Outside was vacant, but the warehouse wasn't. Two seated figures slumped together formed a silhouette to his right. Who else had Dark Kallie dragged into this nightmare?

"Comfortable?" a deep voice asked.

Josh narrowed his eyes, hoping to see something, to match them to the sound that had drifted from somewhere on his left. "What do you want?"

The lights flicked on. Bright, industrial bulbs flooding the room and forcing him to squint. Cade stood at the switch, his wooden staff on the button.

The bulbs stayed lit long enough for Josh to register him, to recognize the murderous stranger he'd never met but knew so much about. Plunged back into darkness, the slumped silhouettes near Josh moved.

"Josh, is that you?"

His stomach dropped. "Sarah?"

He heard her whimper, her tear-stained face coming to life when Cade flicked the switch again. Bound at her wrists and feet, Sarah sat next to an equally tied-up Kered, dressed in his security uniform.

Sarah's blond locks were a tangle of strands. An angry red mark swelled across her left cheek; a similar graze sat above Kered's right eyebrow.

"Are you two okay?" He got the words out before Cade turned the lights off again.

"We're just dandy," Kered's groggy reply echoed.

"Where's Kallie?" Sarah's question squeaked out in a panic-pitched voice.

"Hopefully dead by now." Cade hit the switch one last time, finally leaving his plaything to walk toward them.

The former professor was shorter than Josh expected, but lean, with long limbs and skinny fingers that twisted the staff in his hands as he strode over. The crystals glinted under the bright lights. Would Cade miss them when Josh ripped out and smashed every single one? Probably. He didn't look like someone not used to getting their way. There was an arrogance in his step, in the way he dressed, still like the teacher he'd been before murdering his students, as if he was someone who deserved respect.

"Perhaps you would like to tell the story, Josh?" Cade offered.

"Sounds like you know it well enough." Better to keep Cade talking. Dark Kallie's power still tainted the ropes cutting into Josh's wrists, but it felt weak. If he could force enough energy to his hands, he'd be able to free them. He just needed another minute.

"I understand why you might not want to," Cade said. "It is embarrassing for you." He straightened himself directly in front of Kered and Sarah, gripping the staff like it was a scepter and he was a King.

"You see," Cade raised his voice, ensuring he had Sarah and Kered's attention. "Not only was the Kallie you all knew a... what did you dub them, Josh? A dark half, but she's also the reason you're here.

She delivered each one of you to me on a plate. Not to the place I had planned, but it'll do." He scowled at their dirty surroundings.

"And what reward did you promise Dark Kallie?" Josh asked.

"Nothing really. Just the chance to become whole again—as the dominant half."

Whole again. Is that what Kallie meant by merge? His mind flashed back to what she'd shown him the night Cade accidentally created the first dark half, and it slipped into place. "Dark Kallie would need binding magick for that, right? For the halves to merge permanently."

"You know about binding magick?" Cade raised an eyebrow.

"I know you need it too, so you can unlock the magick in your crystal. I'm sure that means you didn't give Dark Kallie the real box."

Cade's gray eyes ran the length of his staff, pausing on the ruby crystal near the top before he allowed a sneer to touch his lips. "You had an eventful nap. I hope Kallie enjoyed sharing with you one last time."

"Well, I know I enjoyed it." Josh gave him a real smile. "It was *very* helpful."

His bound arms ached, the ropes loosening with each passing second, but he didn't know how many he had left. Especially after Cade arranged himself in front of Kered and Sarah again. Josh lowered his veil and waited for the rush of energies to flood him. They lapped at his feet like a low tide hitting the sand. *That's... odd.*

"So, you two are loose ends." Cade dug a hand into the inside pocket of his coat and pulled out something small and shiny. "Given my history, I can't have those. And I don't waste magick on such useless things."

Oh, shit!

From the way Kered's skin paled, Josh knew the gun in Cade's hand was his.

"You patrol empty buildings, so that thing isn't loaded, right?" Sarah asked her rope-bound buddy, a glimmer of hope in her voice.

"Let's find out, shall we?" Cade aimed the pistol at her and cocked it.

Josh's heart jumped into his throat. He directed his energy into his binds and his skin burned like it was on fire until the rope slipped from his wrists.

"Tell me, Josh," Cade asked without looking at him. "Which one of your friends would you like to see die first?"

"None!" Josh thrust his blazing red hands at Cade, his skin stinging with heat as the energy zapped forward, tinged with all the strength he could taint it with.

The professor flew backward, the gun hitting the floor and sliding into a pile of construction rubble.

"Go!" Josh yelled, tearing off Sarah and Kered's binds.

Cade was only stunned and already climbing to his feet. That push should have knocked him through the wall, or at the very least, out cold. Josh glanced at his discarded ropes. Had the exposure to Dark Kallie's magick done something to him?

Josh pulled Sarah and Kered up, shoving them to his left. "Head for the door!"

"It's the other way!"

Sarah's arm slipped from his grip. "No, I was tied up right near it, at the first brick pillar."

"You were tied up in the middle of the room!" Sarah grabbed his bicep.

Was I? He pictured Cade at the light switch, directly across from the pillar. It had been in the middle of the room. Did Cade move him when he was unconscious?

"What do we do once we're at the door? I saw Cade lock it." Kered's panicked voice interrupted Josh's thoughts.

"I can get it open." He began building power again, letting the red color guide each step they took. It was five before Kered fell.

Yanking Kered up by the collar of his blue security jacket, Josh gave him a push, before the weight of long fingers attached themselves to his arm.

Those fingers spun him around with force, and the wooden staff was pressed against his chest. Cade's clammy hand slapped across

Josh's forehead, keeping him in place as the clear crystal at the apex of the staff lit up.

Its power burned Josh's skin, sinking into his soft flesh and flooding his veins. It burned like lava, ripping through his insides and bringing them back as a prize. The clear quartz turned red, siphoning Josh's energy out of him as freely as rain fell from storm clouds.

Josh searched for the edges of his veil. It could protect him; it could hide his power. It was an umbrella against the storm, but it was flimsy, battered and upturned in the wind; a weak form of shelter. What did Dark Kallie's rope magick do to him?

Halfway down the staff, another crystal lit. It was as black as the one he'd seen in Kallie's vision, the magick within it pure darkness. The crystal was new to the staff, shinier than the others and recently jammed into place. Cade had gathered more darkness. And if he mixed it with Josh's gifted magick, he would have the final element of the casting Melinda died trying to stop. Josh wouldn't let that happen.

He abandoned trying to hide his magick and flooded it to his skin, infusing it with his strength ability.

The staff's remaining crystals grew bright in response. Blue for water, orange for fire, brown for earth and yellow for air. All the elements Cade had collected. All the lives he had stolen. Josh wouldn't be part of it. He placed his palm over the closest quartz.

This is for you, Jerry. Thank you for being Kallie's friend. The blue crystal shattered under the weight of his gift.

For Kallie. For her mom. The orange crystal burst under his left palm, scorching it when hot magick spewed out.

"Stop!" Cade screamed, pulling on the staff and yanking it from Josh's grip.

He tried to hold on, to crush the yellow crystal, but his strength failed and he fell to his knees. Josh might have destroyed two of Cade's elements, but Cade could gather more. He could do it right now using Sarah and Kered. Josh heard them banging on the far door. They'd made it. But what good was having an exit if you couldn't get out? They needed his strength. He needed his strength.

Staggering to his feet, Josh regrouped, taking a step before Cade pointed the staff at him, aiming its sharp tip to spear him like it had Melinda.

Josh lit his hands, covering them with every drop of magick he had left. Cade looked like he was on fire, clouded in the red glow spewing from Josh's fingertips as he held them up in a fighting stance.

As Cade struck his weapon down, aiming it at Josh's chest, Kallie's words rung in his ears; *he's nothing without that staff.*

Redirecting his strength ability into every muscle, Josh's skin hardened like metal armor, as it had that day in the forest when he stopped the tree from crushing him. The crystal at the tip of the staff struck his forearms first, and the quartz shattered.

Cade's whole body bounced backward on impact, his features twisting as he tried to keep his balance. His eyebrows shot up, those gray eyes going as wide as the O his thin lips formed.

It was a shock, but it wasn't enough. Josh hadn't damaged the staff, only one crystal, and Cade had plenty of those.

Josh needed to boost his power. Sarah and Kered were still working on the door lock, too far away to help charge his energy like Dark Kallie had taught him. But Cade wasn't. In fact, he was within grasp. *He might be a snake, but he's a live snake.*

Cade's staff was above his head again, but when Josh reached out, Cade switched tactics, repositioning it like it was a bat and he was about to hit a home run.

"Come on, take a swing at me!"

Cade wound the staff back, twisting his torso and leaving it open. Josh latched on, his energy taking on a life of its own. It leaped at the professor, the red glow flicking out and hitting him squarely before shooting back to Josh. It must have been like an electric shock, given how Cade's eyes bulged.

The professor's body froze, the staff raised sideways. It gave Josh's magick enough time to replenish and power the full strength of his ability.

"There you are." He smiled as the red hue deepened in color and bathed them both. Josh's magick was back. He was back.

Cade swung the staff again, but not before Josh took half a step back. Instead of the wood hitting his head, the end swiped past his face. On the backswing, Josh caught it and snatched the staff clean out of Cade's grasp.

The professor flexed his hands for a full three seconds before realizing they were empty.

"You're just a dumb kid!" he spat at Josh. "You don't deserve magick."

"You think you do?"

"I found it!" Cade screamed. "It belongs to me. It was *my* discovery to share with the world. I didn't let those other witches stop me and I won't let *you!*"

Cade was not a dark half, he wasn't ripped from someone human and filled with blackness, but his essence was the same. The darkness of his soul was just as present in his eyes. It was clear all Cade cared about was proving he wasn't crazy, that he was justified in murdering innocent people, but nothing could make that right. Cade didn't really care about those things. All he cared about was his staff. And he was nothing without it.

Josh brought the staff down and his right leg up, flooding his entire body with power. The crack of the wood as it hit the red energy pulsing across his knee echoed through the warehouse.

Blankness replaced the darkness in Cade's eyes. His pupils as empty as his crystals. Each remaining one shorted out as the break in the staff webbed through the wood, covering it in thousands of tiny cracks.

"What. Have. You. Done?" Cade screamed.

Josh gasped. Cade's fingers wrapped around his neck before he'd blinked, forcing him to drop the remains of the staff. As it clattered against the ground, he clawed at Cade's hands, trying to get free.

Josh willed his fingers to move. He didn't need power in them, not even his strength, he just needed to fight back like any normal person would. But this wasn't a normal situation. It hadn't been long enough.

Only a few seconds had passed since he'd spent all his energy destroying Cade's staff. His body hadn't recovered.

As the air in his lungs dried up, the surrounding darkness deepened and shadows closed in, rocking when an earthquake hit the warehouse. *What was that?*

Josh felt Cade's crushing grip loosen, and he drew in a welcome breath, filling his lungs so rapidly he was worried they would burst.

Bright stars clouded his vision, dancing in front of Josh so thickly it caused him to lose sight of Cade until a blink showed he was clear across the warehouse. The professor had been ripped away by the earthshaking force, the same one that also busted a hole in the building's side.

Dust and broken bricks littered the floor, but so did light. The high moon allowed Josh to see with clarity, and it showed him an escape. The hole was only a few feet from the door Kered and Sarah had desperately been trying to open.

"Run!" Josh shouted at them, attempting to follow. His legs wouldn't move. His body needed oxygen. He opened his mouth and puffed up his chest, choking on the dust he swallowed, but loving that sweet air. With enough recovery time, he'd have his power back, but as Cade stirred from his crumpled heap on the floor, Josh knew he wouldn't get the chance.

"Josh, come on!" Sarah screamed as she and Kered made their way over the debris. The hole created a mountain of rubble, and Kered had almost climbed to the top.

Josh saw Sarah struggling to find her footing, slipping every few steps and grazing her bare shins. She dropped the hem of her dress, but then her ballet flats kept getting caught on it.

"Maybe next time you should think about wearing something a little more climb-for-your-life-friendly?" Josh shouted as he ran toward her.

"The next time I'm kidnapped by a murderer?" Sarah called over her shoulder.

"Yeah. Pants and sneakers would probably be better."

"Thanks, I'll keep that in mind. Maybe the next time you should think about hurrying the f—"

Sarah's voice cut off, snatched out of the very air. No. It was the sound of everything that was taken away. The gray light stole the noise from the warehouse. Josh sensed it before he saw it. The tingle of the energy swept his back, snaking its way along his spine. Quickly, it slipped in front of him, lighting up his field of vision and blocking out the dust, Kered, and Sarah.

It stole his picture of them like it'd stolen Sarah's voice. Then it gave them back.

The flash of the glow reached fever pitch, exploding across the entire length of the warehouse, taking everything with it in a blot of brightness. When that light disappeared, the world came roaring back in blinks.

Kered falling backward as the gray glow knocked him out into the alleyway.

Sarah with covered eyes and slipping feet, crashing into the concrete floor.

Cade and a crystal grasped in his hand, traces of gray spewing from its former prism.

That bastard!

"Josh!" Sarah's pained voice called from the ground; fresh blood streaked across her face.

He ran to her, pooling the little energy he'd built into his fingertips and pushing his healing gift into it.

She swiped his hand from her bleeding cheek. "Save your power."

He barely scowled at her before she turned him around. Cade was on the ground too, his ankle bent at an odd angle, but his hands were injury free and still holding onto the crystal. The gray glow returned. It was the magick Cade used to keep Kallie trapped. He was going to do the same to Josh and Sarah.

There wasn't time to get out of the way.

THIRTY

The gray power shot across the room and something warm crushed Josh's right palm. He glanced down and closed his fingers around Sarah's hand as she trembled. He wanted to whisper it would be okay but didn't want to lie. Not if they were the last words he'd ever say to her.

Josh couldn't stop the power; he didn't have enough of his own to attempt any defense. Cade would win again. Two more victims added to his list.

"Kered got out, he'll get help," Sarah whispered, squeezing his palm tighter.

Even if Kered had found someone already, no one else could help them. Not against magick.

"Josh." Sarah let go of his hand, throwing both arms around him and burying her face in his shoulder.

He didn't blame her for not wanting to see, but he couldn't look away. He searched for Cade beyond the haze of power, a blurry mess still on the floor, crippled by his broken ankle but still beaming because he knew he'd won.

The energy swelled, inches from Josh's nose as his body tensed and his arms wrapped tighter around Sarah. He should have stood in front of her, shielded her, taken it all.

He waited for the power to trap them both so Cade could wreak whatever revenge he saw fit, but it burst before Josh in breaking gray waves.

"No!" Cade's voice boomed.

Josh's shoulder dipped, shifting with Sarah's weight as she turned to look at the warehouse floor.

"What happened, Josh? Did you do this?"

He raised his hand toward an invisible heat. His fingertips hit a barrier, making it shimmer a deep blue. "Kallie."

Another wave of gray burst against the barrier, causing it to ripple like ocean waves. Beyond the blur, Cade dragged his injured leg across the floor to the brick pillar and used its support to keep him upright.

"Get out here now, you little bitch!" Cade's raspy voice bounced around the empty rafters.

The metal door to the alleyway scraped open against the concrete, kicking up dust. It caught in the beams of light pooling through the hole in the wall, lighting the figure Josh had only ever seen before in dreams.

"It's her," he whispered to himself, to Sarah. "It's really her."

"Are you sure?" Sarah's wavering voice asked.

There was no mistaking Kallie's brunette waves. She was even wearing her usual jeans and white shirt. And it didn't matter that her hair was unruly, or that her tattered jeans and bloodied shirt were hanging from her painfully thin frame. It was Kallie. The real Kallie. She'd escaped the tiny wooden room, and she and her power were no longer bound by the shackles Cade had placed on her.

"Well, well." Cade glared. "*You* battled the dark half and walked away? I can't believe she let that happen."

"What she thinks happened and what really happened are two very different things."

Josh backed up a step, waiting for Kallie to bring down her invisible wall, or walk over to him and Sarah. She was so close. Finally, so close. He could see the tremble in her hand as she slipped it into the pocket of her jeans and pulled out a small crystal.

"You were always better at working your power," Cade said. "Tell me, did you let her think she'd killed you or did you play dead from the moment she'd arrived and hide until it was safe to escape?"

Kallie raised her hand, letting the clear quartz glint in her palm. Josh didn't understand what she was doing. He couldn't feel any power coming from it.

"Looks like your crystal's out of juice." Cade sneered.

Josh pressed his hands into the barrier, sinking his fingers into its spongy surface. They should have popped through as if he was breaking a bubble, but blue energy surfaced against him, keeping him in place. "Kallie, let me out. I can help you."

"Why is she ignoring you?" Sarah whispered, her own hands pressing against the glossy blue sheen and rejected just as swiftly.

"I don't know."

Kallie's fingers wrapped around the crystal, her eyelids fluttering to a close. It matched the subtle movement of her lips as she murmured into the belly of the quartz. Her energy flooded it, settling into its center in a dull wash of pale blue.

"There's something wrong," Josh said to Sarah, pushing his hands against the barrier again. "Her energy is off. The color is all wrong."

Kallie's weak hue seemed to be of great delight to Cade. His lips stretched so wide Josh could see all his teeth.

Under Josh's raised palms, Kallie's protective barrier flickered. He searched beyond his veil for her power and realized she was splitting it across the barrier, the crystal, and herself. She needed her magick to keep her malnourished body upright and walking, but was that the entire reason? The blood on her clothes was fresh. "She's wounded." This time he filtered his strength gift into his fingers as he dug them into the barrier.

Crack.

The noise drew Kallie's attention, and she finally looked their way. Cade didn't.

"Watch out!" Sarah's warning came too little too late.

Cade, balancing on his one good leg and the brick pillar, swung a sharp elbow into Kallie's side while she was distracted.

She doubled over, the crystal flying from her grasp and shattering in shiny pieces on the dirty concrete.

The power dissipated and the protective barrier fell away. Josh was free, and Kallie needed to be healed. Blood streamed down her side and mixed with the dust on the floor as he and Sarah sprinted toward her. *How is she still standing?*

One person Josh wouldn't be healing was Cade, whose ankle was bent so horrifically it must have broken slamming into something hard. Maybe Cade hit the pillar, or the pile of broken bricks, gliding through the dust and coming to rest just like…

"Kered's gun," Sarah gasped.

Cade had the pistol. Hidden in his coat and now clutched in his hand, his smug expression was so fixed in place it was like the wind had changed and frozen it there.

"Kallie?" Josh slowed, pulling Sarah to a stop beside him. Kallie was the closest to Cade, an easy target, but she held her palm up to Josh.

"I'm okay. Stay back." She straightened as best she could, clutching her bloody side as she glared at Cade. "You know that can't kill me."

Cade knew. Josh too. Nothing by that monster's hand could end Kallie's life. With only a vengeful smirk to proceed his actions, Cade readjusted his aim.

"Sarah, move!" Josh shoved her as the deafening echo of the gunshot bounced off every surface. They couldn't run, not fast enough to get away from a bullet.

He grabbed Sarah's shoulders and pulled her down. Or did he fall? It happened so fast he couldn't be sure.

He landed awkwardly, pain rushing through his lower body. *Those goddamn bricks.*

A cool sharpness stabbed at his abdomen as he tried to sit up. Sarah was next to him. He could feel her breath on his cheek, small puffs of air rapidly escaping her mouth. If she didn't slow her breathing, he was worried she would pass out.

"Josh." Sarah's hands pressed into his shoulders. If she was trying to keep him still, she was doing a terrible job. Her shaking hands were moving too much.

He couldn't stay down. He needed to help Kallie. To stop Cade. *Why aren't my legs working?*

One of Sarah's bloody hands moved from his shoulder.

"You're hurt." He'd gotten her injured. He tried to spark his power so he could heal her, but now his hands wouldn't move.

"Lie still," Sarah begged, gently straightening his head.

Josh focused on the roof of the warehouse. Orange light bathed the steel beams crisscrossing the space, a blue tinge washing through it. That was Kallie's magick. He'd know that shade anywhere. If she was using her energy, she was okay. *She's okay.*

"Kal..." he mumbled her name, the word lost when his lips tried and failed to slip into a smile.

"She's here."

Sarah's voice sounded weary. She should lay next to him and relax for a minute.

Something heavy hit his stomach, putting pressure on his insides. He opened his eyes. *When did I close them?* Kneeling beside him was Kallie, the ends of her brunette waves brushing against his cheek. He reached up to catch a strand. He thought it tickled his palm before he realized his hand hadn't moved.

"What do we do?"

Sarah's voice again. She needed to calm down. Now she sounded scared. She didn't need to be. He was there. Kallie was there. They would stop Cade. Just as soon as Josh could get his arms to cooperate.

They were playing tricks, and so was his neck. It wouldn't turn his head, but that didn't matter, he still found Sarah. She'd taken off her cardigan and placed it over his stomach. Now that he thought about it, he was cold. Sarah was a good friend. He shouldn't have lectured her about wearing a dress to their kidnapping. It looked nice on her. The cardigan too. It was red. He could have sworn it was white.

"Josh?" Kallie's hand cupped his cheek, her skin was warm, soft. It was also stained red.

"Is this a dream?" He blinked, trying to chase away the darkness smothering the orange sunrise, but he couldn't keep the shadows at bay.

"It's not a dream."

"Good... because in my dream... you got shot."

Beside him, Sarah sobbed.

"Did my dark half tell you about the amulet? How it works?"

"There's power in-in it. Life... death."

"Yes, that's right."

"She said it was... Blackbirch? She could-couldn't find it."

"I sent it here so you could use it."

"How can Josh use it, he can't even move?"

Was that Sarah's voice? It was muffled, like she was talking from the bottom of a swimming pool. He felt the same way. He knew what words to say, but they weren't coming out right.

"Josh, I need your help, okay?" Kallie's hand brushed his cheek again, making his head tremor. *Stop closing your eyes.* "I don't have enough energy built up to save you and deal with Cade. *You* will need to use the amulet on Cade," she said. "Do you understand? The death power will kill him."

Cade. Where was he?

"I knocked Cade out. In a few minutes, he will come to and sit up," Kallie said to Sarah. "When he does, move out of the way. Let Josh have a clear path to him. There's only one dark crystal left on the amulet, he has one shot."

Sarah nodded.

Josh tried to nod too, but his neck muscles still weren't talking to his brain. If Cade was getting up, so was he. *It's time to help Kallie finish this.* His head shifted half an inch and his whole body spasmed.

"I don't understand how Josh is going to stop Cade." Sarah pushed harder on the cardigan, tears free-falling down her cheeks. "He won't make it long enough to do anything."

"Yes, he will." Kallie's energy surfaced on her skin, that familiar blue even weaker than it was earlier, as if she'd drained it, keeping them both going. Josh didn't need that. It was only a few minor cuts, some bruises at most. She didn't need to waste her magick on him. He could heal himself; he just needed his hands to move to reach his back. *It's your stomach that hurts. It's your stomach that's bleeding.* Bleeding? No, he was just cold. That's why Sarah wrapped her cardigan around him and was pressing it so tight.

"You're going to use the life magick in the amulet to save him, aren't you," Sarah said to Kallie.

The life magick? It brought people back from the dead. He wasn't dead. *Not yet.* He didn't want her to do that. She should be using her power to defeat Cade, not save him. "Let... me... go."

Kallie stroked his face, her touch lingering on his skin. "I can't. Only you can stop what's coming." She wiped the back of her hand across her cheek, mopping up her tears before she discarded Sarah's bloodied cardigan and held her glowing hands up.

A tear ripped through the air above them, the amulet sliding through a crack of blue light in a silver blur and landing neatly in Kallie's open right palm.

"Do-don't," Josh begged, his breath snatched away as Kallie's gentle hands pressed the amulet against his torn flesh.

She bent close and kissed his forehead. "You'll know what to do."

The life-giving power of the amulet hit Josh as his final breath escaped his lips, released as Kallie's blue energy weaved into a sparkling crystal. It pushed into his skin and attached to his wound, working to rewind what the bullet had done. Unlike his last death, he remembered being saved this time. Josh would always remember it.

Kallie's essence tainted the magick that seeped into him, becoming part of him in a way that felt right, fitting, destined. The coldness that had infected his limbs thawed, chased away by a source of energy that knew how to bring balance and heal what had been ruined beyond repair. It took the injuries marring his insides and resurrected every shattered piece.

He braced as his stomach clenched, tightness gripping every muscle in his lower body to the sharp edge of agony, yet never quite making it there. He knew Kallie didn't want him to feel the pain. When this was over and he could heal her with his gift, he would make sure to return the favor.

As the final parts of his tattered flesh magically bound back into place, Josh's body rose, pushed into a sitting position by the amulet that still glowed against his skin.

"Are you alright?" Sarah's tear-stained face hovered into view.

Beyond her, the gangly shape of Cade using the pillar and his broken staff to prop himself up drew Josh's attention. His body reacted. His left arm lifting and twisting his hand and the amulet into position. It was automatic. Natural. Like breathing.

Sarah's face contorted, her eyes growing wider than her open mouth. Josh didn't have time to explain. He couldn't. His fingers grasped forcefully around the silver disk, angling it at Sarah's head.

Power flooded uncontrollably to the center of his palm and the red glow ignited the amulet, light once again bubbling from the tiny crystals adorning its tree.

"Move out of the way."

Kallie's instructions echoed between them, but it sounded like his voice saying the words that reminded Sarah of the promise she'd made. Realization swept her features, and she dropped out of the way as a thick stream of muddy power shot forcefully from the amulet's tinted crystal.

Cade didn't budge as it barreled toward him. He barely had time to finish standing.

Josh would have liked to have seen his lying lips twist into a scream, but he didn't witness any of it. The death power didn't allow it. It swallowed Cade whole, disintegrating his bones, his precious staff, and turning them into dust no different from the mess on the floor.

When it was over, it was like waking from a bad dream. The light scattered from the amulet, Josh's palm cooling while the crystal he'd used faded to clear.

As he dropped the silver disc and it rolled to a stop at his feet, Sarah's arms wrapped around him.

"Is Cade gone?" She squeezed Josh's neck.

The pillar was scorched. "He must be." Josh turned to Kallie beside him. He wanted to hug her too. To finally hold her now that his arms were working again. It was because of her that he was alive. It was because of her that Cade was gone. But Kallie's broken body was no longer stitched together by power. Her fatal injuries were free to wreak havoc now her magick was spent—and she was gone too.

THIRTY-ONE

Josh forced his eyes to blink and his hands to move. That's what live people did. That's what Kered was doing. His whole body was moving, while Josh's was crippled in place on the warehouse floor.

Five minutes ago, the security guard had run in with help; Max and his uncle, Rory. Blackbirch really was a small town. The house closest to The Playhouse belonged to its owner, who looked devastated that anyone had been hurt at his business.

Sarah burst into fresh tears when she saw her best friend, their argument forgotten as Max wrapped her in his arms. Josh had to look away. He couldn't bear to see her cry anymore.

Kered's mouth had dropped open at the reunion, the color draining from his skin. It must not have occurred to him that the teens would know each other. He lived outside of Blackbirch, not in a small town.

Now Kered was bending down to help Josh up, but he didn't want to leave. If he did, Kallie would be by herself, and she'd already been alone long enough.

Kered seemed to understand, even if he hadn't been there when she appeared, even though he didn't know who she was or what she'd done. He sat beside Josh, the two of them watching while Max led Sarah out into the parking lot and Rory called for the police and an ambulance.

"I told them it was a robbery," Kered whispered. "That some guy had jumped me looking for money at The Playhouse. I said you and Sarah were walking past, that you tried to help and got nabbed too.

Then we were all dragged into the warehouse to look for tools when I told the robber I didn't have access to the safe."

"Is that true? You can't get to the safe?"

"Yeah."

Maybe the story would work.

"What do I say now about her?" He gestured to Kallie's body without looking at it.

"That she helped too." That she'd done the most.

"We need to go outside." Rory approached them. "I don't trust that more of this wall won't come down."

Josh would have to move his arms to get up, his legs, his whole body. Kered reached out to help again, but Josh kept him waiting. He had to pick up the amulet and slide it into his back pocket without anyone noticing.

He could feel it there, like a weight dragging him down, as he stood in the parking lot next to Max, Sarah, and Rory, watching the police pull up.

The sheriff got out of the police cruiser first, followed by his deputy, an athletic younger man whose complexion was already green. The lightweight hadn't even seen anything yet.

By the time the deputy emerged from the warehouse with the sheriff and Kered, his skin was void of all color. The sheriff was more professionally composed. Removing his dark brown campaign hat, he strode toward them, combing down the thick strands of his chestnut hair.

"Kids, I'm Sheriff Stevens." He nodded at them politely. "I'm sorry about the friend you lost in there, and for what you've been through."

"Thank you." Sarah sniffed, wiping her wet cheeks.

Josh stayed silent, thrown by the sympathetic stare of the sheriff's hazel eyes. Maybe the cover story would hold up.

"Mr. Wheeler, could you join us?" Sheriff Stevens called over his shoulder. "I have his statement." He turned his attention back to them. "Now I just need to hear what happened from the two of you."

Josh glanced at Sarah, who was clinging to Max like her life depended on it. Concrete dust and blood covered her dress and hair. Her eyes were red rimmed. She wasn't in any condition to talk.

"Like Kered said." He cleared his throat, throwing a quick look to the security guard now standing beside the sheriff. "Some crazy guy tried to rob The Playhouse... we tried to stop him, he got hold of Kered's gun and um... forced us to find tools to break into the restaurant."

"How did the wall come down?"

"That was inevitable," Rory answered. "There was structural damage to the wall. I was waiting for a crew to fix it. That's why the warehouse was locked up."

"So, the work site was shut. Is that why you couldn't find any tools?"

Josh opened his mouth and closed it. *Did they say they couldn't find tools?* He tried to look at Kered for confirmation, but the sheriff was staring right at him, awaiting an answer.

"Was not finding any tools the reason the gunman opened fire?" the sheriff asked again.

"Yes," Sarah answered.

Sheriff Stevens made a note on the notepad he was holding and looked at Rory. "Are there any security cameras in the area?"

"Yes, in The Playhouse."

"None in the warehouse?"

Rory glanced at Max.

"Some of the construction crew complained about their personal items going missing," Max said. "I placed one camera where they locked everything up. It's at the back of the warehouse and motion activated. If it's still on, it might have caught something."

A security camera? Josh slicked his hand across his forehead, trying to catch Sarah's eye under the guise of wiping the sweat off his skin. She'd returned her stare to the asphalt. How would they explain what happened if it was caught on tape?

"I'll need you to get me that footage please, Mr. Ryan."

Max nodded at the sheriff. "It's set up to transmit to my computer. I can get it now."

Damn you, Max. Stop being so helpful.

"Jackson," Sheriff Stevens called to his deputy. The poor guy was still as pale as a ghost. Maybe he'd never seen a body before? He was lucky he wasn't one of Josh's friends, he'd have come across plenty by now. Jackson wouldn't just be pale then, he'd be as traumatized as Sarah, as despondent as Kered, as dead as Kallie. *I don't deserve friends.*

"Can you take Mr. Ryan to pick up some security footage."

"I can just run home and get it," Max offered.

"I'll drive you." Deputy Jackson couldn't leave fast enough, turning and walking to the cruiser before Max had extracted himself from Sarah's grip.

How long would it be before they returned? Twenty minutes? An hour? Could he come up with a creative lie by then? If tonight was on that security footage, all the time in the world wouldn't help him think of a plan to explain it. Especially when his thoughts couldn't move beyond Kallie.

She kept flashing through his mind. The softness of her hands, gentle even when her touch caused him pain, and the comforting warmth of her lips on his forehead. He would never feel any of it again.

"Can you tell me what happened after Mr. Wheeler left?" Sheriff Stevens' question drew Josh back to the conversation. "How did your friend die?"

Die. He hated that word. He knotted his fingers together, trying to keep them from going to where the bullet had ripped through his skin. He was so unaware at the time. Now, he wondered if he'd ever forget how it felt.

"Kallie. Her name is… was Kallie Jacobs."

"Of course." Sheriff Stevens nodded, softening his voice. "How was Miss Jacobs fatally injured?"

"It was my fault," Sarah spoke up. "I shouted out, I startled C— the robber."

God, Josh hoped she'd made that up. That it wasn't what she really thought. None of what happened was Sarah's fault. It was his. And

Cade's. "Only the robber is to blame," Josh said. "We all tried to follow Kered out of the warehouse, but that murderer stopped us."

"All I remember is hitting the ground and staying there," Sarah said, her eyes unfocused. "Then we saw Kallie was… hurt." Her voice wavered. "We wanted to help her, but she died so quickly."

"Unfortunately, that's the way these things go."

Sheriff Stevens' tone remained comforting, but his eyes narrowed, sweeping them both from head to toe. Was he suspicious of the dried blood caking them? Did he notice that Josh's shirt was saturated with so much blood that if he walked into an emergency room, a dozen doctors would treat him for a life-threatening injury? Maybe Stevens wouldn't draw that conclusion. Maybe he would take it as evidence Josh tried to do everything he could to save Kallie. Maybe that's the lie that will be believed.

"Do you know where I can reach Miss Jacobs' parents?"

"Her mom is dead. She lived alone in a room at the Blackbirch Motel."

Sheriff Stevens' lips dipped into a frown as he jotted down that information. When he finished, he waved to the ambulance that had arrived.

Josh winced at the flashing red lights painting color across the dark parking lot. Just the lights. No siren. There was no one to come and save.

"You've all been through a lot tonight," the sheriff said. "And I'm sorry you lost a friend. I just need a description of the gunman and then you can go home. Everything else we'll follow up tomorrow."

"He wore a balaclava," Kered said. "None of us saw his face."

The sheriff fixed his gaze on Josh and then Sarah. They both nodded in unison. "Okay. Mr. Wheeler, walk me through what happened when the assailant first arrived at the premises." He gestured for Kered to direct him.

Josh watched their backs.

"Your mom's on the way," Rory said.

The news made Josh flinch. *Grace must be freaking out.*

"Thanks, Rory." Sarah shuffled over to Josh, leaning into him as Max's uncle left them to trail Kered and the sheriff.

"Your mom will never let us leave the house again." He wrapped his arms around Sarah's shoulders. Her skin was ice cold. He almost asked her where her cardigan was.

"Max is back."

The headlights of the police cruiser hit them as it turned into the lot. Josh closed his eyes to escape the glare and hoped more than anything that when he opened them again, this would all be a nightmare.

Deputy Jackson handed Sheriff Stevens a USB drive as soon as he'd put the car in park and released Max from the locked backseat. Jackson couldn't even let Max ride up front? He wasn't a criminal.

"Maybe I should be in the back of that cruiser," Josh muttered.

"What?" Sarah pulled away from him.

"Nothing."

"How did you go?" Sheriff Stevens asked, glancing in their direction.

"We've got footage of the security guard patrolling the perimeter of the restaurant. After that, zilch. Could be the gunman knew there were cameras and took out the feed."

There was Sheriff Stevens' frown again. Maybe he wasn't as accepting of their story as he appeared to be.

"What about the camera in the warehouse?"

"Nothing there either. The motion sensor didn't activate."

"Thank god," Sarah whispered.

Now Sheriff Stevens' frown was a full scowl. He turned in their direction, and it smothered any relief Josh felt in a crippling wave of anxiety. Why was he staring at them like that? Why was he rushing toward them?

"Everyone's fine, Grace."

Huh? Somehow Josh missed the bookstore van pulling up behind him and Sarah, and Grace tearing out of the driver's door.

"Are you two okay?"

Arms squeezed him and Sarah from behind, twisting them around.

"I'm okay." Josh's ribs protested the embrace, as he watched the fear leach into Grace's features when she registered the amount of blood on his shirt.

"Sarah?" Grace patted her down for injuries. "Oh my god, look at your dress, your hands!"

"I'm fine." A stream of new tears flooded Sarah's cheeks.

"What happened?" Grace uncharacteristically barked at Stevens, her arms swallowing Sarah in another hug.

The sheriff recited a thorough version of the events. He had a high level of recall, and a man good at details wouldn't miss anything. *Guess you will take a ride in the back of that police car, Josh.* The truth of the crime scene would be his undoing.

"Oh, Josh. I'm so sorry."

Grace pulled him into her hug. The story had reached the part about Kallie. He was hoping in the noise of his self-loathing thoughts he'd missed it.

Grace's fearful expression shifted up a notch. He'd seen that look in her eyes before. She was worried about how he would deal with another loss. Truth be told, so was he.

"Can we leave now?"

"How about we get the paramedics to check your over first?" Sheriff Stevens suggested.

"No. I'm all good." Josh lifted his bloodied shirt to show he was injury free and walked to the van. He'd answered all the questions he was going to, and he'd stayed covered in his own blood for long enough.

Sarah followed him, joined by Max.

"I'm sorry about Kallie," he said. "She seemed cool."

Max had never met the real Kallie, but Josh couldn't correct him. "Thanks." He patted Max's shoulder.

It was then the two paramedics came out of the ruined warehouse; a body bag tied to their stretcher. It should have been Cade. He should have been the only victim of tonight. *No. It should be you.* It was supposed to be. First his mother and now Kallie had died saving him.

It was a sacrifice Josh couldn't fathom; one he didn't believe he deserved. Then he remembered some of Kallie's last words.

Only you can stop what's coming.

THIRTY-TWO

Sarah's skin warmed on the front porch's stone tiles, the sliver of early morning sun she'd found helping to bring heat back into her bones.

Two days later, she still felt the chill of the warehouse in her limbs and wished she'd dressed in something thicker than a t-shirt, but all she owned was cardigans and she couldn't bear to slip one on. Not another red cardigan, at least. *Or a white one.*

Max's car pulled into her driveway. He usually swung the bright green hatchback in too wide, barely missing the black birches lining the yard, but today he didn't come close to sideswiping them. Why did that bother her? It's not like she wanted him to hit the trees. Then she realized it was because Max almost taking them out was normal. And she needed normal.

"Hey," she called, reluctantly pulling herself up from the heated tiles.

"Hey."

Max looked as if he'd gotten as much sleep as she had lately, which was barely any. Maybe if she slept properly, she could pretend everything that happened wasn't real. That she could erase it by waking up. But it wasn't a dream. It had happened. Right in front of her. And she couldn't get the images out of her head.

"Where's Josh?" Max asked as they stepped inside the house.

"Upstairs in his room." She shut the door quietly in case he was asleep, although she doubted the poor guy would ever rest deeply again. "How are you feeling today?"

Max's question was the same one her mom asked, before Sarah insisted Grace go and open the bookstore. She couldn't spend another day being stared at by her mother, drowned in her sympathetic smiles and worried glances. She knew she meant well, but every time her mom looked at her, it reminded Sarah of that night and started a fresh avalanche of tears.

"I'm okay." She settled on the far end of the couch, leaving room for Max to join her like he usually did. He sat across from her in the armchair, making her wonder if he was still mad at her.

Before she could ask, Max pulled a USB from the pocket of his jeans and put it on the coffee table between them.

"What's that?"

Max's gaze swept her, darting from her face to the table and back again. Was he expecting a reaction from her? His features morphed, the sympathy plastered to it since he got out of his car melting, replaced with what she could only describe as anger.

"This is the security footage from that night."

Sarah gave a longer glance to the USB. It didn't help. Why did Max have it when the feed showed nothing? "And you brought it here because..."

"I wanted to give you the chance to explain to me what really happened in the warehouse."

What did he think happened? Sarah swallowed thickly, studying the USB while her heart thumped against her chest. Her cheeks flushed. This was not the heat she needed. "You said it didn't record anything."

"That's what I told Deputy Jackson and Sheriff Stevens. I saw Josh's face when my uncle confirmed there was a security recording."

"You kept the real footage from the sheriff?" Ice crept along her bones. *That's right, Sarah, you'll never feel warmth again.*

"If you were in trouble, I didn't want to make it worse." Max's anger briefly broke. "But what I saw on that feed..."

She clenched her eyes shut. *No more tears.* She pressed her fingers to her mouth and couldn't decide if it was to hold back vomit or a scream. She couldn't talk about that night. Not to Max. *I won't bring him into this.* He meant too much to her.

"Sarah." Max's hands found hers and cupped them as he slid beside her on the couch and finally took his usual spot. But everything was still off. His voice had an edge in it she wasn't used to, his eyes a harder stare. "Please, Sarah."

He used her full name. Not his nickname for her, the one she publicly hated but secretly loved because it was only Max who called her 'Sar.' "What do you want me to say?"

"The truth." His blue eyes begged. "I want you to tell me what the hell is going on."

THIRTY-THREE

Sarah watched Josh from her seat at the edge of the schoolyard. It was odd seeing him out in the daylight. Odd to see him at all, really.

In the last week he'd never shown his face during their stilted conversations through his closed door and she didn't want to get started on her countless texts that he'd ignored. Each encounter was the same; he insisted he was fine; she knew he wasn't.

"He looks different," Max said, settling beside her with a breakfast burrito in his hand.

"You only think that because you know what he's been through."

"Have you told him?"

"No." It wasn't exactly something you brought up in a text message. Not with Josh. "He barely spoke the few times we did talk. It never seemed like the right time."

They watched him dodge a group playing basketball and slip into the homeroom building.

"Do you think he'll be mad?"

"I don't know." She shrugged. Josh never wanted Max to know.

"Maybe tell him our other big secret. It might soften the blow." Max's arm wrapped around her shoulder and she reveled in his warmth. He'd made the move a thousand times before, but it was different now. Not just familiar comfort from her best friend, but a touch that now gave her stomach butterflies.

They'd been there since the day he came to her house to find answers, and she'd told him everything. When the months of secrets spilled out of her, so did the words she didn't know she was going to say until she did; that she wanted more from their relationship too.

The old Max was back after that, the one who texted her every night before bed. The one whose only for Sarah smile transformed his lips whenever he saw her. Those same lips she'd kissed at the end of their first date, clutching the roses he'd brought her and the box of chocolates with all the caramel ones eaten because he knew she didn't like them. She was so happy after being drowned in such darkness, and she wanted the world to know. Just not Josh. Not yet.

"Maybe…"

Max frowned. "I hate hiding this."

"I know, but the timing still isn't right."

"You were less scared about telling your mom."

"I'm not scared of telling him. He's still grieving her loss, no matter how much he tries to hide it, and I just don't want to go around flaunting my happiness." Max would understand if he lived with Josh and saw first-hand how haunted he'd become. Sarah didn't want to add to that. She wouldn't. She couldn't.

Max's frown deepened.

"Please, a little while longer?" She nudged him gently with her shoulder.

"Fine," he agreed, refusing to smile but then breaking into a small one after Sarah quickly kissed him. It made the butterflies flutter more, adding to her nervousness.

"I'll let you know how it goes." She stood, looping her bag over her shoulder and licking her lips. They tasted liked burrito.

In the homeroom building, she spied Josh at his locker, his shirt wrinkled and dried mud caking the lower edges of his sneakers. It confirmed her suspicion that he'd been getting to school by walking alone through the woods; swapping the walls of his room for trees in his self-imposed cage.

It wouldn't be so bad if the fresh air was doing him good. As Max pointed out, Josh looked different. His hair was longer than it'd ever been, and the tone of his skin had dulled that night and never returned in the same way. He was a little slimmer too. It wasn't from lack of food. He might not sit at the dinner table with her and her mom anymore, but he was still eating most of the food Sarah left outside his bedroom door. She suspected his change in appearance was because of his hikes in the woods. The exercise made him leaner, but she didn't think it made him healthier. How could it when his heart was so scarred?

Josh's heartbreak was as obvious as the dark circles under his eyes. Sarah could hear him through the wall again, during the few hours he slept. It wasn't nightmares of monsters keeping him awake anymore, but the reality he no longer dreamed of Kallie. Her death at the expense of Josh's life was something Sarah knew he'd never move past. And it broke her heart.

"Hi." She approached him, knotting her fingers together.

He closed his eyes at the sound of her voice, as if it physically hurt him to hear it. Was that what she was now? Someone who caused him pain.

When he opened his brown eyes, she could see his ever-present regret. It stirred up her own memories of that night. Of watching Josh bleed to death on the dirty warehouse floor.

"Please don't ask me how I am," he said. "I'm banning that question from ever being asked again."

"Mom special?" Sarah leaned against the locker next to him.

"Yeah."

Her mom hadn't allowed Josh as much distance as Sarah, but he'd still pushed her away too. "Well, that's what happens in our family. Mom backs up her working-mom-guilt by asking the same question a million times."

"Grace doesn't seem to understand I have a personal vow to not involve her in the supernatural shitstorm that is my life." Josh sighed. "No one else needs to get hurt because of me. I can handle it alone."

Alone? After everything they'd been through, he really thought he'd be better off doing things alone? "Well, you weren't alone in that warehouse, and you're not going to be anymore. We're in this together. I might not have any of your special power, but I can still help."

"Maybe I don't need your help."

Sarah shook her head. Wasn't he smarter than this? "You can't do this on your own. If you were alone, Kallie wouldn't have been there to help you."

Josh's face went blank and his body froze.

"Don't bring her up!"

Ah, Anger. So that's the grieving stage he was at. Sarah didn't want to relive what happened either, but he needed to deal with it to move on. "You'd be dead if it wasn't for her. You need to talk about it."

"There's nothing to say." Josh stopped unpacking his bag and started snatching books back from his locker. "Kallie did what she had to." His hands reached for another book, shoving it toward his bag before it dropped from his shaking grip.

The notebook fell open as it hit the floor. Reaching for it first, the pages flipped open in Sarah's hand. Josh's handwriting covered the lines, scribbled paragraphs about the elements and witchcraft that would put the stacks to shame. "Is this what you've been doing all week?" She scanned through the notes, finding a rough map of Blackbirch in the middle. He'd marked out the clearing. Why was he mapping the woods?

Josh frowned at her, grabbing the notebook. "I have to do something."

Wow. He really did blame himself entirely for what happened. She expected that he would; it was Josh, and she knew there was nothing she could say to convince him otherwise, but this? "What do you need? If you're planning something, I want to help."

"Dark Kallie is still out there. She knows I'm here. By now she must know Cade's gone. She could come back, looking for me or the amulet."

"Do you have it?" She braced for the answer, wishfully hoping he'd buried it somewhere deep.

Josh nodded. "There's only two crystals in it that have any power left. It's life-giving magick. It might not be of any use to her, but it's power."

Power would be exactly what that traitor would look for. Would she really come back here though? "If she visits Blackbirch again, are you sure you'll be able to face her? Especially when she looks—"

"They're not the same person."

"I know, but—"

"But nothing! She's a dark half. I'll stop her."

"How?" She got the best of him last time. Of all of them. Sarah absently rubbed her temple. Her skin might have forgotten she'd unwittingly been knocked unconscious by Dark Kallie, but her memory hadn't. "Still, if—"

"I've been practicing some castings." Josh interrupted her. "I've been learning to build up my magick and control my ability. I'll be ready for her."

Sarah wasn't questioning his magickal abilities. She'd seen Josh battle Arden and Cade and win, but she'd also watched him falter. After crushing Cade's staff, Josh barely had enough power to light a light bulb. He might have thought it was his lack of experience, and it was great he was trying to fix that now by learning spells, but she wasn't so sure his theory was right. She believed the energy was more than just something he could conjure and shape into a weapon. It was a part of him, and how he used it was just as much controlled by his emotions as his physical body. "Fine. But promise me if Dark Kallie does come back, you won't face her alone."

"I can't promise that."

She pressed her head against the locker. "Josh."

"I'm not putting you in danger again. We were lucky to live and to get away with it. Other than Dark Kallie, the only people who know the truth and about my power is you and Kered. The three of us can keep it contained. We can keep ourselves safe and this nightmare can end." He glanced up the hallway, lowering his voice. "We can finish high school like normal people and move on with our lives."

Oh, Josh. It was a nice plan. A good plan. One she wanted to happen too. It was such a shame it wouldn't. "Do you really think it'll be that simple? She said there was something else out there. That something was coming."

"I know what Kallie said," Josh snapped.

Maybe they'd be lucky and Dark Kallie wouldn't return to town. Kered was long gone, finding a job closer to home, so he'd never have to step one clumsy foot in Blackbirch again. Even the sheriff's investigation into that night had so far gone smoothly. Was she the only person not willing to let it go? Josh had clearly prepared himself for any other situation. Perhaps she should be backing him up and confessing that Max knew. *Don't hate me, Mr. Control Freak.* "Um, just so you know…"

"What?"

"The camera in the warehouse *was* on that night."

He met her reveal with a blank stare. *Great, he's had a stroke.*

"I can only assume the sheriff hasn't seen what really happened."

"Max kept it from him."

Josh's brow creased. "How much does he know?"

"Everything."

Josh sighed and closed his eyes, a more subtle reaction than she was expecting. "Are you mad?"

"No. I didn't want to get anyone else involved, but I guess it's out of my hands."

"Max handled it better than I thought he would."

"Did you watch the footage?"

"No, I couldn't." Did he really think she would? "He gave it to me, and I deleted it."

"Good." Josh shut his locker. "Thank you."

"Of course."

"Maybe now that you know about Max, we could all get together and talk about everything."

"You really aren't going to let this go, are you?"

She smiled at him. "No, I'm not."

"I'm sure you and Max have better things to do then spend time moping around with me, you know, like going on dates and making out in Max's hatchback."

"Excuse me?" She must have misheard him. Josh didn't know about them. It also sounded like he was trying to be funny, and Josh had zero sense of humor. "If that was a joke at my expense, it was bad," she said.

"I'm out of practice." Josh shrugged, the smallest of grins appearing on his face.

"You know about me and Max?" Mr. Hide-In-His-Room-All-Day had worked it out?

"When you started looking at him the same way he's always looked at you, it became kinda obvious."

Sarah let out a breath. It turned into a laugh. It felt so good to laugh.

"You didn't need to keep it from me," Josh said. "I'm happy for you two."

His admission would be more convincing if it wasn't tinged with such sadness. He couldn't have what she had now Kallie was gone. "I thought I would die in that warehouse." Sarah's smile slipped. "And what scared me the most was never seeing him again." She pictured Max's face, and it forced another laugh, one that caused her eyes to crinkle and push unshed tears down her cheeks. She wiped at her wet skin and watched the sadness in Josh's eyes deepen. "I wish you could have this too. You deserve it. Both of you did."

"Well, clearly there's something out there in the universe that disagrees." Josh sniffed. "It probably wouldn't have worked out, anyway. It's not like I knew her. We met for a few minutes and I was literally dying for all of them."

"Is that what you thought when you saw her? Because I was next to you, and the way you looked at Kallie, the way she looked at you before doing what she did..." Sarah wiped at fresh tears. "It doesn't matter how brief it was. You two instantly understood each other. You *did* know her."

"Yeah, *knew*," Josh muttered.

Sarah reached out, pulling him in for a hug whether he wanted it or not. He'll be okay. Eventually. She knew because he hugged her back.

Above them, a shrill bell split the air and the dim hallway filled quickly. Students flooded around them, more than a few whispering in

huddles when they spotted that Josh was back at school. *Gossipy jerks.*
"Are you going to be okay?"

"I thought I would be, but... can you tell your mom I went to class? I just can't be here right now."

"Depends. Are you going off to do anything crazy by yourself?"

"No." Josh fixed his backpack over both shoulders, straightening up.

"Promise?"

"I promise, Sarah. I just need to be somewhere where I don't feel like an act in the circus. You know, the guy death follows."

"Okay, I'll tell mom. But I want to talk to you later at home. Do you know why?"

"Because you're an annoying busybody who has nothing better to do?"

She pulled him in for another hug. "Because we're family and we look after each other."

For a second, she felt his arm on her back and her shoulders squeezed in a return embrace. Then Josh's arms fell to the side. He might still be a little reluctant to call her and her mom family, but she wouldn't let him forget that he was.

"Nothing crazy?" She took a step back, giving him room.

"Nothing crazy," Josh promised, sliding away from the bank of lockers and getting lost in the crowd.

"Damn." Sarah sighed. If only she believed him.

THIRTY-FOUR

Josh reached his street, rushing down it so he could get inside without his neighbors seeing. The last thing he needed now was word reaching Grace that he couldn't handle one day back at school. He was so focused he didn't notice the police cruiser parked in the driveway until he practically ran into it.

"What is he doing here?" Josh muttered under his breath, eyeing the good sheriff sitting patiently behind the wheel. *Did he see me? Can I run?* He glanced back the way he came. Maybe if his legs hadn't frozen in place.

The driver door cracked open and Stevens climbed out, a pile of folders in the crook of his arm.

"Hi, Josh."

"Hello..."

"Do you have a few minutes?"

"Ah, not really. I'm running late for school."

"Really? Because I was just there looking for you, and the principal told me you weren't in homeroom so you must still be resting at home."

Damn. "You're right. I *was* going to school, but I'm not feeling that great so... maybe we could talk another day? Grace isn't here anyway, and if this is about the warehouse, she needs to be present, right?"

"I know where Grace is." Sheriff Stevens smiled, patting the folders. "And I don't think you want her knowing about this."

The sheriff wasn't there to talk about the investigation? Josh eyed the folders. "What are those?"

"Everything I have on you, Kallie Jacobs, your aunt, your mother, and Blackbirch."

"Excuse me?" *Melinda and his mom? Blackbirch?* Stevens listed them so casually, like he was reciting items on his grocery list. They weren't files. They were people, his family. Josh eyed the manila folders. "I don't understand. You have a file on my mom. How do you know anything about her?"

Instead of an answer, the question seemed to prompt a wave of sadness. There was a dip in Sheriff Stevens' grin, a dimness that touched his eyes.

"You knew her." Josh realized. *How did he know her?*

"Take these." Stevens held out the folders. "When you're done reading them, come and see me and perhaps we can both make sense of this together."

"Together?"

The sheriff nodded, forcing his smile to return. "We both got thrown into this, you see."

Josh swallowed. "Thrown into what?"

Sheriff Stevens pulled his cell phone out of his back pocket and showed Josh the screen. It was a paused security video of what looked like the Sheriff's office. He was sitting at a desk while a stout older man stood on the other side of it. "This Portland detective is in town. If he approaches you, don't talk to him."

Portland? That was where Kallie was from. "Is his name Brewer?"

"Yes. Have you spoken to him?"

"No." Josh studied the cell phone screen. This was the detective Kallie was so scared of? "I'd like to know what he talked to you about."

Sheriff Stevens handed him the phone. "Press play."

"Still hanging around, Brewer?" The sheriff in the video glanced up from his paperwork, his eyes fixed on the round face of a man with dark circles under his eyes and a ruddy glow infused over his plump cheeks.

"I've still got questions," Brewer huffed in a voice so gruff it sounded like he'd spent years pairing cigarettes and whiskey for breakfast. He threw a manila file down on Sheriff Stevens' desk. Across the label stuck to the front was Kallie's name.

Stevens picked it up and thumbed through it. "I've seen the coroner's report. I don't know how you got a copy."

"She died of a stab wound."

"I'm well aware." The sheriff put the folder down.

"There was no knife at the crime scene or enough blood to prove she was stabbed in the warehouse."

"That doesn't mean the robber didn't take the knife with him, or that the blood wasn't there. There was lots of construction damage." Sheriff Stevens shrugged at Brewer. "I'm sure the blood is there under a pile of bricks."

"You don't want to make sure?"

"This was a shocking incident. We don't get a lot of robberies around here, least of all ones that end in the murder of a seventeen-year-old girl. I have dealt with the case and closed it."

"And it doesn't concern you that your whole case was based on the word of a few kids?"

"The story checked out with the evidence at the scene. I have no reason to distrust the witnesses."

"What about the robber?" Brewer asked. "You barely followed up the leads on him."

"Without a description there isn't a lot I can do, you know that." Sheriff Stevens scowled. "The robbery was such a mess it was obvious he was an amateur."

"The robbery wasn't the only thing amateurish." Brewer snorted. "Even the reporting was lackluster. You didn't allow a picture of the girl to be released, never asked for other potential witnesses to come forward."

"And what good would splashing a photo of Miss Jacobs across the front page of the paper do? It's not like she had a family we were trying to reach."

"Or you were afraid someone would recognize her. Wonder why she looked healthy on the restaurant CCTV footage, and then like death only hours later."

"Again, the body is a mysterious place, especially after the trauma hers had been through." Sheriff Stevens' gaze drifted back down to the coroner's report.

"That excuse doesn't fly when her clothes were different, her body malnourished and dehydrated." Brewer picked up the folder and waved it around with his chubby, yellow stained fingers.

Sheriff Stevens rose from his chair and snatched the folder as Brewer whizzed it past him. "I let you hang around as a professional courtesy, but you've outstayed your welcome. This is my investigation and I'll run it how I see fit!"

Brewer glared at the sheriff and reached for his file. Stevens held it back. "Thank you for your help."

"You're an asshole!" Brewer yelled as he slammed the door shut behind him.

Josh stopped the video and handed the phone back to Stevens, knowing he'd never talk to Brewer, even if he was forced to. What he also knew for sure was that a thorough police investigation was only a hole poke away from exposing the lies of their story. "You're covering everything up," Josh said. "Why?"

"Read the files." Sheriff Stevens slipped his phone away, stepping back to his car and opening the door. The morning sun reflected off the window, glinting against the name tag pinned to his uniform.

Josh had never paid close attention to it before, his mind on other things when they'd talked. He made the time to read it now. *S. Stevens.* "S.S," he said the sheriff's initials out loud.

Sheriff Stevens raised a curious eyebrow at him.

"Did you ever carve your name into the bottom of a wooden bench at the high school?"

Stevens' smile appeared again, genuinely this time. "I believe that was your mother." He climbed into the cruiser and started the engine.

Holy shit.

Josh watched the sheriff wave before driving off and held tight to the folders as he jogged up the front steps. In the house, he made himself comfortable on the living room couch, stacking the manila folders onto the coffee table.

It was a thick stack, some with labels that didn't seem important. But this was Blackbirch; the shiny gloss was on the outside of the hidden, darker inside.

The first set of papers he pulled out were Kallie's. The only way Josh had dealt with her death was by reminding himself he didn't know the real her.

Their time together hadn't been long. Brief moments caught in dreams; even briefer moments drenched in blood. But as he looked at her name, typed neatly on the sheet of paper in his hands, none of that mattered. Sarah was right. One look in Kallie's eyes, one touch of her fingers on his skin, one second of her lips pressed to his forehead, were moments that lasted forever. Josh had barely met her, but he felt as if he'd known Kallie all his life. And it crushed him that he only got to know her for the last few moments of hers.

His eyes scanned the first page and learned what he didn't know about the girl that had saved him. She had no known father and no middle name. Her mother was fifteen when she had Kallie and worked as a manager at a steakhouse until her death in the house fire for which Kallie was the prime suspect. The investigation was headed by Detective Tom Brewer, but his line of inquiry into Kallie was dropped when he was removed from the case.

Kallie had also been the suspect in a Brewer-led case when her neighbor, Melinda Tucker, was killed during a bungled home robbery. Kallie had been linked to the crime after her DNA was found at the scene. Three weeks later, Brewer was stood down pending an internal investigation and named as a suspect in Kallie's disappearance. Josh paused reading. He'd seen everything that had happened to his aunt. Cade's DNA had to have been all over that scene. The memory of Brewer in the sheriff's video flooded his mind. Even after her death, he seemed to have such a high level of interest in Kallie. *Why?*

Josh moved to the next page in the file; a list of missing items from Melinda's house compared to her insurance records. According to the notes, these objects were the reason a robbery was suspected. *Jewelry, a wooden box listed as a family heirloom, and a rare collection of books.*

The heirloom box must have been the one Melinda put Cade's binding magick in, and he wondered where it was now. Cade didn't give the real one to Dark Kallie, and he didn't have a box on him in the warehouse. Maybe Sheriff Stevens could help Josh find out? If he truly was on their side.

The last few pages of the file were printouts detailing Kallie's house fire, the drowning of Jerry Miller, and the attempted robbery of The Playhouse.

K.M. Allan

Stapled behind the printouts was a sheet of hand-written notes on Sheriff Stevens' letterhead. *Survived fire and brutal home invasion. Perished in robbery. Fatal injuries consistent with damage caused by a deep stab wound from a long blade with a serrated edge. No knife found at the crime scene. Condition of body malnourished. Clothing and weight do not match CCTV footage of the victim at The Playhouse earlier in the evening.*

The notes here questioned everything. Sheriff Stevens didn't trust their story, yet he was publicly acting like he did. Why? Because he was high school friends with Josh's mom? There had to be more to it.

Josh shuffled through the rest of the files, hoping they'd have a clue. He came across a series of juvenile records for shoplifting and break and enters. These weren't his, or Kallie's, but with all the names blacked out in thick marker, he didn't know who they belonged to. It was no one recent. The date marked on the file was from twenty-five years ago. Sitting in the same folder was an eerily similar juvenile record with a name he did recognize—Eve Thomas.

What? While Josh wasn't surprised Eve had her name on a file in the Sheriff's office, why was it grouped with these folders? No one outside of Josh and Sarah knew Eve had a connection to him, especially now that she didn't work at the bookstore.

Did Sheriff Stevens know something Josh didn't, or was he smarter at reading people? Josh had seen Eve kill Arden. He knew she was messing with magick when she convinced Sarah to help her cast that glimpsing spell, yet he ignored it. He took his own newbie-magick search, and a search conducted by a dark half, as proof that Eve had no power—dismissing how badly Eve wanted it and the lengths she would go to keep such a secret hidden.

Someone had salted the earth in the clearing and taken Arden's place. Someone who knew exactly what spells to cast. If Josh asked Sarah if she thought Eve would bring a tree down on him, she'd say yes without hesitation.

Josh needed to talk to Eve again, and this time he wouldn't write her off like everyone else always did. Like he already had.

The next folder was full of photocopied pages of a book. Josh scanned the printed paragraphs, ready to dismiss them until the author

238

caught his eye. "Oh my god." It was Cade's textbook. The one he'd written about power and the elements when he was a professor.

Josh hurried to pull the pages free, hearing the front door creak open just as he'd emptied the folder. It was probably Sarah using her free morning study period to check on him, and for once he wasn't annoyed at her clinginess. "You'll never believe who was waiting for me in the driveway," he called to her, his eyes afraid to leave the pages in case they somehow disappeared.

"Who?" a male voice asked.

That's not Sarah.

Josh shot up, dropping the photocopies as an unknown visitor stood in his doorway, dressed in a big overcoat with a baseball cap pulled down over his features. "Who are you?" Josh stepped forward; the floorboards creaking under foot. He paused at the echo that followed, realizing too late that someone was behind him. *No one ever locks the doors!*

Josh barely turned before the pain of a heavy hit splintered his skull and his vision plunged toward unconsciousness.

Two. He tried to remember before his thoughts slipped away. *When I wake up, there will be two of them.*

Josh twitched his fingers, the smallest body part he could wiggle. The tips buzzed with pins and needles and the prickly sensation spread throughout the rest of his hand, waking it up.

He tried to sit, but the only thing he could shift was his neck. It lugged his head to the side and rewarded it with a bout of searing pain that stretched from temple to temple.

Maybe my eyes will work better? He cracked open a lid and cringed at the sunlight pouring through his bedroom window's half-raised curtain. It's okay. He was at home.

Home?

He knew that. He'd been in the living room when someone broke in. Not just a someone. Two people!

Both eyes flew open and the familiar walls of his bedroom took shape. "How'd I get here?" His hands stayed put when he tried to stand, yanked back by the rope keeping him chained to his own bed.

He summoned his power, waiting for it to burst through the nylon and set him free. The red energy instantly recoiled when it touched the fibers. He'd seen that trick before.

He scanned the room and stopped at his open closet. The smooth wooden door faced him, moving slightly on its hinges as someone—or something—rummaged behind it and through his things.

"I doubt I'd have anything that would suit you, Dark Kallie. I don't shop in the evil section when I get new shirts."

"Too busy shopping in the lame joke department?" She stepped from behind the closet door, clad in jeans, a dark fitted shirt, shiny midnight-tinted boots, and the jacket he'd lent her that cold night in the alleyway.

Hadn't she taken enough of his clothes? "Yeah, yeah, I can't make good jokes, I can't move my hands,"—he tried again to raise his arms—"and I can't believe *you* showed your face again in Blackbirch."

"Did you miss me?"

"I don't know? Do people miss the worst person they've ever met in their life?"

"Aww, come on, you met Cade." She pouted. "Surely he's worse than me."

"I killed Cade."

She stretched those rosy lips into a huge smirk. "I figured you did."

The closest door bumped on its hinges again.

"Who's your friend?" God, he hoped it wasn't a tied-up Sarah.

"Someone who is very interested in meeting you."

Dark Kallie stepped away from the closet, her partner rounding the door and stopping at the edge of the bed. He wasn't in an overcoat or hiding behind a baseball cap anymore. Instead, he was in Josh's clothes, standing in Josh's bedroom, yet Josh couldn't believe who he was staring at. It had to be a mistake. He must have bumped his head when he was knocked out, or he was still unconscious and having a nightmare.

What. The. Fuck.

"You were right." Dark Kallie's partner nodded at her, pointing to Josh. "My other half looks exactly like me."

Thank You!

Thank you for reading **Blackbirch: The Dark Half.**

If you enjoyed it, please leave a review at the place of purchase or on Goodreads (even just a sentence or a star rating will do) and recommend the book to a friend. Reviews get the word out about independently published books and are very much appreciated.

The Blackbirch Series will continue early 2021.

Acknowledgments

An author writes by themselves, but they aren't alone when they create a book. *The Dark Half* would not be what it is without the encouragement and support of some wonderful people.

Thank you to Donna and Derek, who read my first drafts, listen to my complaints, and tell me things are good when I think they're bad.

Thank you to M.L. Davis, who convinced me to keep writing this book when I was once at a point so low, I was going to give up. Your words, encouragement, and friendship are an awesome thing to have on this writing journey.

For my writing friends who've read various versions over the years and pointed out what was working and what wasn't, thank you Ruth Miranda, Amelia Oz, Lorraine Ambers, and Bryan J. Fagan. I wouldn't be the writer or person I am today without knowing you guys.

Like this book, these acknowledgments would not be complete without a shoutout to the #6amAusWriters crew! Thank you, Belinda Grant, Sandy Barker, Veronica Strachan, Emily Wrayburn, Emma Louise Hughes, KD Kells, Lyn Webster, Anna Whateley, Helen Edwards, Deb Hannagan, Natasha O'Connor, and Naomi Lisa Shippen. I was editing this book when I joined our little group and got through the endless rewrites with all the help the right GIF on a cold, dark morning can muster. I'm in awe of everyone's talent, and so thankful for the support, friendship, and Zoom tea catchups. When I needed extra readers, you stepped up at short notice to give the feedback I needed to make this book the best it could be, and I'll forever be grateful for that.

Last, but not least, thank you to my family, friends, blog readers, and social media buddies for supporting the release of my first book, *Blackbirch: The Beginning*. It totally blew me away and I hope you liked this book just as much, even with *that* cliffhanger.

About The Author

K.M. Allan is an identical twin, but not the evil one. She started her career penning beauty articles for a hairstyling website and now powers herself with chocolate and green tea while she writes novels and blogs about writing.

When she's not creating YA stories full of hidden secrets, nightmares, and powerful magic, she likes to read, binge-watch too much TV, spend time with family, and take more photos than she will ever humanly need.

Visit her website, www.kmallan.com, to discover the mysteries of the universe. Or at the very least, some good writing tips.

CPSIA information can be obtained
at www.ICGtesting.com
Printed in the USA
BVHW081745070720
583154BV00001B/105

9 780648 773023